The FAMILY
JEWELS

The FAMILY JEWELS

CAROLE HART

HEAT

HEAT
Published by New American Library, a division of
Penguin Group (USA) Inc., 375 Hudson Street,
New York, New York 10014, USA
Penguin Group (Canada), 90 Eglinton Avenue East, Suite 700, Toronto,
Ontario M4P 2Y3, Canada (a division of Pearson Penguin Canada Inc.)
Penguin Books Ltd., 80 Strand, London WC2R 0RL, England
Penguin Ireland, 25 St. Stephen's Green, Dublin 2,
Ireland (a division of Penguin Books Ltd.)
Penguin Group (Australia), 250 Camberwell Road, Camberwell, Victoria 3124,
Australia (a division of Pearson Australia Group Pty. Ltd.)
Penguin Books India Pvt. Ltd., 11 Community Centre, Panchsheel Park,
New Delhi - 110 017, India
Penguin Group (NZ), 67 Apollo Drive, Rosedale, North Shore 0632,
New Zealand (a division of Pearson New Zealand Ltd.)
Penguin Books (South Africa) (Pty.) Ltd., 24 Sturdee Avenue,
Rosebank, Johannesburg 2196, South Africa

Penguin Books Ltd., Registered Offices:
80 Strand, London WC2R 0RL, England

First published by Heat, an imprint of New American Library,
a division of Penguin Group (USA) Inc.

First Printing, March 2009
10 9 8 7 6 5 4 3 2 1

LIBRARY OF CONGRESS CATALOGING-IN-PUBLICATION DATA:

Hart, Carole, 1965–
The family jewels/Carole Hart.
p. cm.
ISBN 978-0-451-22637-2
I. Thieves—Fiction. I. Title.
PS3614.E66F36 2009
813'.6—dc22   2008034894

Set in Centaur MT
Designed by Ginger Legato

Printed in the United States of America

To Victoria Hobbs

Chapter One

"You're not dressed for it, are you, darling?" said André, looking with drowsy speculation at Olivia's flimsy halter top. His faint German accent was tinged with the British tones he'd picked up in his English private school, and there was a cultivated decorum even in his lustful glance. Everything about him, in fact, was painfully upper-crust, as it should be. After all, André *was* the thirty-fourth Count von Fremberg-Asp in an unbroken line going back to— Well, Olivia wasn't sure what. Did they have Neanderthal man in Austria? André had mentioned the Holy Roman Empire, but she wasn't sure where his family fit into it, or in fact what it was, though it certainly sounded impressive. André was also unsettlingly handsome, dazzlingly charming, a man who could kiss a girl's hand without looking silly. His melting, hypnotizingly sleepy brown eyes were just the finishing touch to a physique that had been entrancing Olivia—a little too much—for five days now. It was certainly going to be hard to leave André behind.

"Do you want a leg up?"

"Oh—no, thanks." Olivia eyed the horse distrustfully. Dorset was a lovely pale gray Thoroughbred, almost silvery, an elegant animal—but enormous. Could the size be normal? Was it a special breed of giant horse ridden by the aristocracy? Every time he lifted one of his hooves and let it drop again, sounding like a hundred pounds of dead weight, Olivia had to grit her teeth to keep from flinching. The groom was holding the bridle with a perfectly blank expression, which only made Olivia more convinced that he was onto her. The instant she trotted off on the back of this dinosaur, she was certain the groom would be confiding his suspicions to André. He was an annoyingly attractive man, too—a big hulk of a blond man with big strong hands. It was all wrong for a man like that to dislike her; it was against nature. But, hell, as long as she survived long enough to be thrown out, she would be relieved at this point.

The worst of it was that the horse had taken a dislike to her on sight. He had immediately begun to nip at her and irritably kick at nothing in particular. She shouldn't take it personally, André explained. "Dorset doesn't like women—probably because of Mama."

It was all her own fault; she had thought it would be better to pretend that she had grown up with horses, because she was posing as the sort of Ivy League girl who did. And after all, she had ridden a horse twice, when she was thirteen. She couldn't have forgotten everything. In the car on the way here, it had all seemed so easy, such an adventure, like trying out white-water rafting for kicks.

"Sure you don't want that leg up?"

"I— Maybe." Then, inspired, Olivia blurted out, "I guess what I used to ride was more, like, ponies?"

André burst out laughing, making the horse toss his head again, rolling his eyes back superstitiously at Olivia. André said, "He's not so awfully big for a jumper, you know."

Olivia stopped herself just in time from crying out, *He's not going to jump with me on him, is he?* She took a deep breath and said, "Well, leg up, then."

André put out his interlocked hands, and before she could think any further, Olivia stepped into them, grasped the saddle, and swung herself up into the air and on.

Immediately she was surprised by how alive the horse felt between her legs. The feeling of him dancing under her, combined with being so high up, made her feel instantly elated. It was like the moment when the roller coaster begins to move. She looked off up the road, with the bridle path that ran alongside through a copse of trees before taking a turn into an Alpine meadow. Once she was out in that clearing, she knew, there would be a view of snowy mountain ranges against a piercingly blue sky. Already in the day she'd been here, she had come to love the Austrian Alps, and the idea of riding through the meadow with the mountains rising above her now made her heart swell. "Well, got up here, anyway," she said, a little breathless.

André smiled up at her and let one hand drift onto her bare

thigh. "I shouldn't let you ride without boots, really. I'd hate to see you get scratched up. Your skin is so lovely. I know you don't think so. . . ."

Olivia smiled a little weakly. As a natural blonde, she had pale skin that would only take a tan out of a bottle—and even then it was more likely to come out in tiger stripes. "Do Austrian girls all have this colorless skin?"

"You don't understand what you have," André replied.

Then the groom was reaching up the reins to her and she was taking them in both hands, tightening them with as much care, as much sensitivity as she could. Meanwhile Dorset had begun to edge to one side—it was a feeling uncomfortably like being in a car when it skids on ice. The combination of André's appreciative looks and the simple physical sensation of the horse between her legs gave Olivia an unwanted, unexpected surge of heat through her belly, ending in a fiery point of desire in her cunt. She looked down at André, finding the shape of his muscles under his polo shirt, the deep, powerful chest he had, the—

The horse turned his head entirely around to stare back at her in disbelief and outrage. Then he reared slightly, sprang forward, and was galloping at breakneck speed down the road with Olivia clinging to his mane for dear life.

André was very wrong to accuse Olivia of not understanding what she had. There could hardly be a girl in the world with as exact an appreciation of what she had. There was what she could make men do. There was how absentminded they became when she was in the room. And finally, most crudely, there was her bank account, representing the amount she'd been able to steal over the years, with the unwitting help of men who had been beguiled by her looks and her sexual prowess. She had long pale blond hair, blue eyes, and a cherubic face with deep pink pouting lips—looks that made both men and women stare at her, even when she was wearing a sweatshirt.

When she was dressed with flirting in mind, the stares were of a different nature. Olivia had had generous, rounded, D-cup breasts since she was fifteen. The rest of her body was always a little chubbier than she would like, and her skin a little whiter. But men never seemed to notice, or care. Once, when she and her sister, Lee, were watching *Heroes* on television, Lee had said, "What would your superpower be?"

"My superpower is being blond with big breasts," Olivia said without thinking.

"Nothing like knowing yourself!" Lee hooted.

Olivia opened her mouth to protest, but shut it again. Lee was grinning at her knowingly. "Well, you're actually prettier than me," Olivia muttered at last.

Lee started laughing. She said, "Oh, okay. That means a lot."

"It does!" Olivia said.

"Never mind," Lee said. "No one could make better use of it than you."

Then Olivia laughed, too, and had to admit that that was true.

Olivia had always been boy crazy in the filthiest way. She didn't just like men's bodies; she loved men's bodies, and men's habits, and men's clothes, and men's deep voices. She loved the moment when a man kissed her and she felt the telltale signs that he was losing control, the moment when she knew she was going to sleep with him. She loved most of all the moment when he first pressed his dick against her pussy, and paused, and then shoved into her. When she forgot everything and hung on for dear life. She always felt half in love with a man she was fucking, or in fact with any good-looking man she met. When they broke her heart—half broke it, anyway—she didn't hold it against them. She broke hearts all the time, and there were always more hearts where they came from. That was what her life was about, at least half of the time.

The other half of the time her life was about extremely expensive jewelry that wasn't exactly, in the eyes of the law, hers, but which could be spirited away from its owners in a delightful variety of ways. If no alarms had been set off in obtaining it, it was simply hidden in her overnight bag, usually in a box of Tampax. If alarms were ringing, it might be buried in an out-of-the-way place against a future opportunity. Once she had even used a trained dog, to whose sweater she had added a clever compartment; and then there was the unhappy occasion on which in desperation she had stuffed her pussy with a Van Cleef & Arpels diamond necklace—ouch, never again.

Beautiful jewelry, like beautiful men, appealed to her dreamy, romantic nature. While it remained in her hands, she would look at it again and again. So many of the pieces were originally bought as pledges of love; some of them had wild stories of fatal passion attached to them, typically about a man who impoverished his family to buy an elusive mistress the trinkets she coveted. And back in the day, before Olivia had started planning for the future, when she was still drunk on her newfound wealth and freedom, she had worn the jewelry sometimes. She would fly to some out-of-the-way place—Costa Rica, Stockholm, or even just Montana—so that she could wear her purloined rubies and emeralds with impunity. Then she would find herself sitting at a bar wearing cool, brilliant jewels against her skin and little else; the gems seemed to radiate passion into the surrounding night, the strange city. Sooner or later a man would sit beside her at the bar and ask what she was drinking. Then she would encourage him to touch the gems, his fingers brushing against her cleavage, her neck, her tender wrists, until she was tingling all over with the cool-hot desire. "Do you like my necklace? The earrings match. Feel them—the stones are real." It could end in bed, or it could end in a doorway. Either way, the jewels made her utterly fearless, shameless, as if they were all-powerful weapons. She would always be wet with an electrifying sensitivity that made coming seem almost cosmic, like thunder in the sky. Fucking while wearing only gems—stolen gems—was a high unlike any other sex in the world.

Just that morning she had convinced André to open his mother's safe and drape her with the ropes of pearls—three of varying lengths, pink, white, and black—his mother, Belinda, had received as a wedding present from his father. André was mainly fearful that Belinda would return and find them naked on the Persian rug in the study. While he opened the safe, Olivia began to strip for him, saying, "I want to feel them against my skin," which was true—but also ensured that he wouldn't notice the keen way her eyes followed his movements as he worked the combination lock.

She was wearing a short wraparound skirt and a halter top both in the same blue linen that set off her eyes. It was all held up with bows, so first she undid these so that the linen just gently clung to her skin, remaining in place until she began to dance, freeing it to flutter away onto the floor. Then André was scrabbling through jewelry cases with his eyes on her trembling breasts, their pale pink nipples stiffening under his gaze. Olivia gave up trying to think about the gems, the money, the job, and let herself respond to André's intent gaze, his brown eyes raking up and down her body, lingering on the little strip of pale blond pubic hair she'd left above her pussy. By the time he stood with the long ropes of pearls in his hands, her pussy was aching with lust. He slung the longest string of pearls around her neck, and the chill stones made her shiver all over. As he pressed himself against her, the strings were crushed into her breasts almost painfully. The shape of the erection in his jeans made her feel her own wetness clearly. He was saying, in his deep, serious voice, "You're so sexy in those, they should belong to you. And you should belong to me."

Then he suddenly reached between her legs and slipped two fingers inside her. Olivia gasped and he simultaneously leaned down and took her nipple in his mouth, sucking it while he finger-fucked her. And then she felt him working a string of pearls into her and cried out involuntarily at the cold, slick touch. The pearls were slipping over her clitoris and in and out of her vagina, helped by his strong fingers.

She whispered, "Fuck me. Please, with the—"

"Yes," he said, and he was pulling his jeans down and she felt the tip of his cock pressing against her, the heat of the sensitive skin there making her dizzy beside the chill of the stones. And then he was fucking into her, the pearls moving around his cock in a complicated swirling that set off immediate spasms of orgasm. She was against the wall without knowing how she'd gotten there, and André was driving his thick cock into her, overfilling her with the slipping, unpredictable stones like a hundred tiny orgasms filling her cunt. Then, as he pressed into her one last time, shouting out in a hoarse, loving note of climax, Olivia's eyes drifted languidly, gratefully, to the open safe, and the tumbled boxes there. Everything was going to be perfect.

The von Fremberg-Asp jewels were renowned among connoisseurs. The stones were of extraordinary quality—especially a certain flawless blue sapphire that was the largest of its quality in the world, and a diamond that was relatively small but had belonged to Marie Antoinette. Some had been exhibited in museums. The settings were of exceptional artistry, which wasn't usually important in Olivia's business. It could even be bad, psychologically. You didn't like to be the one responsible for destroying a beautiful piece of craftsmanship when the gold, silver, and platinum were melted down and sold as metal. But with antique jewelry of the very highest class, collectors would pay through the nose for a piece that could never be worn in public, or even seen by anyone but the owner.

Olivia never walked into a job blind, and she already knew what she was likely to get for this heist. It would net her half a million dollars—give or take fifty thousand. It was a dream job made all the dreamier by the fact that it involved seducing and reseducing the very beautiful and athletic André.

There was only one problem. It was a problem Olivia had had

before, but perhaps never to such a degree. André was sweet, a little in love with her, a darling in every way. She was a little in love with him, too, especially with his body, which was lean and powerful from the tennis he played semiprofessionally. He had a tennis player's quick physical intelligence, and she never stopped being impressed by the way he moved. How could a man move beautifully even when on all fours, looking for a lost earring, completely naked? Most of her targets had been impossible narcissists, or threw temper tantrums, or at least they were rude to waiters. There was *something* to dislike about them, apart from their being unforgivably way too rich. There was something to latch on to when her conscience acted up, some straw to grasp. With André, there was nothing. He was a wonderful person, and a mind-blowing lover. Finally, he was already having a hard time. Because, as she had learned in the past week, the last count, André's uncle, had frittered away the family fortune on card games, horses, and gold diggers. Every medieval stone of the castle was mortgaged; the grounds, the art, and the furniture likewise belonged to the bank. Unless some miracle occurred, André and his mother would be moving out within the year, never to return. The horse that was currently running away with Olivia, nearly pitching her into the mud with every leap, was the last thing in the world that André von Fremberg-Asp owned free and clear.

After the first shock, Olivia managed to get a grip on the horse, holding on with her legs and tangling her fingers deep in the thick mane. She even managed to catch the reins, which had slipped from her grasp at the first leap. Leaning down so that the pommel of the saddle pressed into her stomach, she inhaled the sweetly earthy scent of the horse's skin, and her panic began to settle into a wild thrill. Dorset was taking off along the exact path she had planned—probably the route he knew best. The trees flashed past, one branch zipping by hazardously close to her ear. Her heart was pounding as Dorset came out into the clear and the two of them galloped at breakneck speed along a path that skirted a pale and spacious valley, with wildflowers tingeing the light green April grass. The scent of the meadow was intoxicating, and Olivia just had time to sit back a little, taking in the sweep of the distant mountains, when the horse stopped dead. She went sailing, head over heels, over Dorset's head.

For a moment she was simply knocked flat, her whole body ringing with the splat of her fall. Her fingers were stinging where the reins had slid through them at lightning speed. She sat up gingerly, and was relieved to find she could still move all her limbs. In fact, apart from having the wind knocked out of her, the only pain she felt was in her fingers, and where the string of her halter top cut into her neck. She felt for the place, a little worried that her neck had been sliced into. There was no wound but there was no halter top either. Her eyes flew open, and she stared down at herself. In fact, she was sitting topless in the grass with her skirt flung up over her waist. Dorset was calmly grazing a few yards away.

The next thing she saw was a tall, thin, black-haired man staring at her from the woods with mingled concern and appreciation. When she snatched her top and covered herself, he shook his head and smiled. The next instant, he was gone, and the instant after that, André came running along the bridle path, shouting.

"I'm all right!" she shouted back to him. Dorset raised his head, looking haughtily at his approaching owner, and neighed expressively. Olivia laughed and said in an undertone, "Well, I wasn't fooling you, was I?"

Then André was in front of her, falling to his knees and saying anxiously, "You're all right? Are you sure? You're not hurt?"

"No," she laughed. "My top was—"

"Oh . . ." He actually blushed as his eyes went to her breasts. She couldn't help it; she blushed, too, and she felt the presence of that black-haired man in the woods. Somehow she knew he was still spying on her, and instinctively she arched her back slightly, as if to let him get a good look.

André leaned over her then and kissed her gently on the cheek. He said, "I was so frightened." And then he was moving on top of her, asking her gently, "Are you sure—is this all right?"

"Yes . . . I'm fine," she said, and the excitement of the ride on the runaway horse came back with a rush as she reached up under his shirt and felt the smooth muscles there. Then he was kissing her, his tongue twining expertly around hers and reminding her of what it was capable of down below. His hand found her breasts, triggering little memories where the pearls had left the slightest possible bruises. Her nipples ached with them, and she let her hands skate down the muscled landscape of his back to his firm buttocks. He pressed her down to the soft grass and she felt his erection hard against her thigh, making her moan out loud. He pulled her panties to one side and entered her for the second time that day, her cunt receiving him grate-fully, and sending surges of pleasure all through her body. She lay back, spreading her legs as wide as she could to bare her clitoral area to his thrusts, the shaft of his penis slipping down past her clit again and again, faster and faster, teasing the pleasure into flame. The sensations seemed to leap one over the other, a hot intensity that made her whimper helplessly and grip André's buttocks ever harder, pulling him into her again and again. His cock carved deep into her, strumming vibrations of joy through her thighs and stomach as well as her hypersensitized cunt. At last he cried out and pressed her to him, crushing her tender breasts against his smooth, hard chest and driving deep, opening her into an ecstatic climax. The feeling shocked her eyes open, and the intense blue of the sky became part of the intense sensa-tion, a pulsing sky-sized pleasure. Her orgasm easing, she turned her head away. Her eyes rested on the dark sage green and shadow of the forest.

Then she saw that same lean, black-haired man watching from a little nearer in the woods. He was wearing a T-shirt, and his crossed arms were powerful, big out of all proportion to his lean frame. His face had a sculpted elegance, a pretty-boy face that seemed in contrast to his careless, butch stance—and his eyes were knowing and friendly in a way that rang all too many bells.

Chapter Two

Olivia's mother had died when she was only four years old, and her sister, Lee, was two. Her father, Mitch, had never remarried. As he said, things being like they were, it would have had to be a rich lady, and no rich lady was likely to want him, with his struggling hardware store, his bad debts, and his two rambunctious girls. Lee and Olivia had both worked from the time they were thirteen: babysitting, paper routes, addressing envelopes while sitting in front of the TV watching *Buffy the Vampire Slayer*, season five, again and again. Mitch Stewart was a good, old-fashioned father, which meant that there were rules for everything. Since the girls were left on their own a lot of the time, he tried to set strict boundaries to keep them from getting into trouble—which was, unfortunately for Mitch, all Olivia had ever wanted to do from the time she was old enough to walk.

Olivia had read that older siblings were supposed to be the obedient ones who toed the line, while the baby of the family tended to be a rebel. In her family it was just the opposite. A typical scene from her teenage years was of her crawling in the bedroom window at two a.m., tousled and drunk, to find her little sister asleep with her head cushioned on an open chemistry textbook. By the time Olivia was fourteen, there was no point in Mitch grounding her. She would just nod very seriously, go to her room, and clamber out the window. It was silly pretending to ground someone, Olivia believed, in a one-story house. A naturally gentle man, Mitch was reduced to giving her stern lectures and withholding her allowance. Again, Olivia simply adjusted to circumstances and did without an allowance. Even when her wages from her various jobs fell short, a sympathetic boyfriend, suitably impressed by her tales of her tyrannical father, would always step in to buy her the shoes or the hot fudge sundae that she needed. The Stewarts lived in a town on Cape Cod where the average income was nearly ten times Mitch's, so it seemed completely reasonable to Olivia that the community should be paying for her manicures and her leg waxing and her first guitar. It was an early foretaste of her later dedication to the redistribution of wealth.

But on one point she would not defy her father, because she couldn't bear the thought of really breaking his heart. She would stay out till all hours, and smirk through the dressing-down she got over breakfast the following morning. She borrowed a little

Kawasaki dirt bike from a boyfriend, kept it in a clearing in the woods, and rode it for a month without a license. When she was finally pulled over by the cops, her father's pale face at the police station made her cringe, but she couldn't say she was honestly sorry. And her bad grades, which Mitch considered a criminal waste— Well, Olivia just knew better. She wasn't the studying type; there was nothing she could do about that. There were plenty of other ways to succeed in life, and she was firmly convinced that Mitch would eventually come around to her point of view once she proved herself.

But she knew that if her father thought she was sleeping with guys, it would kill him. He was from a Baptist family, and though he never went to church himself, there was no mistaking the sheer terror in his eyes when he asked her, uncomfortably, "You aren't getting in trouble with boys, are you?"

She would promise she wasn't, and wouldn't—at least, if trouble meant going all the way. On this point alone, she exercised complete self-control. Mitch seemed to understand the difference, because her avowals always reassured him. And even though she could have had a sneaky affair with one of the seasonal residents—whose sons she drank with most every summer night, after all—something stopped her. Perhaps her father's fear had infected her a little, in fact. There was such unfeigned terror in the way he talked about "fooling with boys," while never going into detail about how one went about that, or why it was bad.

So it was long steamy kisses and caresses in cars, on yachts, on the leather couches in the architectural homes of the summering classes—and then excuses and explanations while her whole body screamed at her to *Go ahead, let him, let him*. It didn't help that she was the acknowledged hottest girl in her school. By the time she was sixteen, she would sometimes meet boys on the beach and be told, "Yeah, I heard about you." Then her body would burn with the knowledge that wherever she went in public, boys—and men—were sneaking looks at her, following her body with their eyes and imagining stripping her, touching her. *Let him, let him*, her body chanted. Her pussy would ache with lust, and her breasts would tighten until she felt as if her nipples were rubbed raw. But she would say, as coolly as she could, "I don't do that with anyone."

If she couldn't sleep with boys, though, she could make out with as many as she wanted. That was her rule. Perhaps her semicelibacy made her all the more obsessive about sex. The last three years she spent at home, she couldn't remember thinking of anything else. Living in a beach town meant that there was an ever-circulating supply of boys and men, and Olivia made a study of the exact nature and limitations of the power she had over them. She never had a boyfriend for more than two weeks; once she phoned to break up with her current boyfriend from the open-top car in which she was about to open her blouse and let her next boyfriend do exactly what he'd been dreaming about—up to a point. But she wouldn't rest if any of her exes was angry at her, so the jilted lover would get a phone call the next day, too. Then a visit, and eventually, inevitably, another tour of Olivia's naked but cruelly inaccessible body.

There was a night when she'd had too much to drink and it

was three boys: prep school boys she'd been hanging out with for a few days, cracking silly jokes and then talking intensely, drunkenly, about how adults didn't understand what it meant to really cling to your dreams. Two of the boys, Nick and Charles, were football players, and Olivia had fallen so much in love with them that she actually confessed her love to the third, Zack, a more bookish type who immediately said, "No, you're supposed to be in love with me." So Olivia obligingly looked him in the eyes, and finding them to be beautiful and tender, said truthfully, "Oh, you're right—I am in love with you, too, I just hadn't realized it till you said that."

The night it happened, they had gone to the basement of Zack's parents' house, because it had a pool table. They were playing pool; then somehow they were playing strip pool. Olivia was at a disadvantage, not only because she wasn't a great pool player, but because she was only wearing two things: a dress and a pair of pale pink lace panties. Once she lost the dress, all thought of pool vanished from the boys' heads.

Olivia found herself standing with the dress around her feet and all three boys staring at her with a look of stunned need. Her cunt was tight with desire, and she could feel every inch of her breasts responding as if they had been teasingly caressed. The thin lace of her panties was soaked; she could feel the wetness rich there when she shifted her weight from foot to foot. She was simultaneously frightened of what might happen, and longing for all three of them to just take her, hold her down, and make her do what she really wanted to do. Finally Charles said, in a pained, husky voice, "Olivia, I'll do anything for you, anything you want, if you'll let me touch you."

"I can't—I can't fuck you," she whispered.

Zack started to laugh. "Don't worry. Don't be afraid, Livy. We're still your friends."

"I'm not," said Nick.

This time all of them laughed. Then Olivia swallowed, trying to control her voice—if they knew what a state she was in, they would never let her get away without taking all three of their cocks in her untried pussy. . . . The thought of it made her shut her eyes hard. Then she found herself saying, with her eyes still shut, "I can't fuck you. But you can touch me any way you want."

She kept her eyes shut and waited. So she didn't know whose hand it was that first touched her—on the cheek. It stroked her cheek comfortingly, then traced a line down her neck, her collar-bone, and finally ventured—by now trembling—onto the ample curve of her left breast. One finger tickled across her nipple, making her gasp. Then the hand cupped her breast and squeezed it appreciatively. At the same time, startling her, another hand cupped her other breast, crushing it hungrily, so that she made a noise low in her throat and licked her lips.

Then there were hands all over her, slipping down the taut flatness of her belly to teasingly, lightly test the surface of her panties, pressing gently against her flimsily covered clitoris so that she moaned and reached out blindly to be supported. Then she was being carried and set down on top of the pool table. The hands were feeling under her panties; fingers were slipping into her while someone began to suck her breast, tenderly at first, but then more fiercely, nibbling at her hypersensitive nipple. She was moaning regularly now, and her pussy was beginning to spasm around the anonymous fingers inside her—two different hands were there, the fingers sliding past one another as they finger-fucked her at different rates. One of them began to slip his thumb across her clit rapidly, back and forth, at the speed of her racing heartbeat. And when she came, under the eyes of those three near-strangers, it was a force that pressed her hard against the pool table, that made her give out a strangled cry and buck her cunt up, welcoming the hands. At the last second, the or-gasm seemed to start all over again from a new plateau as she imagined clearly, to the point of feeling it, their three cocks, one in her hand, one in her mouth, one in her pussy. . . .

Not just that night of excess, but even simple make-out sessions left her feeling as if she'd run a marathon. Her body went through so much longing and pleasure and cheated longing again that she got home feeling limp and helpless. Sometimes it felt as if her skin was a paradise all to itself. Her pussy was an over-whelming presence in her life, with its sudden zinging desires, its keen pleasures that blotted out everything, and the sleepy sloppi-ness she carried around with her most days, the wet pussy always aware of the cock she wouldn't let it have. And no matter how worn-out she felt, as soon as she got into bed at home, or even just into the bathroom, she had to reach down and make herself come—once, twice, three times, imagining what it would have been like if she had let her lover of the evening go all the way and sink his dick— Oh, God!

Part of her understood that this couldn't go on forever. It wasn't realistic to expect her to stay a virgin until marriage, and nothing less would really spare Mitch's feelings. Was she really willing to marry at eighteen? And would that even help? Wouldn't she keep on wanting more and different men, the way she did now? Wouldn't she always be fickle and lovesick for five men at once? Still, she was only sixteen—seventeen—eighteen. She had only just finished high school. Surely she didn't have to decide yet. There was no hurry yet.

Then she met Paul.

The Austrian Alps were shimmering in the clear sunlight as Olivia and André walked back, leading Dorset—who still occasionally tossed his head with an impulse of self-congratulation. The groom laughed when told, and gave Olivia a friendlier look. She smiled at him with the sincerity of one of her instant crushes, and he met her eye with a frank hunger that made everything comprehensible. He wanted to fuck her, of course. He was angry because he thought that girls like her were only for rich guys. Well, maybe she would have a chance to cure him of that unhealthy cynicism.

She let her eyes go languid as she told the groom, "I'm sorry I wasn't up to Dorset's standard."

He shook his head.

André said, "You're forgetting Jenz only speaks German."

"Oh." Olivia cocked her head and, without thinking about it, licked her lips. Then she was rewarded by an intensifying in the groom's blue eyes. She said, awkwardly, *"Danke schön,"* and the groom and André both laughed.

"Your accent is very sweet," André said.

Olivia smiled. "I guess I'll take that as a compliment. Though I know very well it's not . . ."

The Schloss von Fremberg-Asp was not a proper castle, not anymore. The castle with its fortifications had been destroyed three times in three different wars. The current *schloss* was really an eighteenth-century mansion. It was a heavily decorated building, more overtly opulent than equivalent palatial homes in England or the United States. Its floors were polished honey-colored granite, and the pilasters that ornamented every room were of a forest green stone. Paintings in heavy, fantastically carved frames hung in three rows, from ceiling down to just below eye level. The furniture was the only thing that betrayed, here and there, the dilapidated state of the family finances. The velvet on one sofa was worn through to an unhealthy shine on the arms. A table leg, gnawed by one of the family's deerhounds, had been left with its splinters showing, unrepaired. Some rooms had only a few pieces of furniture left, the most valuable pieces having been sold to make mortgage payments.

Also, if Olivia had been here the year before (André had explained with a grimace on the drive up), there would have been a three-course lunch prepared by a chef; there would have been a waiter in white gloves to serve it. Now there was only his mother, Belinda, gamely cooking for the first time in her life.

"If you cut off the burned parts," she was saying now, "the lamb may yet be edible. I'm not promising anything, you understand." She was a lean woman of about fifty who looked thirty-five, her glossy brown hair still hanging halfway down her back, her chiseled features smooth, and her body still gracefully slender. André had warned Olivia that his mother was renowned for her frankness, even rudeness. She had been the daughter of a notoriously debauched British marquis who kept his estate full of concubines recruited from local cashiers and bank tellers, and her irregular upbringing had made her into an irrepressibly, cheerfully shocking person. She had greeted Olivia by saying, "Oh, exactly what we need! A really stunning girl without any money for my son to marry! That's wonderful, André. I shall be delighted to share a one-bedroom apartment with Miss Stewart. She is a pleasure to look at. It will gladden our poverty."

"Mother, you promised," he said in an exhausted voice. "What nonsense, really."

"Oh, for God's sake, can't you laugh at a joke anymore? It is the only pleasure left to us, after all." And she said to Olivia, taking her hand, "But you really mustn't marry him, darling. It would be too thoughtless. He is pretty enough to find an heiress, and after all, heiresses are getting more attractive every day. It's not like when I was a girl—they were like the chorus in a painting by Hieronymus Bosch."

Olivia forced a laugh, adding another item to her private list of things to Google. She said, "Any special kind of heiress you would like?"

"Oh!" Belinda grinned and put a hand up to straighten her hair. "I think anything with a Learjet is fine. Money doesn't stain."

The delightful—to Olivia if not to André—outspokenness of the count's mother also bore unsuspected fruit. As they gave up on the charred lamb and all had double helpings of chocolate ice cream, Belinda remarked, "I think you were nosing about in my jewels, Count—"

"Don't call me 'Count,' for God's sake," André muttered. Olivia was amused to see that even an aristocrat could be turned into a five-year-old boy by his mother.

"Well, then, Your Excellentness," Belinda went on, unabashed, "I think Your Excellencehood has been at my jewels. I didn't have time to do an inventory, but I do hope you haven't been making any impulsive presents."

"Of course not, Mum. And if you can't use my name—"

"Oh, but I mean it as an endearment. It's like 'sweetheart.'" Belinda turned to Olivia sweetly. "You see, I don't begrudge you it, and I'm sure those jewels would suit you better than anyone else, especially"—she narrowed her eyes as if forming a mental picture—"mmm, yes, the pearls. I think the pearls."

André looked at Olivia rather desperately, shaking his head. She was desperately trying to stifle a laugh.

Belinda went on. "But, you see, the trouble is they don't belong to us, do they, darling?"

André broke in in a dry, factual voice. "They do belong to us, but only in trust. They can be worn, but they can't be sold. They don't exactly belong to anyone unless I have children."

"Female children," Belinda added. "My brother-in-law, the last Count von Fremberg-Asp, was a poisonous bastard. When he turned out to be infertile, it nearly made me believe in the existence of God. The creature absolutely hated me. If he'd lived long enough, though, he might have liked André. I think he secretly fancied boys—he was that sort of womanizer. But you were still at school, Your Excellent—"

"Mother, *müsst du*—"

"Don't you know it's rude to speak German in front of your friend? Perhaps Adolf wouldn't have liked you after all." She turned to Olivia. "That was the late count's name. Adolf. Born in 'thirty-eight. A delightful family, all around."

Olivia said, "But surely you don't . . . I mean, André's father . . . ?" Then she blushed, afraid that Belinda was going to say André's father was another womanizing bastard.

But Belinda smiled. "Oh, he wasn't like that. He wasn't like that at all. But you see, he was illegitimate. It was the masculine line where the trouble lay, and he and André are both as charming—well as charming as a certain film actor who used to be a regular visitor to this house, many years before you were born. That's pure speculation, of course—there's no knowing whether the actor was the culprit. André's grandmother entertained widely."

Meanwhile, Olivia felt relief coursing through her. She had just realized what this meant. In stealing the gems, she wouldn't even exactly be robbing André—just his notional female children, who might never in fact exist.

It was past midnight before Olivia let André fall off into well-earned sleep. By that time he had fucked her for the third time that day and fallen asleep gratefully only to be awakened by the expert ministrations of her hand; fucked her again, sleepily, side by side this time and heroically managed to come a second— or fourth—time; fallen asleep; been wrenched out of sleep, less happily, by her mouth making him hard again, and come a third time, barely, without ever having really woken up. It was a formula that Olivia had found absolutely foolproof over the years. The key was to withhold oral until the third time. Otherwise they wouldn't wake up for it, and you were stuck with an imperfectly sedated lover. With this method, she could count on André to sleep through anything up to and including a tornado tearing the house down all around him.

There had been one occasion, with a particularly objectionable Wall Street trader, when she'd foregone all this in favor of a simple dose of sleeping pills crumbled into a (very) dirty martini. But then she'd found herself developing hypochondria on his behalf, and spent the next two hours checking his pulse obsessively. Usually she preferred to rely on her own hard work and dedication. It had the convenient side effect that—so far—no man had ever suspected her. Some of them had provided a hurriedly concocted alibi for her in the belief that she couldn't possibly be guilty and therefore shouldn't have to be investigated. No man could believe that a woman who had loved him up *that* enthusiastically could have any motive for doing it but true passion. The masculine ego had been her safety net through two dozen heists, large and small. It probably helped that she generally did have a delicious crush on her poor targets. Her passion was real, and there were a few men she'd continued to sleep with for months after relieving them of their diamonds.

But no passion would ever get in the way of her work. When it came to work, there were no favorites and no exceptions. Olivia could have fallen in love, gotten married, and stolen a display case full of engagement rings from her husband on their wedding night (something she had once contemplated when introduced to an unusually suspicious—and sexy—man who owned an up-market jewelry store). Somewhere in the back of her head, she was convinced that if she'd explained the entire situation to these rich men, they would have offered her the gems out of the goodness of their hearts. She just didn't believe it quite *enough* to ever try asking.

Now she slipped out of bed and went to her little Coach travel case—a sweet thing in soft mustard leather, with a few clever modifications of her own invention. The lining, which still *appeared* to be stitched neatly to the leather, was in fact only attached with Velcro, and now, pulling it free, she revealed a generous secret compartment. She pulled out a little toiletries bag and weighed it in her hand. As always, she had to pause to fully absorb the excitement. It was a shame that there would be no one there to really *share* the experience.

Her mind went to the black-haired man she'd spotted in the woods, and she frowned, all the excitement turning to anxiety. She shook her head as if to free it of unwanted thoughts and pressed the compartment shut again, rising and heading to the corridor. She hadn't been sure until that instant whether she was going to dress. Now she went off nude out of instinct. If Belinda woke up and caught her before she arrived at the study, the nudity would be its own alibi. No one would go to crack a safe in the nude, after all. Also, there was just the slightest chance that she would find an old friend already there. In that case, her nudity would be her ambassador, as it had been in a hundred tight spots before. Finally, crucially, the nudity made the entire theft into a sexual act.

As she walked, her breasts trembled, and the cool night air seemed to explore her body, setting off chills over her buttocks and along her slightly raw labia. She was especially aware of her bare pussy, still luxuriously wet from the sexual marathon she'd just completed. Her body was full of afterglow, and every movement had a slight aphrodisiac overtone; every step reverberated in her cunt like a memory of a cock driving in. She passed Belinda's bedroom with a practiced, achingly slow cat tread. The door to the study had been left ajar, and she slipped through sideways. On being closed, it squealed gently and gave out a click that sounded like a rifle shot to Olivia. Then she turned the bolt to lock the door, a second rifle shot. Olivia held her breath and waited.

Nothing. She smiled and her body seemed to fill with electricity. Her knees were weak for a moment and then she took a deep breath and turned to the safe.

It took only a few seconds for her to turn the combination lock, and the safe popped open with that beautiful welcoming gesture. It always reminded her of someone pulling her into a kiss for the first time. It said: *Come and get it.* She opened the safe with a broad, meltingly satisfied grin on her face—and froze.

It was empty. She stared into it, registering for the first time how very deep it was—how many jewels must have fit in here! It was as big as the Fouriers' safe in Monte Carlo had been. But this one was empty.

A little scrap of paper lay in the center of the empty safe. She picked it up, already furious. Written on it was:

Darling, So sorry to leave you with the blame.
Call me—but not from jail. 212-555-3419.

Paul

Chapter Three

At first, Paul had just been another hot guy on the beach. In Penntucket, there were two beaches: the Scott Memorial Public Beach, which was always crowded to capacity, and a cleaner, almost deserted stretch of beach that ran in front of the homes of the wealthiest families in town. Theoretically there were nine different private beaches there, but in practice, if you were welcome on one, you were likely to be able to cross them all without disturbing anyone. It was a tight-knit, old-money community where the first families had been inviting one another to parties, marrying one another, and being buried in the same little graveyard, overshadowed by ancient oak trees, for hundreds of years. So a Blake son could happily wipe out his surfboard on the Markleby beach, while the Markleby daughters, when they went running on the beach, would do a double circuit of the private waterfront, stopping short of the boundary to the public beach, where profane eyes might see them.

Every year there were new faces at Scott Memorial—people who were staying in the bed-and-breakfasts in town, city people from Boston and New York who had rented summer cottages. While some of these people were even wealthier than the local aristocrats, they would never be welcomed onto the hallowed sand that fronted their mansions. Until the year she turned eighteen, Olivia had never been welcome there either. She sometimes swam past and spied on the forbidden paradise—occasionally seeing a Markleby mother yawning in a deck chair, or a Harker father throwing a stick of driftwood for an Irish setter.

But the year she was eighteen, she became best friends with Athena Markleby. They had had a boyfriend in common, whom neither of them liked. One drunken night, they had started by doing imitations of him, progressed to confidences, and Olivia ended the night sleeping on the huge sofa that Athena had in her bedroom. That sofa was Olivia's first lesson in how the rich were different. It was the kind of thing that made sense after you saw it, but which she could never have predicted before seeing it. Olivia's bedroom had nothing in it but a bed, a dresser, and her sister, Lee.

Athena was a redhead with a slim, lithe body that seemed made for designer clothes. At home, on the beach, or in a Pizza Hut, she would be wearing some Marc Jacobs minidress that made both the boys and the girls stare. It wasn't clear to Olivia why she was suddenly Athena's favorite. After that first night, she seldom saw her alone; it was always a cocktail party on the

private beach, or a sailing trip with assorted brothers and cousins on Nantucket Sound. She sometimes felt like a stray dog that
Athena had adopted because it was cute. Over time, Athena began to dress her, too; Olivia was sent home with bags full of last
year's fashions until she had accumulated an entire wardrobe of
ex-Athena clothes.

So that year started out as the Athena Year, the time when
Olivia first slept in a ten-thousand-dollar bed and realized that
even the sleep was better when you were rich; when she first realized some people routinely spent two hundred dollars on a bottle
of wine. It was the first time she ever saw someone in real life
wearing diamonds on anything but an engagement ring. It was
the year of realizing, for a confused moment, that if she married
a Markleby type, she would never have to work again—that she
could wear Marc Jacobs dresses and drink champagne every
night, and never worry again. All Athena's parties were full of
boys in clean-smelling, expensive clothes who were eager to corner Olivia and whisper compliments into her ear as a prelude to
kissing her with a skill her old public-beach boyfriends could
not match. There was always some Harvard freshman unbuttoning her blouse with all his arrogance suddenly turned into abject
need. These boys bought her her first gold jewelry and expensive
perfume. And there was something dizzying about knowing any
one of them could change her life. In that way, these horny kids
had the powers of gods; they could make all her problems disappear by simply speaking a sentence.

By the end of the year, though, she knew she would never take
that route. Perhaps it was the feeling that she would always be

beholden to someone, would owe him something she could never repay. More likely she just wasn't the marrying kind—at least not at eighteen. She loved men plural, or men serially. To win her heart, a man needed two qualities: a modicum of good looks and being in the same room. Giving up men plural would have been like turning her back on her true love. But before she realized that, it was the Year of Rich Boys, a summer laced with dreams of an easy life.

It was only later, in retrospect, that it turned into the Year of Paul.

He had appeared first, as all new people did, on the public beach. Olivia was there with a boyfriend of the moment, which one she didn't remember. Paul was alone.

It often happened that Olivia would be startled by some new man's beauty on the beach. She would think that, finally, this was the most handsome man she had ever seen, that she would ever see. Then she felt as if she were programmed from birth to find The Most Handsome Man in the World, and pursue him with all her might, as if that was what she was born for.

But the man would smile and show crooked yellow teeth, and close up, he would turn out to have bad skin. On inspection, his legs would turn out to be skinny and have a strange stripy pattern of hair. These details would not stop Olivia from hunting him down, flirting with him mercilessly, and falling into one of her desperate, dreamy spells of heavy petting with him. . . . However, she liked to think that, deep down, she was an aesthete. And as soon as she saw the skinny legs, a little part of her would

detach and start looking again for The Most Handsome Man in the World.

When she saw Paul, she was so ready for disappointment that her heart sank ahead of time. He had beautiful thick black hair that had grown out a little too long, just like she liked it. His body was strong and tanned, and he had a delicious breadth of shoulder tapering to a muscular but lean waist and hips. When he stood up, his ass was something amazing—it was perfect, round and taut in a way that made her gulp. So she was sure, absolutely sure, that when she met him in person, he would turn out to have a lazy eye, or pockmarks, or just be so hopelessly idiotic that his good looks would be spoiled.

But she didn't meet him. Whenever she went to the public beach, he was there. He was always alone. He never talked to anyone she knew. He never met her eye.

She didn't exactly become obsessed with him. Not exactly. She did, perhaps, begin to neglect Athena a little bit. She started to have an unaccountable preference for the crowded, dirty public beach and to find the private beaches—on all of which she was now welcome, as a domino effect of having become a friend of one of the big families—well, to find the private beaches a little too private, to the point of boring. And when she did go down to the public beach, she would always look for the black-haired man. More and more often, she went alone.

At first, she decided he must be an actor; he was too beautiful to be anything else. Once she saw him walk down to the water, though, and dive in with a powerful and careless agility—no, she decided on the spot, he was an athlete. Probably a professional athlete; he had a sports injury and he was here recuperating.

Then she saw him having a conversation with an ice-cream vendor and decided that his face was too intelligent for that. He was an entrepreneur, a millionaire genius. Or—as time went on and she became frankly infatuated and even obsessed—he might as well be a prince in hiding. If not a god.

One day, when the patch of beach next to him was free, she went, with her heart pounding, to spread her towel next to his. He continued to lie still, with his eyes closed, for an hour. She wondered whether she ought to give him a shove. Perhaps he had fallen asleep, and she could be the one to save him from a terrible sunburn? She could say something; she could say, "Are you asleep?" Even if he wasn't, it would be all right. She would look like a compassionate person, someone who noticed the problems of other people.

No, she would look like the hundredth girl that week who had tried to get his attention. Why was it that this one man was so impossible to approach? He was older, but not that much older. Maybe thirty, at most. And usually Olivia didn't have a problem; she would walk right up to someone and ask him—but what did she ask men? Now that she really needed a line, she couldn't think of anything. "The ocean is beautiful today." Stupid! "Are you from the city?" Boring! "You're motherfucking gorgeous and I want to get naked with you." Well . . . no, she was losing her mind.

Olivia sighed but continued staring frankly at him. To her despair, close up he was just as beautiful as he was faraway, with the difference that he was close up, so the power his looks had was overwhelming. She was almost afraid of touching him, as if it would turn her to stone. His skin was too smooth and his tan too golden. His chest was too perfectly molded, and the way his flat stomach led down to . . . Then he opened his eyes and he was looking straight at her.

She gasped. His eyes were blue. They were an icy cornflower blue that she wouldn't have guessed from his tan, his black hair. As he smiled, she realized fully for the first time how beautiful his mouth was. Then she realized that he was smiling at her. All she could think was that he was motherfucking gorgeous and she wanted to get naked with him. Surely honesty was the best policy?

Before she could say anything or even smile, though, he was on his feet. He strode off down to the water and through the shallows, then dove in with that careless masculine grace.

For the next hour, she was lost in a sexual fantasy. He was going to come back out of the sea and walk straight up to her. He would take her hand without saying a word and she would follow him through the crowd, up to the parking lot. They would get into his car and— No, this was taking too long. She jumped the fantasy forward to them arriving in the driveway of his house, which was in a secluded place, deep in the forest. He got out of the car and came around to her door. She knew in the fantasy that once she stepped out of the car, she would have to give herself to him—there would be no going back.

He opened the door. She got to her feet and then he was pressing himself against her, his tongue in her mouth, his hands pulling off the bikini top. Then pulling down her bikini bottom. His fingers were playing in and out of her cunt as she moaned and whispered to him that he could do anything—anything.

Let him just come back. He could do anything. She couldn't wait any longer to give her virginity to him. She needed his cock. Somehow she knew this was the one.

Olivia waited for three hours. The beach crowd was thinning out and she had developed a burn on the tip of her nose when she finally gathered her things and crept off home with her tail between her legs.

He never came back. For the next three days, Olivia went to the beach and hung out for an hour or so before giving up. Then she would just stop there in her car on her way somewhere—to Athena's again, most often, now that her obsession had up and gone. She would get out of the car, do a quick circuit of the beach, and buy an ice cream on the way out, for cover. Half the time she would throw the ice cream away. She had actually lost her appetite. She had lost five pounds that summer, and she felt ridiculous that her worst-ever case of lovesickness should be for a man she had never met.

Two weeks passed, and she began to recover her equilibrium. He had obviously been on vacation, and now he had gone back home. It happened all the time—it would have been amazing if he hadn't gone back home. By the time he came back, if he came back, it would be the following year, and Olivia had already planned to move to New York City with Athena. She was crazy, but she wasn't crazy enough to give up her whole life plan for a man— Oh, God, that man! If only she knew he was coming back, she would give it all up without a second thought!

She next saw Paul at a Fourth of July party thrown by the Harkers, who lived next door to Athena. The party was held indoors, with an excursion planned to the beach in time to watch the municipal fireworks. Olivia was staying the night in the Harker house; she was a great favorite with Mrs. Harker, a chubby unpretentious woman who lived for her garden. Olivia had won her over forever the day she had been taken on a tour of that garden and blurted out in the middle, "I can't believe anything real could be so beautiful!" with actual tears in her eyes. Mrs. Harker had developed the idea that Olivia must live in some impossibly seedy hovel, and could never be made comfortable again with the thought of sending her home.

What prevented Olivia from taking more advantage of this was her antipathy for the Harkers' daughter. This daughter insisted that everyone call her Mystery because she hated her real name, Ann. Mystery was a dumpy, plain-faced girl who could never forgive Olivia for being sexy. She liked to make waspish remarks in Olivia's presence, such as "Maybe going around with your boobs showing works for some people, but I'm not that desperate" or "I feel sorry for girls who look pretty now, but you can tell they're going to be saggy and ugly at thirty." Mystery was always dressed to the nines, and wore an ever-changing selection of jewelry, usually emeralds, to set off eyes whose greenness she was insufferably proud of, in spite of the fact that they were more muddy than emerald.

Olivia was sorry for her at first, as she was for all girls who were ignored by men. The few times she had been rebuffed by men had been stunningly painful. She would stay up all night afterward, rehearsing everything she had done and said, and feeling completely gross. But then she could get up out of bed and go stand in front of the mirror, and feel better. Even in her darkest moments, when she thought her eyes were so close together she looked inbred, and her nose had a bump that made it look broken—she simply, undeniably, had a great body. And though in more romantic moods she would have rather had Lee's delicate and exquisite face, it was Olivia the boys stared at and fought over, not Lee. And emphatically not Mystery, who was a laughingstock for her airs, who got called Mystery Meat behind her back. So Olivia tried to be sympathetic, but the fact was that lots of girls were ordinary-looking without being nasty. Mystery wasn't the sort of girl who was hopeless in the looks department, anyway, just mousy, square-jawed, profoundly unsexy. If she'd had a good personality, she would have done okay. Olivia finally felt justified in hating her right back.

The party started out as pure pleasure, nonetheless. Olivia was given a bedroom that overlooked the sea; she embraced Mrs. Harker with real affection and enthused about her new magnolias. The Irish setter, Leo, kept following Olivia around and grabbing a mouthful of skirt to insist that she scratch his belly. There was the usual crowd of Harker cousins, who drifted through all summer long, and an assortment of Harker business associates looking bored or looking at Olivia.

Olivia was wearing an olive green baby doll dress with asymetrical layers of crepe; it had a low neckline in front and showed her legs almost to the hip. Athena had insisted she take it because it made her blue eyes look almost aquamarine. "It's a crime to leave you in those Gap clothes," Athena had said. "You're a princess, and you have to dress like a princess, at least when you're with me."

Olivia had laughed. "Don't you mean that you're a princess, and that's why I have to dress up to be with you?"

Athena looked at her narrowly, a little sadly. "No, that's not what I mean."

"You're just a naturally generous person," Olivia said, looking at herself once more in the mirror. "You can't help it." Her slim arms did set the dress off wonderfully, and against the dark green her hair shone. She could imagine herself as a princess, wearing this. Even though her father would disapprove. It was the sort of thing he said looked like a nightie, and wasn't decent to wear in public.

"No, I can't help it," said Athena, softly. "But I don't think it's so unusual. It's always nice to give things to nice people."

Tonight, when Athena arrived, she'd gone straight to Olivia and kissed her on the cheek with her usual graceful cool, saying, "Such a relief to see you, princess. I thought we might lose you again at any minute."

"No." Olivia blushed. "No, I'm back to stay. And soon in Manhattan . . ."

"Yes," Athena looked away at the big bay windows in the

main room, where the sun had just begun to streak the sea with red and gold. "Manhattan, of course."

"You're not having second thoughts?"

Athena continued to stare at the ocean, distracted. At last she said, "It's like a nice dream, isn't it?"

"We'll have an apartment on the thirtieth floor. Or something." Olivia smiled, trying to catch Athena's eye. "You look beautiful tonight. I wish I had your eyes."

"Oh, I guess," Athena said, looking at Olivia again with a sleepy smile. "But the freckles make me look like a beagle, really."

"That's ridiculous." Olivia scowled—but just then a group of Athena's brother's friends came in and had to be introduced to Olivia. And then they had to be taken out to the beach, and then they had to clandestinely pour drinks for the girls from a bottle of Maker's Mark they'd brought—and by then the issue was completely forgotten.

The party continued in that lighthearted vein, the young people mainly gathering out on the beach, where they could drink on the sly. The music of the hired string quartet drifted down from the house, mingling with the crashing of the breakers. A couple of the girls had set up a net and were playing beach ball in their party dresses, having left all their shoes in an elegant heap.

As usual at these parties, Athena kept close by Olivia's side. Olivia was always grateful for that. The presence of so many people who took wealth for granted made her feel shy; she felt as if she was going to be unmasked. With Athena there, that all went away. And whenever a particularly awkward question was asked, Athena would smoothly answer it for her, making it seem completely natural. If the answer wasn't always exactly true, that

wasn't Olivia's fault. For instance, Athena had once told a particularly obnoxious Ivy League type that Olivia's parents had
died while attempting to become the first husband-and-wife
team to climb Everest. Tonight, Athena was sweetly tipsy, whispering in Olivia's ear funny comments about the other girls or
about the friends her older brothers had brought home. "That
girl is already engaged, but the fiancé is extremely, extremely gay.
Apparently they have an agreement that she just gives him head,"
Athena would say, before greeting the girl in question in the
most pleasant way imaginable. Or a man who had just given her a
rough hug before moving off down the beach would earn the com-
ment, "So manly. I have to go wash the testosterone off of me."

Olivia was just considering whether it would be possible to
sneak off with one of the guys, or if Athena would be offended,
when she saw him.

It was the man from the beach, wearing a flawless suit with a
white shirt that seemed to shine into Olivia's eyes. She was so in
love she almost lost her balance, even though she was standing
still. He looked better than ever, and because she'd only ever
seen him in swimming trunks, to see him fully clothed felt painfully intimate; she knew what he looked like under his clothes.
To look at him was to undress him mentally. And when she got
to the trunks (which she imagined him still wearing under his
suit), Olivia kept on going. She could imagine his dick, ripe and
thick, just beginning to swell in his pants as she pulled the
trunks down, letting it spring free and . . .

"Livy, are you all right?" Athena said.

"Huh?"

"Are you all right?"

"Of course I am.... I'm fine."

But she wasn't all right. She had just seen who the god of the beach was with. Mystery Meat Harker. He was laughing as he nuzzled her mousy head, and slung one beautiful arm around the place where a waist should be.

"Are you sure?" said Athena. "I'll go with you if you want to go lie down."

Olivia took a deep breath, trying not to watch as Mystery, her beady eyes shining with excitement, grasped the love god's head with both hands and pulled him in for a deep, lingering, disgusting kiss. It was so wrong; it was like watching a cow try to mate with a gazelle. Her mind immediately sketched the unwanted picture of Mystery unzipping the god's pants, taking his delicious cock in her hand, kneeling down.... *Apparently they have an agreement that she just gives him head.*

No, it was impossible. But he was holding Mystery's shapeless form close against him, rocking her back and forth. Olivia knew that gesture and she could feel exactly what Mystery must be feeling: the secret shape of his hard-on pressing against her stomach, that pledge of pleasure to come. She, Olivia, would have taken that pleasure—for the first time, too!—from him. How could he give her prize to that awful, bitter...

"Oh, you're right," she said suddenly, taking Athena's hand. "You're right. I do— I should lie down. Let's go in."

And she staggered, with Athena holding her hand all the way, up the beach. She gave the offensive couple as wide a berth as possible, but she couldn't help stealing a glance.

The man was following her with his eyes, staring over Mystery's shoulder with a smile of sensual recognition.

Chapter Four

Call me—but not from prison.

She read again, her eyes narrowing in frustration and disbelief. She mouthed, *Bastard! Rotten stealing bastard! Thief! Thief!* The obvious illogic of this made no difference at that moment. Every fiber of her being was telling her that Paul had stolen *her* jewels, and if it took her the rest of her life, she would get them back. For the first time, she understood what people meant when they talked about seeing red. She was literally seeing everything through a veil of scarlet heat. *Robbing rotten thief!*

She took a deep breath and let it out slowly. There was no time to sit here seething at her ex-lover. Jewels or no jewels, she would have to cover her tracks.

For a minute she considered the pros and cons of simply going

back downstairs, putting her little bag of tricks back into its secret compartment, and getting a good night's sleep. But it was no
good. As soon as the loss was discovered, she would be a suspect.
Then she would need an alibi, just as badly as she would if she
had the loot.

She shut the safe quietly and opened her toiletries bag. In it
there were two coils of what looked like thin rope, of two different
colors and widths. She took out the first one and began to work.

Ten minutes later everything was exactly as she'd planned. As
usual, the plan that had seemed flawless and foolproof when she
was inventing it turned out to be ridiculous and risky now that
her liberty was at stake. Of course the fuse would be used up
much faster than she expected. The explosive would turn out to
be a dud; her fingerprints would then be left all over everything,
and she would be exposed not only as a thief, but as an incompetent, stupid thief. The abseiling rope would break, and she would
be found on the cobblestones under the window, probably with a
broken back. In prison, she would be wheelchair-bound, a cau-
tionary tale for other would-be incompetent thieves. What had
ever made her imagine she was an explosives expert?

While her mind raced, she worked, molding the plastic explosive into the lock of the safe exactly as Paul had shown her
once, long ago. She spent some time fussing about, arranging the
fuse along the marble floor so that it avoided anything fragile.
Somehow it was easier to contemplate robbing someone's diamonds than it was to knowingly and willingly make burn marks
on their Persian rug. Finally she opened the window and paused
again, listening. In the night outside, an owl was hooting, mak-

ing her imagine Paul standing under a tree in the woods, watching her. *Bastard*, she mouthed again, but with an involuntary longing. Then she lit a match and held it to the end of the fuse, muttering a prayer, as she always did, to Saint Nicholas, the patron saint of thieves.

One minute later, she was standing on the stones beneath the study window, her knees a little scuffed where she'd scraped them against the side of the house. The sensation of being out of doors, naked, made her forget her troubles again. A joy as spacious as the Alpine night seized her. A rogue part of her mind was pulling her out into the forest, where possibly Paul was waiting. But she knew she had to hurry; she had to be in bed with André when the charge went off.

Moving swiftly and soundlessly, she crept along the side of the house toward the back door, which she'd unlocked before going to bed. From there, it was only two flights up on the old servants' staircase, and she would come out right beside André's bedroom, with a minute to spare. The night breeze ran over her skin, cooling and reviving her, and as she tiptoed across the lawn, she startled a little fox, which jogged away with a slightly affronted air. It all added to Olivia's longing to stay out here—to lie in the grass and have Paul come out of the darkness to join her.

Now she was at the door. Her breath caught as she tried the knob—if anything had gone wrong . . . but it opened smoothly, with only the tiniest ticking noise. She was in, and running up the stone steps easily, home free.

Then the lights suddenly came on. Jenz was standing on the landing in front of her, as naked as she was, and scowling in astonishment. His brawny body, roped with muscle, at first gave her an instinctive thrill of fear; there was no way she could get past him. Then, as he looked down at her body with a subtle change in his face, she felt hot all over, and she knew what she was going to do, without even knowing if it was the right decision.

She was about to seduce someone, out of nowhere, a game she had played for years without ever growing tired of it. She put her finger to her lips and let her mouth fall open, just a small suggestive fraction of an inch. Jenz took a sharp breath. Then they were standing, staring at each other. Neither of them made any gesture to cover themselves. Olivia let her gaze dip to look appreciatively at his thick chest, his body well muscled from work. His cock was already stiffening, lengthening, in that semierect state she loved, and she couldn't help licking her lips. From where he stood, two steps above her, it was almost on a level with her mouth.

When she met his eye again, his look was one of despairing hunger. He muttered something in German, and then she stepped up, one step, two steps, and laid her hands lightly on his shoulders, resting her tender breasts against his chest. He groaned and she inhaled deeply, suddenly realizing she'd been holding her breath. She said, in the faintest whisper, into his strong neck, "Jenz..."

Then he turned to her and kissed her violently, forcing her head back, his huge arms closing around her. She let herself melt against him, arching back as he leaned over her. His cock was growing now against her belly, and she reached down to find it, letting her fingers close and slip along its hot length. Then he reached down, and with offhand ease, lifted her off her feet, and was carrying her through a doorway and along a low-ceilinged hallway. As he carried her, he leaned down to nibble at her breasts, and she responded by pressing kisses on the sweat-salty back of his neck. Then they were in a dimly lit bedroom, and he was lowering her onto a bed. He paused to stand over her, looking her up and down. His mouth formed a word, and at that moment, she heard the distinct cough of the explosion upstairs.

Jenz started. She sat up immediately and bent to take the tip of his now rock-hard cock in her mouth. At first her only thought was to distract him, and she made her tongue slip and play around his glans with an intense and skillful concentration, reaching under to find his firm balls and squeeze them in rhythm with her mouth's activity. Soon she was rewarded by feeling his thighs relax and then tense again, pressing his cock forward into her throat. She was soon distracted herself, as the sweet thickness of his cock slid deeply into her throat, her tongue appreciating its shape and exquisite hardness. He had a wonderful faintly sweet taste that made her want to suck him forever, and the exact shape of his dick, curved slightly left of center, felt perfect in her mouth. Olivia, no matter how she tried, could only open up and deep-throat a cock that felt right to her, and she was relieved to feel her throat relax and accept Jenz almost gratefully. As she continued to fondle his balls with one hand, she found his firm ass with the other, and pressed him farther in, her throat stretching as he moaned and fucked her mouth harder, the muscles of his ass straining with the intensity of the sensations. She kept her tongue in action, torturing the sensitive underside of his dick, and finally she could feel the specific telltale tightness in his erection, the subtle ripe fullness in his testicles, that told her he was about to come—but it was still a shock when he did come, deep in her throat so she had to struggle, swallowing around his dick so it was forced slightly out, causing him such excruciating pleasure that he let out a slight scream—as the door was flung open and a horrified André stepped into the room.

Chapter Five

The Harkers' house was lit up all along the ground floor, and Athena and Olivia had to slip through the ongoing party, responding to greetings as they passed. Olivia gave everyone what she hoped was a careless smile; though, superimposed on everything, she could still see that beautiful black-haired man wound into the awful tentacles of Mystery Harker. Mrs. Harker held them up for an agonizing five minutes, telling Olivia all about the new flower beds she was putting in. Then there was a young man who wanted to accompany them, and had to be dissuaded by a dishonest hint about "someone waiting for us upstairs." It seemed to take them forever to make their way to the stairs, and only when they'd escaped to the relative peace and quiet of the second floor did Olivia realize she didn't know where they were going. Athena paused, too, looking along the row of doors with a preoccupied frown, as if trying to remember something. "Oh, right," she said, and led the way into one of the rooms, finding the light switch without hesitation.

They were in what must have been Mystery's bedroom, a spacious room with a huge canopied bed and windows overlooking the sea. Clothes were strewn everywhere, evidence of Mystery's difficulty in choosing an outfit for the party. Athena unceremoniously cleared the bed of a few slinky dresses and sat down, gesturing for Olivia to join her.

Olivia sat and then lay back, groaning as she shut her eyes. Athena was laughing at her with a note of commiseration. "Oh, thank you," Olivia said. "I don't know what happened to me back there."

"Do you want me to guess?" said Athena in her usual voice, detached and warm at the same time.

Olivia didn't answer. The darkness of her shut eyes was already filling with images of the black-haired man on the beach in his swim trunks. Him pulling the trunks down. Mystery reaching... "Aargh," said Olivia clearly. Then she opened her eyes and both she and Athena laughed.

Athena put a hand on Olivia's bare knees, saying, "You can tell me, you know. I won't tell anyone. I think it's fair to say I can keep a secret."

"I know that," said Olivia, though it had never occurred to her before. She had never had any secrets, exactly, or only from her father. And that hardly counted. Now she looked into Athena's serious hazel eyes, admiring their thick fringe of auburn lashes with half her mind while the other half continued to suffer and sulk. She said, "Well, it's just a man. It isn't even anything."

"Just a man," said Athena with an odd lilt. "Well, that's what I suspected."

"It's not even a man I know," said Olivia. "It's just someone I was seeing around . . . on the beach. And then I got this idea that I should lose my virginity with him. It's stupid."

"Yes, that's okay," Athena said, seeming very far away.

"Then . . . he was hooking up with Mystery . . . Ann. . . ."

At this, Athena started laughing, and Olivia couldn't help but smile in response. Athena said, "Oh, that hurts. But then he can't be all that good-looking."

"You didn't *notice?*" said Olivia, scandalized.

That made Athena laugh even harder. Tears came to her eyes, and her hand on Olivia's knee gripped hard, making Olivia squirm as it tickled.

"Cut it out," Olivia said, pulling her leg free. "Cut it out! How could you not notice him? That's just . . ." She shook her head.

At this Athena turned away sharply, her arms crossed, her back to Olivia. Olivia sat up. "Athena? What's wrong? Oh, you did notice him, didn't you? Do you . . . Is it 'cause you have the same crush? I mean, it doesn't matter, does it? If he's with Mystery Meat?"

"Don't be an idiot," Athena said in a low voice. "I can't stand it." She turned to look at Olivia, and her eyes were filled with tears. "Why do you have to be so blind? You could at least have the grace to reject me. But you . . . don't see."

"Oh," said Olivia. Suddenly everything made sense. She felt not just like an idiot, but like an insensitive, coldhearted idiot. "God, Athena. If it's what I think it is . . . I'm sorry."

"Well," said Athena, "be sorry then."

"You mean—I mean, I just want to be sure you mean what I think you mean—"

"*Ssh.*" Athena put her finger to Olivia's lips. "Don't say any more, please." She pressed her finger gently against Olivia's mouth for a second, then took it back and folded her hands, looking at the floor with a frown. She said softly, "I want you so badly, Livy. I know you don't understand. But it still hurts."

Olivia caught her breath. She said quietly, "What makes you so sure I don't understand?"

"I'm sure," said Athena with a trace of bitterness in her voice.

Olivia sat looking at her friend's back, the delicate tracery of her spine clear under her fine pale skin. A light dusting of auburn freckles covered Athena's slender shoulders, and Olivia was lost in a confusion of feelings and desires. It wasn't clear to her how much she was responding to Athena's lust for her; how much she was still inflamed by her crush on the gorgeous stranger; and how much she was genuinely attracted to the other girl's graceful waist, the curve of her breasts in her gray satin halter dress. At last she decided it didn't matter. Other people were careful about sex, but she couldn't be. Whenever she'd tried to curb her passions, it felt as if she were trying to crush her own heart. Now she had to kiss her friend—she suddenly simply had to.

Olivia put out a hand and touched Athena's back lightly. Athena flinched and looked back at her with a miserable passion in her eyes.

"Athena," said Olivia, "what makes you so sure I couldn't understand?"

"Oh, you're straight, that's all. A little detail like that." But

Athena was looking at her intently, the energy of hope returning to her eyes.

"But I don't know how to put this. . . ." Olivia thought, while Athena watched her face intently, desperately. At last Olivia gave up trying to think of a good way to put it and simply said, "I'm a slut."

Athena smiled. "You're not, though. You're a virgin slut, at worst."

Then Olivia leaned forward and her lips met Athena's. For a moment they remained like that, completely still, the shock of raw adolescent lust pouring through them. Then Athena moaned and put both her hands into Olivia's hair, kissing her deeply, her tongue slipping and turning around Olivia's. Olivia put her hands on Athena's waist and pulled her close. Their breasts met with a tender shock and were pressing together, the surprise of the softness making Olivia's body tense with anticipation. "You're beautiful," Athena was murmuring into her neck. "Livy, I've wanted you so badly—you just don't know."

Then Athena's hand closed on Olivia's breast. The thin fabric only intensified the feeling, the slight friction against Olivia's nipple sending shock waves through her. Then Olivia had to try it. She let her hand slip up from Athena's waist, all the while half pretending to herself she wasn't really doing this, that it was all part of the fantasy she'd had about the man on the beach. But when her fingers found Athena's soft breast, smaller than her own and more pointed, firmer, she gasped with the eroticism of it, the feeling of sweet transgression.

Then Athena had pressed her back to the bed and was lying on top of her, and their hands were slipping everywhere, the girls exploring every inch of each other's bodies. "God, I do want you," Olivia whispered. "I do. I don't know how I didn't notice."

"*Sssh,*" said Athena, and she was sliding down Olivia's body, and pulling up her thin skirt. Athena's fingers lightly grazed the inside of Olivia's thighs, making her hold her breath with excitement. Then Athena was nuzzling into Olivia's pussy, her mouth pressing against the damp crotch of Olivia's panties. Without removing her mouth from Olivia's cunt, sending subtle vibrations into her, Athena murmured, "Can I? Will you let me?"

"Yes," Olivia breathed.

Then Athena was pulling the cloth of the panties aside, and her tongue was poking in between Olivia's labia, dipping and flicking around her clitoris and the sensitive slit of her vagina. Olivia was squirming and her breathing was coming out as a gentle moan. The pleasure was indescribable. Athena kissed her clitoris hard, sucking slightly so that the sensation made Olivia tense all over. It was as sharp a thrill as orgasm itself. And as Athena returned to licking her rapidly, up and around her clit, letting her tongue slip into Olivia's pulsing cunt again and again, the orgasm came to chase it, lifting Olivia's hips up off the bed and making her cry out hoarsely as her pussy exploded in bliss. Then again. For a moment Olivia was aware of Athena's mouth poised just above her pussy, the light breath an excruciating threat of further pleasure. Then the all-powerful tongue descended again, releasing yet another round of coming from Olivia, who found herself burying her hands in Athena's cool, smooth hair, the memory of its gorgeous russet gleam mingling with the pleasure to make her feel the first romantic love she ever had for another girl.

When it was over, she opened her eyes to find Athena sitting up again, one dress strap slipping down her arm to expose a perfect pointed breast with a deep rose nipple. Athena was gazing at her with a softness, a vulnerability Olivia had never seen on her face. "Are you okay?"

"No, I'm not okay," said Athena. "I'm in love."

Olivia swallowed. She wanted to say she was in love, too. But she was afraid of what that might mean to Athena. How could she explain what love meant to her? Her mind ran through the options; she even tried to imagine herself, ten years in the future, settling down and maybe not needing men anymore. Athena was certainly the best friend she'd ever had. At last she blurted out, "I can't love just one person. I think I told you that before?"

Athena smiled and nodded. With some of her old cool assurance, she said, "But I can be one of them?"

Olivia sighed. "That's not enough, is it?"

"Oh, no. That's plenty."

Athena stood up and Olivia was surprised to find that her heart sank. She had assumed that she would have a turn pulling down Athena's panties, exploring her pussy—and though she was a bit nervous at the prospect, worrying that she would do it all wrong, now that Athena was turning away, she was keenly disappointed. She said, "Did I do something wrong?"

"No," said Athena, pulling her dress back into place and leaning down to kiss Olivia briskly. "No, don't even think that. No, I just need to go be alone for a minute. You know how it is, sometimes?"

"But in a good way?"

"In a mostly good way. In a good enough way that you can

just rest here and forget about me." Then Athena was slipping out the door, before Olivia could even reassure her that she would never forget Athena, not for a second.

The door closed. Olivia relaxed and she noticed herself in a mirror opposite. Her dress was in disarray, one nipple peeping out from her décolletage, her skirt crumpled up above her hips. Her panties were still bunched up to one side, and for the first time, she realized that her pussy itself was beautiful, a pale pink rose with a fine frosting of pale blond hairs on top. She held still, admiring herself, imagining with a weird mix of lust and sympathy how she would have seemed to Athena, how Athena would have desired her. For the first time she could see how the rounded plumpness of her thighs could be alluring. Then, out of the corner of her eye, she noticed the slightest movement, like a flickering of the light. She had tracked it down to a copper doorknob when the door opened and the black-haired man stepped out of Mystery Harker's closet, a smile of appreciation on his beautiful, beautiful face.

Chapter Six

"Olivia!" André said with that particular catch in his voice—all too familiar to Olivia, who immediately hated herself keenly, violently, in a way which was also sadly familiar. *Slut!* her mind accused her. *God almighty, are you ever going to learn?*

In the second that it took Jenz to pull out of her mouth, scramble down onto the bed and cover them both hastily with a sheet, she had time to condemn herself and justify herself five times. By the end she had concluded that she would make it up to André somehow, someday. But sparing his feelings was really not worth the prison sentence she would have faced if she didn't have an alibi for the moment that the explosion went off. She might have made her way back to André's room in time, sure. But she would have been left without an explanation for why she was wandering through the castle stark naked in the middle of the night, just as the explosion happened. Now she had the perfect explanation: she was a horny bitch with no conscience whatsoever. If—in an entirely unrelated incident—a robber had not blown the safe and made off with the family jewels, she would have gotten away with it, too.

The hell of it was that she would never be able to tell André the truth. She gave him a sick, unhappy smile—then wiped her mouth hastily. He was shaking his head. He said something in German, and Jenz got up and grabbed a bathrobe from a hook on the back of the door. In a second, the groom was gone and André and Olivia were alone.

André sat down on the edge of the bed, his eyes still shocked and a little uncomprehending.

Olivia said, "I'm sorry. I'm really sorry—"

"No." André put a hand to her mouth. "Don't apologize."

She kissed his palm, but he held her mouth firmly. Then his other hand began to stroke her throat. For a moment she actually worried that he was going to strangle her—who knew how Austrians regarded these things? But then his fingers moved down to toy with her bare breast. She felt a sudden wave of delicious weariness as her breast responded, seeming to glow dreamily in his palm. He was squeezing first one firm pillowy breast, then the other, as she shut her eyes and let her body go limp. Then he took his hand from her mouth and pushed her onto her back. She stretched out gratefully, admiring from below his tousled dark hair and the lines of his strong chest showing in the opening in his bathrobe. When he turned her on her side, she moved as his hands bid her, curling up as if to go to sleep. Meanwhile

he began to stroke her ass, letting his fingernail tickle against
the smooth skin, and across her exposed pussy. The shaved labia
were hypersensitive, and she fell into a semihypnotic state where
nothing existed but his fingers playing across her buttocks and
cunt, the fingertips darting inside her pussy for a split second,
raiding the wetness there, and setting off a jolt of excitement at
the intrusion.

The only warning was the roughness of the bathrobe, rubbing for a split second against her ass, and then his prick was
finding her, parting her pussy lips and slipping in, filling her. He
was fucking into her from behind and above, his cock in her
sideways, and hitting her at an unaccustomed angle that woke
swooning helpless tingles from deep inside. With every thrust,
he swiped her clitoris, sending an extra firework of pleasure cas-
cading over the ongoing spasms inside. Meanwhile, he continued
to clutch her breasts, fondling them with a connoisseur's appreciation, and he bent over her, the size of his strong body pressing
her to the bed, making her feel still more pampered and helplessly used. His thrusts became faster, and the sensations in her
pussy were tumbling over one another, as if her pussy was full of
a hundred vibrations, all clashing and harmonizing and fading
only to rise again in an almost unbearably thrilling cacophony.

Then he pulled out of her with a suddenness that made her
gasp. She almost opened her eyes, but that felt wrong somehow;
she bit her lip and let herself go limp yet again as she felt his dick
nosing gently at her anus. The lubrication from her pussy was
more than enough to ensure easy entry and she cried out only
gently as the discomfort of being stretched almost painfully gave
way to the specific pleasure of being sodomized. His cock slid

into her slowly, delectably, remorselessly, until she had taken its full length in her ass. Then he withdrew and plunged in again, harder, making her gasp. And as he pulled back and thrust still harder, deeper, she felt as if pleasure were being forced into her without any possibility of resistance. And her body's resistance melted, giving way to a volley of orgasms that André rode out, buggering her evenly and powerfully as she whined and held on to the bed for dear life, her pussy, asshole, and belly all lost in a storm of sensation. When he came, she felt herself relax a final notch into utter quiescence, moaning into his gruff moan. He clasped her in his arms then and they rode out the aftershocks together like people clinging to a raft in rough seas.

At last there was just the silent room and the wildly mussed sheets and the peaceful sound of their breathing in time with each other. Olivia twisted her head around to kiss André on the mouth. He met her kiss, and they lay intertwined, their lips resting together for a minute. At last André pulled back and said, with a fond wryness, "My mother thought you were trying to marry me."

"Why would I want to do that?" Olivia said, before she could think better of it.

André laughed. "Well, people do. Want to marry me, I mean."

"Oh, because of your count-ness," Olivia said. "And, I mean, your other qualities. Your—"

"You flatter me," André said.

Then they both started to laugh. For some reason, the events of the night now struck Olivia as impossibly, supernaturally funny, and once she started to laugh, she couldn't stop. Then

André's penis was forced out of her by the laughter, which struck him funny, and he too laughed until tears came to his eyes. They were both gasping and clinging to each other like teenagers with the giggles. When they'd finally calmed down, he said weakly, "I should be relieved. I was so worried about how to let you down easily."

"Oh, you were going to break up with me?" Olivia said, irrationally stung.

"Shocking of me, isn't it?" André smiled at her with his accustomed fondness. "It wasn't because of you—though I'd have to say now you might be a little too casual with your favors for a countess. . . ."

"Oh, I think that would be good in a countess," Olivia said. "'Nymphomaniac countess' sounds good to me. But perhaps I have American ideas about those things."

"The point is," André said, "that you haven't got the money to save the castle. That's the real point. So that's why I say it's just as well that you're brazen and a terrible liar."

"I'm sorry."

"Didn't I tell you not to say that?" He smiled at her sadly again. Then he made a face. "It's a shame I can't tell my mother, though. It would have made her feel better, I suspect. Though she did like you, she's been trying to get me to marry a certain oil heiress for months."

"Why can't you tell her?" Olivia said. "I don't mind, if that's all."

André gave her a funny look. "I can't tell her you were fucking Jenz."

"Not fucking technically," Olivia said with dignity. "And

why not? Not because he's the groom? Do you mean she's a snob about things like that?"

André laughed again. "Hardly. Jenz isn't really the groom, Olivia. Isn't that obvious? We can't even afford a cleaner more than once a week."

"Oh!" Olivia said, the light dawning.

"Exactly," said André with a wry expression. "He's my mother's boyfriend."

They both went off into peals of laughter again, and Olivia felt a weird relief flooding through her—Belinda, anyway, was just as depraved as she was. Riding on that feeling, she said with innocent ease, "By the way, what woke you up? I thought I heard something, like a piece of furniture being knocked over."

"Oh, you don't know. Of course you don't." Andre shrugged. "Someone's gone and stolen the jewels. The jewels I was showing you today."

"Oh, my God!" said Olivia in practiced tones of amazement and horror. "Stolen them? All of them?"

"All of them. Don't worry. He seems to be long gone, whoever he is. I've been all over the castle. I thought he might have made off with you." André laughed weakly.

Olivia had to look away. The words seemed designed to taunt her; after all, that was exactly what had happened when she'd first met Paul. He'd made off with her, effortlessly—as if she were a particularly tasty diamond left on a dressing table. Olivia looked wistfully at the darkness in the window, as if she might see Paul running off into the mountains with a bag of loot over one shoulder. And the number he'd written on the scrap of paper kept running through her annoyingly well-trained mind.

The paper itself had been burned with the same match she'd used to light the fuse.

She shook herself out of her reverie and put a hand on André's shoulder. "God, I'm sorry. What a night. I really am so sorry."

"Oh, no need to be," André said. "It might even be a blessing in disguise. The jewels are insured, you see. We're not certain, but we might be able to keep the insurance money, if we just keep very, very quiet."

Olivia felt a delicious flood of relief. She hadn't needed to feel bad after all! And if all went well, André's troubles would be over. The relief was immediately followed by a niggling pang of regret. Somehow she felt that this proved the jewels were meant to be hers. It was so unfair! She looked back at the window with the desperate clairvoyance of desire, until she could really almost see Paul: beautiful, infuriating, still one step ahead of her after all these years.

Chapter Seven

The black-haired man stood for a moment in the closet doorway, looking down at Olivia with a calm grin of admiration. He had his suit jacket over one arm, and in the other hand, he carried a white plastic shopping bag. He was stunning, and he had the magnetic presence of a man who understood the effect he had on women.

After the first second in which she realized she wasn't alone, and the next second when she realized who it was, there came the third second—the one in which she realized that two seconds had passed and she hadn't made a move to cover her naked pussy, her exposed nipple.

And then, she didn't know why or how, but she stayed exactly as she was. Leaning back on her elbows, her knees spread and the diaphanous green skirt mussed up around her waist, she watched the stranger look at her, beginning to tremble slightly. His eyes went, without any bashfulness, directly to her cunt, and his smile became deeper, drowsier, more sensual while nothing else about his posture changed. She felt his gaze there as a kind of magnified nudity. Her cunt was dripping wet after Athena's attentions, and she was painfully, or ecstatically, aware that he must have overheard her saying that she wanted to give her virginity to him.

He was about to come to her, bend over her, and kiss her. Perhaps he would do it quickly, just pulling down his pants and entering her roughly, enjoying her pussy unceremoniously—she wouldn't stop him. She wouldn't say a word. Or perhaps he would lock the door and take his time with her. His strong fingers would penetrate her, testing her readiness to take a cock for the first time. He would fuck her carefully, gently, the first time—then hours would pass while he introduced her into all the mysteries—

Here her fantasies stopped, and she came to her senses with a clear mental image of Mystery Harker.

At that moment he said, in a deep and slightly raspy voice that made her weak with heightened desire, "I can't stay. I'm sorry, but I actually have to be going." His grin had vanished, and his blue eyes, so striking in his deeply tanned, smooth face, were hungry and frank. "So I can't take you up on your kind offer."

She stared at him. He must mean . . . She snapped her knees together, and was rearranging her dress with clumsy haste. When she was covered again, she found that she couldn't meet his eye; she meant to look at him, but just ended up staring at her own silver sandal, which seemed pathetic now somehow, as if it were a piece of armor that had been pierced in the first assault. She couldn't for the life of her think of what to say.

Then he said, in a low voice, "Oh, God."

She looked at him, startled. He was regarding her with compassion now, and with a sensual familiarity that made her certain, suddenly, that he'd watched the whole scene with Athena—he'd seen her pussy being licked, her squirming and coming under another girl's tongue. "I could go with you," she said, in a fevered whisper.

He took a sharp deep breath. For the first time, she knew she'd caught him off guard. He was looking at her body again, and she saw that his pants had a telltale bulge. It was exactly like every fantasy she'd ever had about him, and it seemed wrong that she couldn't fall to her knees then and there and find the shape of his hard cock in the cloth, let her cheek rest against it and her mouth mold it; find his zipper and expose his cock—the beautiful big cock that would . . . it would be like . . . it would actually be inside her. His cock—she could barely breathe, and she had to look down again at her sandals. They were cheap plastic sandals that she'd bought for herself, twenty dollars at K-Mart, in fact. Again they made her feel ridiculous. She was just a kid. It was stupid to think that she could leave with him just because seeing her half naked had turned him on. She was such an idiot.

But then he said—and his voice had become a hoarse, needy whisper—"You can come with me, beautiful. But you can't come back."

Olivia got to her feet. In an equally faint, throaty voice, she said, "Yes, then. I'll come with you."

Then he had grabbed her by her shoulders and pulled her against him, kissing her fiercely. His mouth fit hers with a strange force. Her strength coursed out of her with the wayward beating of her heart, and she was drooping, her head spinning. Suddenly he let her go, and she caught his shoulders to keep from tripping. They were both staring at each other with wonder, as if to ask: *Did that happen to you, too?*

Then she said, "Only—I can't come back. That doesn't mean you're going to kill me, right?"

He laughed. "I can't absolutely promise you won't get killed, where we're going," he said. "But not by me."

She breathed, "Let's go."

Because most of the party guests were in the rear of the house, the part that faced the sea, Olivia and her new lover only had to pass a few people, who mostly ignored them completely. Only Mr. Harker looked up with his eyebrows raised as Olivia passed. She said vaguely, "I'm going home to get a jacket."

Mr. Harker called after her, "Don't you leave without seeing my wife, that's all." And as an afterthought, "What's the jacket for? It's warm. It's boiling!"

Olivia just waved to him and kept on walking.

The car was an anonymous American-made car, probably a Ford, remarkable for its complete lack of character or characteristics. She got in in a dream, and when she closed the door, it seemed to cut the last ties to her family, her friends, her former life. She remembered with a strange detachment how she had wanted to call after Athena and swear she would never forget about her, not for an instant. An instant later this man had stepped out of the closet and everything—not just Athena but everything else in her life—had become indistinct and meaningless.

He got into the driver's seat beside her, and his mere presence there made her tingle all over. He settled that plastic bag in his lap, and she again thought of his cock, and wondered how far they would be going before they could stop, whether she would lose her virginity in this car. "Nice car," she said as he started the engine, feeling that someone ought to say something.

He laughed. "It's the cheapest rental I could find, actually." He backed the car out and started down the narrow road back towards town.

"I'm poor," she said, stung. "I guess all new cars look nice to me."

"You're poor?" he said, with an odd inflection. He looked away from the road for a second, meeting her eyes. In the dark, she couldn't make out his expression, but a chill passed through her lips at the memory of him kissing her.

"Yes," she said, "I'm poor. I'm not like my friends."

"You were poor," he said, looking back at the road with a certain grim humor. "Five minutes ago."

"What do you mean?"

He lifted the plastic bag and handed it to her. She took it with an odd foreboding, and was immediately surprised at how heavy it was. Opening it, she reached in a little gingerly. Her fingertips met something cold and slithery, and she pulled out a handful of Mystery Harker's emerald jewelry.

"Oh, my God! Oh, my God!" she said, dropping the whole bag into her lap and staring at him. "You—you robbed Mystery? Of course! You were in her closet! I'm such an idiot!"

He had burst out laughing at her first panicked shout. With every word out of her mouth, he laughed harder, until his booming laughter filled the car.

She started laughing, too, but added, "You actually—you did, you stole her emeralds. I didn't even wonder what you were doing in the closet! God."

"I'm sorry," he said, still grinning. "But the fact is, *we* stole her emeralds. Unless you want to get out of the car right now. It's not that far to walk back, but I can't give you a ride. I hope you understand."

"Oh, well." She looked down at the plastic bag, but didn't move to look inside again. He had stolen . . . They had stolen . . . She sighed. "Well, at least you weren't really hooking up with her."

He laughed again. "She's not one of your rich friends, then?"

"Oh, I guess not. No. We stole Mystery's emeralds."

"Seriously, though," he said, and again his eyes sought hers. As they passed under a streetlight, his face lit into beauty for the space of a breath, and then dimmed again. He said, "Do you want me to let you out? I got carried away back there. . . . You did offer me your virginity." His deep voice was full of the humor of the situation; he looked back at the road. "You don't even know my name yet. There's no harm done."

She stared at him, and as they passed under another streetlight, she put out her hand to touch his face—The Most Beautiful Man in the World, the one she was born to chase and break her heart for. *You're not poor anymore, Olivia,* she told herself, but she didn't care. The money, the danger, none of it honestly mattered to her. All that mattered was the knowledge that she would kiss him again before long; he had as good as promised.

"So what's your name?" She said it quietly, firmly.

"Paul," he said. "But call me Michael if we get stopped. Fake driver's license."

"I'm Olivia," she said. "When can we have sex?"

Two hours later, after a seemingly endless drive in which Paul kept his hand tantalizingly on her thigh, they arrived at a deserted marina. Only a handful of sailboats bobbed in the water beside a few warped docks. There was no guard, no one around, and as they walked down the docks to his boat, the sea smell and the solitude made her feel once again the extremity she'd arrived at. She'd left her father and sister behind, her friends and her planned future with Athena; and if she was honest with herself, it was just for the sex she was about to have. She didn't regret it in the slightest, though. The sex seemed to be made of stars and the ocean that smelled of distance; sex was both the black horizon they were headed into and her own body, so small and warm and ready as she walked down the docks with him, holding a small carryall he'd handed to her. He had tossed the bag of gems into a cooler (next to a couple of bottles of white, she noticed) and was carrying this and a suitcase, walking ahead of her so silently that at moments she thought he was a ghost. He might disappear into thin air.

He leapt onto the boat with practiced ease, and as it rocked slightly, he moved with it, leaning down in the same motion to gently drop the suitcase into the cabin below. She paused to take off her sandals, and he watched her closely; she was conscious of his eyes hunting along her cleavage, her bare legs. When she set her bare feet onto the cold damp wood, she wanted to laugh with the freedom of it all. She hopped onto the boat easily, then lost her balance slightly and found herself in his arms. The carryall fell to the deck and he was lifting her, spinning her around as he pressed his lips to hers.

Again, that sensation of electrical connection, of some magnetic energy that lit and raced through her whole body and back to his. Being held against his chest was overwhelming; she could have screamed, or fought like a tiger, or fainted. But instead she held still, with her mind falling through eternal space and her body burningly here, here, here. He carried her toward the rear of the boat, and then he was letting her down on a soft surface—a sleeping bag was all it was—and lying down beside her.

"I'm sorry. It's not the Ritz."

She gazed at him, wanting to bury her face in the soft black hair that hung almost to his powerful shoulders. He was leaning on one elbow, and her heart hurt just to look at him. She said, in a shy whisper, "Do you mind if I unbutton your shirt?"

"No, I don't mind," he said without moving. He reached out and began to stroke her hip; she caught her breath and began to unbutton the white shirt. Soon she was reaching in and stroking the hot skin revealed, letting her hands explore down his stomach and over his muscular chest.

He had begun to gather the fabric of her skirt into his hand, and now he pulled it up completely, baring her legs and hip and already much-abused panties. Sitting up, he shrugged his shirt off, and her eyes followed the perfect lines of his chest and back as he moved himself down to press his lips to her stomach. He kissed and licked his way down to the limit of her panties, and licked along that boundary before snagging them and rolling them down off her, down her thighs and over her knees. She kicked them off and by then his hand was over her pussy. He let one finger slip inside her while the others played around her labia and clitoris, triggering sensations everywhere at once so she immediately began to writhe and whimper. And again, that uncanny electricity seemed to flow between them, so that involuntarily she moved her hips to bring his finger in deeper. Her body instinctively followed even the tiny motions of his fingers.

Then he leaned down and she felt his breath stirring the little patch of platinum pubic hair she left unshaved over her pussy. His breath hovered for a moment, cooling her moist cunt and adding its note to the tangle of pleasures that was slipping over and in and around her. Then he suddenly touched her clitoris, on the very tip, with the strong and deft tip of his tongue. She gasped and cried out; her body rang with a pleasure that was beyond orgasm, that was like a distillation of the desire she'd felt for this man ever since they first met. And in a second he was kissing her cunt and licking in and out of it, strumming her clitoris with his tongue, then his thumb in such quick interchange that she couldn't follow it, and fell into a whirlwind of pleasure that seemed to lift her into some realm where even her body disappeared. Then she was coming, and it all stopped. He watched her orgasm, only the breath continuing—and her cunt was left out on a limb, as if the orgasm was reaching for the onslaught of feelings that had been going on before. Her cunt spasmed and spasmed, chasing something—and he let her go completely and moved on top of her, parting her legs and pressing his cock into her in one graceful, powerful motion.

She shrieked at the sharp pain, and then the orgasm seemed to turn from white to black. But continued. The pain eased, but was still there like a drumbeat underscoring the pleasure of his entry, of the way he now began to slowly fuck her—fuck her—she was being fucked. She opened her eyes, trying to see through the bewildering ecstasy and hurt to him. He was looking at her with a dual seriousness, a grave concern darkening the look of sensual attention—it was the fulfillment of the look he'd given her over Mystery Harker's shoulder, of the look he'd given her when he stepped out of the closet. And as his blue eyes fixed on hers and he whispered something—"How I needed you, God"—she came again in an obliterating way that seemed to be compounded from all the orgasms that had come before. And she found herself making a sweet, prolonged cry, as he fucked her harder, faster, whispering her name.

Chapter Eight

The morning after the debacle with André's safe and André's "groom," Olivia woke in André's bed—with André himself nowhere to be found. She showered and got into jeans and an only slightly see-through blouse, figuring that wearing revealing clothes might be in bad taste after the events of the previous night. Looking in the mirror, she noticed again the few little crow's-feet that had begun to show at the corners of her eyes—really unfair in someone who was barely twenty-three. Too many hours on the beach. Or else, too many worries, now that her father had died. Now that it was her responsibility to put Lee through college.

She told Lee sometimes, "I'll put you through school, and then you can support me for the rest of my life, all right?"

"No," Lee would say, laughing. "No deal. I'll pay back what

you spent on me. But the way you live, I can't afford you, even if
I *do* get to be a doctor."

"Come on, be fair."

"But you like your job anyway. You're always saying how you
get to travel and meet people."

Olivia had rolled her eyes and said nothing—there was nothing she could say. She'd always told Lee that she worked as a
Realtor, dealing in expensive vacation homes in far-flung places.
She wasn't even sure a job like that existed, but it provided her
with cover for her movements and her income—at least cover
enough to fool her bookish twenty-one-year-old sister. It was a
relief that Lee was old enough that if Olivia's cover story was
blown, she could simply resort to the carefully prepared fallback
lie that she was a bimbo who accepted money from very rich lovers. Or (if the cover story was blown in the wrong way at the
wrong time) she could tell Lee the whole truth—from prison.
But that was a given of her life. It had become like knowing that
you would grow old someday—something that you didn't think
about unless you were really, really down. Something that lay in
wait for you on sleepless nights. Or when you woke up realizing
you'd been caught cheating on your lover, and the jewels you'd
been counting on to pay the next year's bills were gone ...

She shook her head at herself in the mirror and headed out
to find André. As she came down the honey-colored granite
steps, she heard unfamiliar voices. Her heart sank. Of course she
should have remembered the police would be here still. Last
night, André had asked them to let her sleep; now she would
have to talk to them. She swallowed and that shadow of prison
flitted over her again. It was generally hard for Olivia to believe

that anyone would really want to punish her for stealing gems. It was such a charming and elegant crime, and it hardly seemed reasonable to regard gems as anyone's property. They were too magical altogether for that; it would be like owning humming-birds or waterfalls. (She was perfectly well aware that there must be people who owned those, too, but *still*.) All it took was for a policeman to introduce himself, however—"I'm Officer Blame, blah blah, and this is Detective Nightmare"—and reality washed over her with the force of a ten-martini hangover.

She decided on the spot that she would have to say she was catching a five o'clock plane out of Innsbruck. All it would take would be a chagrined face, and André would believe she was flee-ing because she felt bad about the scene with Jenz. Belinda could be told whatever mothers are told in such situations. ("We broke up, Mum. No, I don't want to talk about it.") And Olivia could get back all the sooner to the serious business of tracking down *rotten bastard thieving* Paul, and parting him from the gems. At least, half of the gems. At least, half of the money from the gems, which he was probably off-loading to some sleazy dealer right now. (Not that her dealer was any less sleazy, of course, but it was the principle.)

When she arrived in the parlor, Belinda and André were sitting on the slightly worn sofa that was currently Olivia's favorite thing in the world—it was the length of a pool table, and uphol-stered in golden tan leather that was so soft it felt almost pow-dery. It had soaked up so much of Belinda's perfume over the years, it gave off a permanent base note of civety musky sandalwood. On Olivia's first day in the castle, before Belinda had come back from seeing her bank manager in town, André and Olivia had spent a whole long afternoon on that sofa, adding their own note of musk and ocean to the leather.

Across from André and his mother, in a huge Chesterfield armchair, sat an unusually tall, rangy man with close-cropped brown hair. He wore a business suit whose immaculate cleanness and obvious quality took Olivia aback; it was the most uncoplike garb imaginable. Perhaps this was just what plain clothes looked like in the Austrian Alps, she thought. It couldn't be good news, anyway. Any policeman who could afford that suit must be higher up in the hierarchy than was strictly healthy for Olivia.

"Oh, hello, sweetheart," Belinda said as Olivia came into the room to sit next to André. "Bad luck, isn't it? Those jewels you liked so much are gone. Though at least you're still here." And she gave Olivia a bland, innocent look that informed Olivia that she'd been comprehensively seen through. And added, "This very charming gentleman is an investigator from the insurance company."

"I've been telling Mr. Taylor that you were with me when the explosion happened," André hastened to add, giving his mother a poisonous look.

"Olivia Stewart, yes?" Taylor said, nodding to her. "Pleased to meet you."

His British accent seemed to go with his gaunt good looks and his air of impervious calm. Olivia couldn't help noticing, with that gourmet's reflex that made all men fascinating to her, that he had unusual pale green eyes and sat with a certain careless ease that hinted at physical strength, agility—and being good in bed, more to the point. She sighed privately and tried to concentrate on his being a— What was it?

She said, "You're an investigator for . . . I'm sorry. I just woke up." She smiled brightly at him, stifling a wish that she'd worn something low-cut. It would be just the moment to pluck at her décolletage and bite her lip.

He said, "I work for Berniers Insurance Group, which holds the policy on the Fremberg-Asp gems. And also on the recently stolen Axton jewels, as I've been explaining." He smiled with a polite coolness that made his frosty eyes all the more wonderfully aloof. "I've just come from the Axtons' London house last night."

"Last night, you see," André said to Olivia. "He had a tip-off."

"Not a tip-off, a flight itinerary," Taylor said. "It's surprisingly straightforward to trail people nowadays, once you know the name and a few other facts."

Olivia blinked. She happened to know that the Axton jewels were Paul's last job, implying that this really very likable man was after Paul, not her. She said, "So you knew he would be coming here?"

"Why 'he,' darling?" said Belinda.

"I wouldn't know. Aren't most jewel thieves men?" said Olivia, looking with a certain naive interest at Taylor, who looked back at her without a flicker in his polite, distant expression.

Then there was a long, long silence. André was scowling at his mother, who lit a cigarette blandly and stared into space as she smoked it. Taylor was looking at Olivia while she—frustratingly, horrifyingly—began to blush. Unhelpfully, the sensation of heat spreading down her throat and burning in her cheeks made her imagine Mr. Taylor's hands following the color, gradually leading him down her neck and into her cleavage. Now it was circling her breasts and going . . .

"Why, you're blushing," Belinda said. "Or is that allergies?"

"No, it's blushing," Olivia said. "I blush very easily, you know."

"You've been heroic, then, in not blushing all this week," Belinda said, flicking her ash into an empty vase. "I applaud you."

Taylor was observing her with what seemed like detached curiosity, and Olivia smiled at him foolishly, wondering if fucking him would make prison more or less likely. She said, with a slight stammer, "Well, I was just thinking that I have to catch a plane. And here I'll be leaving you all in the middle of this . . . this disaster. I feel like a rat."

"What a surprise," Belinda said.

André loyally lied, "Well, I've known Livy was leaving today all week, Mum. The plane's at— When is it, Livy?"

"Five from Innsbruck."

"Five," said André. "That's right—it was five."

Here Taylor got to his feet with a fluid grace and said, "That's rather handy, Miss Stewart. I was just about to get back into my car—to Innsbruck. So if I can offer you a ride?"

"I can drive you, Livy," André said stiffly.

"But I'd particularly like to talk with you. It would be an opportunity to speak candidly," Taylor said. Then he added, as if it was an afterthought, "About anything you might have seen or heard. Since I won't have time otherwise."

Olivia put one hand up without thinking, and combed it through her smooth hair, letting a tress fall over her blouse at the strategic point where the translucency of the fabric was most telling. Although her more rational side reminded her that this was bad, bad, bad news, and the less she saw of Taylor, the better, she couldn't help hoping that this was a ploy to get her alone for some more pleasant form of interrogation. Possibly involving handcuffs, but in a good way.

"All right," she said. "I'm happy to help, of course. I'll go get my bags."

"You might give it a minute," Taylor said, looking at his watch. "Someone will still be looking through your things, I expect. Local police, you know. You'll appreciate we have to do that."

Belinda gestured airily and said, "It is unpleasant to be suspected, of course. But I'm sure Olivia understands. Perhaps Olivia's been through this before?"

Ignoring this, Olivia said, "Oh, that's interesting. Of course, I hope it won't take too long? How funny . . ." And she smiled at Taylor while seeing nothing but a little toiletries bag wedged into a fat wad of plastic explosive. In her mind's eye she watched it blow to pieces several times, but in her mental picture, a big shard always flew away from the flames, bearing a perfect fingerprint. The fact that this never, ever happened in real life wasn't enough to convince her now. It never happened that Paul stole her jewels; it never happened that she ran into a naked gigolo on the stairs when fleeing the scene of the crime; and it never, ever happened that she was interrogated by a policeman, private investigator, or meter maid, for that matter. Olivia always got away clean.

Nothing in Olivia's belongings was found suspicious, and ten minutes later she was loading her bags into the trunk of a massive BMW and crawling into the backseat. The partition between the front and backseats was tinted glass, apparently soundproof—the driver pressed an intercom button to introduce himself, and nothing further—not a rustle, not a cough—was heard from the front seat again. When Taylor got in, he nodded at her companionably and set his briefcase on the seat between them (much to Olivia's chagrin). As he shut the door, the car moved. Taylor said, "You'll see, we'll be in plenty of time."

The car drove from the forest cover and out to skirt that vast meadow, beyond which the mountain range was bewilderingly huge and exquisite, peaks giving way to peaks that were faintly silver in the misty distance. For a minute they were both silent, looking out at the mountains. Then Olivia said, in her softest, most intimate voice—the voice of a shy child asking for a kiss—"What did you want to talk about?"

"Why don't you look at me?" Taylor said.

She turned around, a little shocked and wondering if, after all, he simply wanted to fuck her. But he looked as cool and professional as ever, his blue-green eyes unreadable. He said, "Do you know a man named Paul Breakness?"

"No," she said easily.

"Paul Jessop?"

"No."

"Michael Stark?"

"No, are these all jewel thieves?" she asked innocently.

"In a manner of speaking, yes," he said. "Do you like jewels, Miss Stewart?"

"You can call me Olivia. Being Miss Stewart makes me feel very unmarried, somehow." She sighed dramatically, although she'd never had any special desire to be married. It just made her feel more respectable when she pretended she did. It also, she had found, embarrassed men horribly, and she could use any advantage she could get.

But Taylor just said, "Did you answer my question, Miss Stewart?"

Nettled, she looked out the window again. The car had entered another little wood, and the den of shadow comforted her. She said, "Do I like jewels? Well, I like good jewelry. I like beautiful things a great deal."

"Beautiful things? What about beautiful people?"

"Strange question," she said, still gazing into the sable shadows of the wood. "Doesn't everyone like beautiful people?"

"And if there was a beautiful man offering you beautiful things, to speak purely hypothetically, that would be hard for you to turn down."

Olivia found herself scowling. She turned around to give Taylor a sarcastic look. "Are you suggesting that someone was trying to pay me off? That I looked the other way? Or"—again she put one hand to her hair, and let it trail down onto her chest—"are you yourself about to offer me something?"

"I've always found it remarkable," Taylor said with a pleasant smile, "how many attractive girls think being dim-witted adds to their appeal. It's refreshing when something serious happens, and they suddenly talk sense."

"Bitchy," said Olivia. "And you haven't answered *my* question."

"I'm not about to offer you anything."

"What a shame," she said, and looked pointedly at his crotch, then back out the window at the woods.

He continued in the pleasant voice of someone telling an interesting story. "My partner and I have been investigating three robberies connected to this Paul Breakness, or Paul Jessop, or Peter Rabbit, or whatever other names he may choose to go by. And we have a theory. It seems to us that in every case, a girl has been staying in the home from which the jewels were stolen. A girl who has recently—very recently—become romantically attached to the gentleman of the house."

"Really?" said Olivia, a sudden irritable idea forming in her mind. "At the Axtons' house, too?"

"Yes."

"So—" she said, with a lump in her throat. "If you don't mind my asking—who was this girl at the Axtons?"

She had looked at him again, and was surprised to catch him looking at her breasts. The momentary relief vanished when he said, "So you understand that I'm saying the girl in both other cases was you?"

She was genuinely surprised. "*Both* other cases?"

"Could I be mistaken? You weren't staying with Nelson Jaubert in Paris last August?"

She caught herself before she could blurt out, indignantly, *But that wasn't Paul's job at all! That was mine!*

She stammered, "Well, I'm . . . I was, but was there a theft? I haven't seen Nelson in ages. I haven't heard from him about any theft."

Taylor sighed as if he was deeply disappointed in her. Then, startling her again, he reached over and took her hand. "Olivia," he said, in a voice that was suddenly tinged with feeling, "if

you've been put under any pressure ... if you're afraid to talk ...
I can assure you that you'll be protected. This man isn't part of
any organized-crime syndicate, and—"

"No, wait," she said, and clasped his hand firmly. "That's
crazy. There's nothing like that going on. But ... thank you for
being concerned." She smiled foolishly and, in a sudden, impetuous gesture, lifted his hand to her lips and kissed his fingers before releasing it.

He blushed this time, and actually put the hand in his pocket
as if fearing for its safety. "Well, that's clear, anyway," he said.

"Yes, that's clear. Oh, look, we can see the Alps again."

For a moment they looked at the view again. The sun, broken
up by high dense clouds, was sending broad shafts of light down
into the valleys. "Listen," she said, after a moment of contempla-
tion. "You think there's a girl accomplice who might be me? Let's
not mince words."

"It's a hypothesis."

"But at the Axton house, someone else."

"Mr. Breakness is a very personable chap." He took his hand
out of his pocket again, and ran it through his hair, as if the mention of male good looks had made him conscious of his own.

Olivia smiled. "I have no doubt that he is."

"Ah, of course. You've never met him."

Here Olivia looked back at Taylor, making her blue eyes
wide. With a childish, confiding gesture, she reached out and
took his hand again. Well, he had taken her hand first—why
not? He flinched but let her keep it.

"I would like to be friends," she said. "Clearly there's been
some misunderstanding, so I may need a friend."

Taylor said coldly, "I don't know that that's appropriate."

"I'll just leave that on the table for you to pick up or leave, then," Olivia said sweetly. "But listen. Let me help you as if you were my friend. I have a rival hypothesis."

"And is it worth my hearing?" Taylor looked at her skeptically.

"Oh, very much. Now listen. Suppose that this Paul had nothing to do with the Jaubert theft. Suppose instead that this girl—it wasn't me, you understand—met Nelson Jaubert at a party and they hit it off." She moved his hand to her lap and began to stroke his wrist with her other hand. "He offered her a ride home, and they got into a pretty involved conversation in his car—just like me and you. So he ended up driving her back to his house instead of taking her to her apartment. It happens."

"Yes, it happens," said Taylor, and his voice was a little softer than before.

She had let his hand drop now on the inside of her upper thigh. And Taylor, although he kept his hand stubbornly stiff and unresponsive, didn't resist. Meanwhile his eyes had fastened on her face with a slightly fearful surmise.

"But why would she go home with Nelson Jaubert?" she said. "He's forty-five years old, and although he's not bad-looking, he's really no Romeo. But maybe I'm prejudiced. To be honest, I don't much *like* Nelson Jaubert. Did you like him, when you met him?"

"No," Taylor said, and his voice sounded far-off. He continued to study her face closely, and she noticed that in an unguarded moment, he licked his lips.

"He's self-important. I think that's what I don't like. Really self-important. So if I had gone home with him, he wouldn't have been surprised. Or if this girl— I'm assuming she must have been young and good-looking, right? Well, Nelson wouldn't think there was anything strange about that. He wouldn't suspect that she had an ulterior motive. Like that she intended to steal two hundred thousand euros' worth of jewels from his wife's safe."

"Is this a confession?"

"This is a proposition," said Olivia. "If I can have you for fifteen minutes, I'll tell you anything you want."

"Have me?" Taylor's voice was still calm, but when she met his eye, he looked shaken.

Still holding on to his hand, she began to unbutton her blouse. He watched intently as if the key to solving his crime lay in the exposure of her creamy breasts, now trembling with the gentle vibration of the car's motion. She pulled down her left bra strap and teased her breast out of its cup so that the nipple rested over the bra, stiffening in the car's air-conditioning. "I want you to suck it. Please?"

Her voice was actually thin and weak with desire. Taylor perhaps thought she had some complex scheme to throw him off the track. Olivia had nothing of the kind. It was her Achilles' heel not just as a criminal, but in life. She had fallen for this man Taylor now, and she was determined not to let him get on any plane in Innsbruck. They should go to a hotel in Innsbruck, for a day or a week. She would welcome his cock—which must be long to suit his long body—into her in every way she could think of, let him work out whatever frustrations lay behind that chilly exterior by fucking her to his heart's content. Beyond that— She would cross that bridge when she came to it.

He cleared his throat. "I'm afraid I can't do that."

"Can I suck you, then?" she said pleadingly.

"No, you can't." He swallowed and obviously made an effort to control himself. "I think you should carry on telling me what you were telling me."

"But I made a deal. I'll only tell you if you give yourself to me."

"Is this what you said to Nelson Jaubert?"

She laughed. "Don't be ridiculous, Mr. Taylor. Why would I say that to Nelson Jaubert?"

"You might have wanted to make a trade with him, too." His gaze had strayed back to her trembling nipple, and his jaw clenched. "Perhaps he agreed to . . . I don't know."

"Do me a favor," she said. She lifted his hand and pressed it against her bared breast, shutting her eyes for a split second as she felt the delicious crinkly crushing of her hard nipple.

"Stop it," he said. But he didn't try to drag his hand away, and when she turned it in hers to flatten it against her breast, he caught his breath and gave in. His hand molded itself to her breast and the fingers sank in, appraising, relishing it.

She was murmuring, almost inaudibly, "I'm yours, Taylor. I just want you, don't you understand? It's not about anything. I'm just saying whatever I have to say. I want you."

He pulled the briefcase out from between them, and as it clattered on the car floor, he was on her, kissing her deeply as he pulled her blouse down over her shoulders. Then he had unhooked her bra and he was playing with her full breasts, his breath harsh and rapid with lust. She let her hands run over the smooth expensive wool of his suit, opening the jacket and feeling for his hard stomach, the wonderful prelude to—his cock. His almost impossibly long cock, which was already rock hard in her hand. First she held it through the suit pants, compressing its length in her hand and tugging gently at it until she was gratified to hear him groan with longing. Then she found the fly and slowly, teasingly slowly, pulled it down, letting him feel its progress all the way down his hard shaft. It was the work of a second then to pull down his brief and free his dick from his fly. She gasped as she felt its hot, impossibly fine skin; its first dry glide through her hand was rewarded by finding a generous drop of precome at the tip. "I want to suck you," she said. "God, I'm dying to suck you."

"Do it. Suck me."

She was bending to take his dick in her mouth when an incredibly loud honking noise came from overhead, startling her. When she looked up, a trucker was leering down at them from the other lane. Taylor looked up in horror and in an instant the beautiful cock was gone, hustled back into his briefs, the zipper up, the jacket pulled firmly down. She swallowed her pride and put her bra back in place, buttoned her blouse. Then they were sitting side by side, shamefaced, Olivia miserably conscious of the sloppy wetness in her panties.

"Listen, I could tell you that story in a hotel room," she said.

"But would it be anything more than a story?" he said, with a certain sadness that was now intimate—like the voice of a disillusioned lover.

"You mean, am I just trying to fuck you?"

He smiled unhappily. "Something like that."

She pondered, looking out the window. Now there were occasional houses at the roadside, and she realized they would be coming to the city soon, and the airport shortly thereafter. "I'll tell you the story now. At least, then, I have a feeling, I'll see you again.

"Now this is just an example of something that could happen. I go home with Nelson Jaubert. He expects to sleep with me, and I don't disappoint him. He takes me to his bedroom—his wife is away and there's no one to disturb us. And while he's in the other room getting us drinks, I strip completely. When he comes back into the room, I'm lying on his bed with my legs open, and two fingers slipping in and out of my cunt.

"I'm sorry if that shocked you. This is just a story, remember.

"Nelson puts the drinks down and forgets everything. He comes over and, standing beside the bed, begins to kiss my body up and down. He sucks my breasts, harder and harder until I'm begging him to be gentle. He bends down to my cunt and begins to kiss my clitoris, kiss it and then lick it in circles, while I continue finger-fucking myself at the same time.

"And then I let him fuck me—from on top, from behind, standing up. I let him take me in the ass. I make him come three times—he's forty-five, but he's a healthy forty-five. And then we drink. We have four drinks and then I decide to wash his dick in a vodka martini—for hygienic reasons, you understand. So I do, and then I can't help wondering what his cock will taste like. So he's come in my pussy, he's come in my ass, he's come in my mouth. He's had me in every way he can, until I'm sore—and I don't mind admitting I've come time and time again myself. After which the gentleman falls into what is probably the best sleep he has ever had.

"And I'm sorry to say that was the last time I saw Nelson Jaubert."

Taylor was looking at her with a pained, cheated languor. "And Mr. Breakness was taking the jewels while you were . . ."

"I know no Mr. Breakness," said Olivia with dignity. "And I'm getting a little insulted by your insisting on talking about him. . . . Perhaps I'm a prima donna, but I am trying to talk about myself. Because, Mr. Taylor, there was no one else in the house that night."

Taylor looked at her appraisingly. Olivia realized, with mingled irritation and relief, that he didn't believe her. Why couldn't she steal jewels by herself, without any man's help? Well, she did! She had! Nelson's gems were scattered around the world now, and the money safely ensconced in one of *her* safe-deposit boxes, waiting for laundering by *her* associates, one of whom she hadn't even met through Paul at all! So there! But she knew she should be grateful that he hadn't believed her. It was really part of her intent in playing this risky game: that he should not only continue to work Paul into his calculations, but he should become jealous of Paul, should take it personally. Though perhaps the thinking behind this tangled scheme was nothing more than boy craziness overruling her common sense yet again.

He said, "So, what if I call the police right now? Suppose I have you arrested."

She said carelessly, "That sounds very thrilling. But you can't, can you? I'm just fooling with you, telling you stories. Still I do hope you'll take up my invitation to share a hotel in Innsbruck?"

"Can't do it," he said. "I have to get on a jet and fly to New York right away. Seeing the girl from the Axton house."

That brought Olivia back to reality with a shock. That girl at the Axton house must be the one who had replaced her in Paul's favors. And she couldn't help feeling stung and inconsolable at that thought. She didn't mind Paul finding new girlfriends, but the idea that he had a new partner in crime was inexpressibly offensive.

"So," she said in what she hoped was a nonchalant voice, "at the Axton house, who was it? Who was the girl?"

"You have reason to think you would know her?" Taylor said, back to his easy aloofness. "Funny, since you don't know the robber himself."

Olivia shrugged. She was suddenly too tired to play games.

"Well, since you're interested," Taylor said with his cool facade completely restored, "I think you do know her—very well in fact. It was one Miss Lee Stewart. Who I understand is your only sister."

Chapter Nine

The day after running away from home—her first day as a fugitive—Olivia woke in the cabin of Paul's sailboat alone. From the movement of the boat, she guessed that they were at sea, and vaguely imagined them crossing the Atlantic Ocean to some hideout in France. She could hear Paul clambering around overhead, and shut her eyes again, remembering the night before. Her hand reached down instinctively and found her cunt, pressing in gingerly to try to find the difference, the change where she was no longer a virgin. But all she found was a sense memory of him fucking her that sent a pang shooting up through her body, making her vagina tighten and ache. When they'd finished fucking the first time, she had stroked his cock with possessive wonder, memorizing every contour. When it stiffened again, she continued to stroke it and nuzzle it for a long time, just studying it hard the way she had studied it soft. Then he had turned her around and curled himself around her spoon fashion, cupping her breasts and kissing her nape lazily while his hard cock pressed against her pussy from behind. He let the rocking of the boat gradually work the length of his cock into her. Every slight movement of the boat sent shock waves through her. The stinging where her hymen had been torn was sometimes painful like a blister, but then would suddenly meld with the pleasure and bring her to the brink of another orgasm. He wasn't thrusting into her but just rested inside her, and the sensation of his steely hardness, that presence in her of his straight erect cock, seemed almost too good to be real. Meanwhile she was gazing at the moon reflected on the water, the spectral outlines of the other boats floating, rising and sliding downwards in unison with her, with him, with the whole starry night.

"So you're my hostage now," he whispered into her ear,

"Shouldn't we be running away?" she asked. "Won't they be after us?"

At this he thrust into her, making her gasp with the intensity of the feeling, composed of pleasure and pain and—she could swear—a dizzying sensation that was purely that of being free. And he said, as he began to fuck her again, "Yes, we should be running away. They'll be after us, and we should be running away. Right. Now."

Then she was lost in a series of orgasms that hurt exquisitely, her cunt closing on his dick with excruciatingly delicious force, as if trying to catch it, stop it from pulling out again—and in— while they should have been escaping . . . and the water and the silver light that tickled over its million ripples, and the million stars, and the million pleasures all turned into one trance in which he plunged into her a final time and cried out in a kind of dazed triumph.

Now she stretched and looked around herself at the cabin, a tiny chamber paneled in oak, with a kitchenette so shiny clean she suspected it had never been used. The platform bed she lay on took up most of the space. While the rest of the cabin was immaculately clean, the bed was a jumble of sheets and quilts, and she vaguely remembered waking in the middle of the night to find him stroking her all over—she had begun to kiss him all over, still half asleep, and the salty memory of his skin, of licking the sweat from his belly, licking her own juices from the end of his dick and holding him in her mouth for the first time—and then what?

She sat up trying to remember, and was startled to feel the weight of a dozen necklaces jangling against her collarbone. Across from her on the mini fridge was a cheap mirror with a magnetized back, and in it was reflected a shocked blond Venus wearing ropes of emeralds, gold, and sundry jewels all over her throat, arms, and hands. Then she remembered Paul dressing her in all of Mystery Harker's gems the night before, the shiver the cold metal sent through her as he put on each piece, reverberating with her newly awakened flesh, the soreness in her pussy. And at the end he'd gone down on her, licking her into orgasms that were almost too much for her to bear, her body crying out for rest, and for more at the same time. The last thing was her sucking him again, and his final ejaculation into her mouth, the taste of him becoming a dream as he went up top to hoist the sail and begin their escape. . . .

The girl in the mirror was gaping at her, jaw wide-open, eyes naive and big. Could this have all really happened? A jewel thief—losing her virginity—escaping by sea in the middle of the night? But she was undeniably in a sailboat wearing an improbable number of emerald necklaces. The smell of ocean, mingled with the fishy scents of sex, was already intertwined with a hundred blissful memories, and she leapt out of bed and crept up the stairs, needing to see him again. The Most Handsome Man in the World—hers for the small cost of everyone and everything she knew.

She came out into brilliant sunlight, and saw him immediately, wearing a pair of cutoff shorts and a stray emerald necklace, standing at the helm with a dreamy expression, as if he, too, were involved in memories of the night before. Looking around, she saw the dim smudge of the coast to the right of the boat. There was nothing else to see but the open water and the distant off-white sketch of a sail far behind. She was imagining that as the police sail when he called out to her.

"Hello, angel."

She was immediately aware of the picture she made, standing on the deck of a boat wearing only jewels. A little unsteady on her feet, she moved toward him. She'd been intending to embrace him, but when she got close, she was suddenly stricken with insecurity. Weren't men supposed to lose respect for you the morning after? Was this the part where he would try to get rid of her? She had a sudden image of herself standing naked on a beach in New Jersey, with no jewels, no Most Handsome Man, and with hell to pay back in Penntucket.

She ended up sitting on the edge of the boat, looking at him from about a yard's distance, with an anxious smile.

"What?" he said. "Having cold feet?"

"No, not at all," she said, confused.

"Then you're crazy," he said, laughing. "You need to wake up more, because you *should* have cold feet."

"No, I was just wondering . . . I know this is going to sound stupid, but, are we boyfriend and girlfriend now?"

He squinted at her with a complex doubt in his eyes. At last he said evenly, "No, we're not. We're something far more committed than that. We're accomplices."

She sighed with relief and managed a smile. "You mean . . . partners in crime?"

"We'll see," he said, shrugging so that the muscles faintly rippled under his tanned skin. "Of course it would be ideal if I could put you to work. But to be fair, we hardly know each other. Though at a first impression"—he looked down at her body and that dreamy expression returned—"I am favorably impressed."

She looked at his face—his utterly beautiful face, familiar to her from countless wasted afternoons on the beach; a face that was tied up with the endless roar of breakers, the endless whisper of daydreams. It was like walking into a fantasy and finding that it contained a further secret chamber of fantasy . . . and another, and another. Chambers encrusted with jewels, chambers in which gorgeous naked men lay on top of you and murmured your name. She tried to quell the fear of losing all this by reminding herself that no matter what, he would at least kiss her again, and she would feel that specific strange electricity again, their joined lips sparking. There was no way he could avoid that. But she couldn't help worrying that he must have other girl-friends. There was no way she could ever be as special to him as he was to her.

At last she asked, "Am I the first partner in crime you've had?"

He smiled as if he saw through the question, and again raked her naked body with his eyes, calling up recollections of the night before. She caught her breath and was aware of a blush spreading over her body, hot against the cool strands of emeralds and the cool breeze.

"You're so beautiful," he said. "I don't know how I'm going to keep from fucking you all day. I want to fuck you right now."

She caught her breath and, without thinking, glanced toward the shore, as if she might see the forces of the law—the boats of the law?—massed in pursuit. The sea was empty—even that distant blur of a sail was gone—and she found that her pussy was already tight and growing damp in response to his gaze. "But we have to keep going—right?"

"Right," he said. "So I'll answer your question. I have never had a partner, male or female or nude goddess. And I would never willingly have a partner, because it makes no sense. A part-ner could turn me in to the cops at any time. A partner could confide in a close friend, just one close friend, and the gossip would spread, and I would wake up in handcuffs. It would be stupid to have a partner. Suicidal."

"So . . . why?"

He smiled. "Sad thing about jewel thieves. Not known for

our great impulse control. That's how I got into this business, seven years ago. I had a rich girlfriend with extraordinary diamonds and a habit of insulting me in public. A very convincing Persian gentleman told me what the diamonds were worth to one of his clients. It took me ten minutes to decide what the girlfriend was worth to me, and within another twenty I had lost her but kept all the trinkets she was wearing. And a gold cigarette lighter just for old times' sake."

Then, for an endless minute, they were gazing at each other while the boat bounded over the sea. It felt as if they were riding on the wind itself. Olivia pulled a long chain free, where it had hooked around her nipple, and put its emerald pendant to her lips, thinking. His blue eyes were burning into her, and she felt that in a moment she would have to touch herself to release the tension in her pussy. She needed him again. They had to . . . The words "impulse control" began to repeat dimly in her brain as she said to him, "Once more? Just once more?" and he was striding down to take her in his arms, crushing all the gems into her flesh.

Their immediate destination was an island off the coast of North Carolina, where Paul had a cabin in a tiny village of thirteen vacation homes and a general store. The island was connected to the mainland via a bridge that was closed six months of the year. The population in wintertime was zero, or one when Paul was there lying low. His cabin was a semifurnished wreck with a fireplace, a bed, and a camp stove. They spent their first week together in the bed, while Paul taught Olivia everything he knew about sex, jewels, stealing, and the very rich. In between furious bouts of sex, Paul told tales of heists—diabolically clever robberies involving the collaboration of computer hackers and geologists; and wildly daring ones that required hand-to-paw combat with three Alsatian dogs; and a few simple stickups. Olivia was alarmed at first to discover that he assumed she would be doing robberies with him, but then reflected that if he *hadn't* wanted her to, she would have felt cruelly left out.

He also gave her a crash course in gems—the four Cs by which the stones were judged (cut, clarity, color, and carat); the treatments some gems were subjected to to imitate the appearance of costlier stones; and the different standards for judging pearls and opals. He demonstrated some simple techniques of gem switching, in which a cheaper but similar stone was left in place of a superior one. "Very few owners of gems really know what they have," he said. "If you had a day alone with their stones, you could really replace them all with rhinestones. Though I've never done more than one at a time, and I leave diamonds for diamonds, rubies for rubies. They're just ugly, muddy diamonds of the same carat and cut. No one ever notices. It's a victimless crime, in fact."

The first day, she'd called her sister and explained in a rush that she had run away with a man, and she couldn't come home for a few weeks, but she was all right, and—could Lee tell their father not to worry?

"Oh, like that's going to help," Lee said with a sixteen-year-old's habitual disgust. "Everybody's gone crazy here."

"They have?" said Olivia, with a secret prickle of gratification. "I didn't think anyone would miss me that much...."

"Well, someone stole Mystery Harker's jewelry that night. So you can tell me now if you ran away with the thief," Lee said, with an extra helping of teen boredom, "or just one of those gross college guys."

"What's gross about them?" Olivia said, caught up in spite of herself in an old sisterly squabble. "You'd be happy enough to go out with one of them, if they were interested."

"Yeah, right," Lee said. "Anyway, Dad's furious at you."

"He's not worried?"

"Come on, Olivia. Nobody thinks you're going to be kidnapped or anything. You disappeared for two days last Christmas."

"I did not disappear. *You* just didn't tell Dad where I was!"

"That's so not true!"

"Well, tell him this time!"

"Have fun with your little male harem! You're such a slut, I don't know why—"

And Olivia hung up, her face a mask of rage. For a whole day afterward she contemplated sending Lee five thousand dollars cash with a snide note, but she finally realized that she couldn't do anything that suggested she'd suddenly come into lots of money. So it was her father she wrote to, in the end, with Paul's participation. The letter said she'd fallen in love "with someone you would really like, Dad." She knew he would be upset that she wasn't finishing high school, but her grades were so bad, anyway. It was Paul's idea to claim that she was going to get her real estate license. "People are always ready to believe you've earned a fortune in real estate," he said. Thus the cover story that Olivia would live with for years was born.

Paul, for his part, had never given his parents any reason to suspect that he had money. His father and mother were extremely respectable suburban people who had wanted their eldest son to join his father's law practice. Paul had gotten through one year of law school. As soon as the second semester was over, he went home and told his parents that he was never going to be a lawyer, and in fact he was moving to Hawaii to live on the beach for six months. That was where he had met the snotty rich girl who had launched him on his career of theft.

Since he left law school, he had been the black sheep of the family, and he saw no reason to change his status. "Sometimes I write home to tell them I've got a job as a lifeguard or something," he told Olivia. "Every year or so I ask my father for money, and he says no. When I go home, my little brother always takes me for a walk to give me career advice. Last time he suggested I get a degree in library science. Lots of careers in library science, apparently."

Five days after they'd arrived on the rocky beach in front of his cabin, a Mercedes pulled up in the driveway, and Olivia made the acquaintance of Mr. Bezin, the "very convincing Persian gentleman" who had originally led Paul astray. He was an extremely tall and thin man of about sixty-five, with impressively perfect posture and dazzling white hair. He wore—to Olivia's great admiration—a pale yellow linen suit with a white rose in his buttonhole. On seeing Olivia, he immediately claimed that Paul had stolen her on his orders, and set her price at a million dollars. "Above rubies," he said with aplomb. Paul had asked

Olivia to hang around while they did business, to get an idea of what was involved. As far as she could tell, what was involved was endless low-grade bickering, with the occasional rousing temper tantrum thrown in for spice.

Occasionally, to rib her, Mr. Bezin would turn to Olivia and ask her opinion about the pricing of some item. He would say in his slow, accented drawl, "Perhaps Miss Stewart thinks an emerald with so many inclusions should not fetch so much?" Or: "Miss Stewart would not want to rob me so shamelessly. Can I appeal to Miss Stewart for a second opinion?"

The worst argument erupted over a matching set of sapphire earrings and pendant, which Mr. Bezin insisted was the only thing worth having in the lot—and which Paul refused to sell.

"I need it as bait for the next lot, if you really have to know all my business," Paul explained finally, exasperated, after Bezin had threatened to leave, torn the rose out of his own buttonhole, stamped on it in fury, and accused Paul of dealing with "that slave-dealing Norwegian cretin, Tordahl. I can see it in your eyes!"

"Olivia and I are going to fish for better gems," Paul further explained. "And you know damned well if I ever see Tordahl again, I'm going to break his neck."

"Then showing me the sapphires is the act of an unfeeling scoundrel," Mr. Bezin said mournfully, actually dabbing his eyes with a linen handkerchief. "And when I see Mr. Tordahl, I will convey to him your regards."

At the tail end of his visit, Bezin took a series of photographs of Olivia, in order, in his words, "To fit mademoiselle for her first counterfeit passport." And when he left, he suggested to her soberly that in the future she do business with him separately.

"This man will only burden you, Miss Stewart. He is a bungler and a reprobate."

When the door closed behind him, Paul smiled at her with a certain irritation in his eyes. "He always manages to get to me," he said. "Reprobate, yes. Bungler? That jackass has been living off of me for years."

Two days later, a messenger came to the door with two dozen white roses and an envelope containing Olivia's first passport—real or fake—in the name of "Isabel White." Paul tossed the roses into the fireplace, and studied the passport critically, commenting, "You even look good in a passport photograph. It's actually kind of spooky."

Paul decided that their first heist together would be a jewelry store. He targeted a high-end jewelry store in Toronto, the place where the old money of the city would go for anniversary presents and engagement rings. It was intended as a trial run; Paul had said (rather insultingly in her opinion) that the Canadians were less sophisticated about security, and therefore she stood a chance. "Also, their prisons are nothing like as bad as the American prisons, so in a worst-case scenario—"

"Well, if you're so perfect, how do you even know that?" she'd retorted.

"Think for a minute," he said. "If I'd been caught, with the kind of crimes I've committed, I wouldn't have gotten out until I was fifty years old."

"I guess this means you're not that old?" she said, squinting at him skeptically.

He laughed. "When you're as old as I am, which is *twenty-eight*, you will realize that everyone knows Canadian prisons are better than American ones. It's not some kind of insider criminal knowledge."

"Oh," she said, and sighed. "Anyway, on to glamorous Toronto . . ."

They drove (in another cheap rental car, which Olivia persisted in finding luxurious, although she knew better than to say so this time) all the way to New York, where they stayed in a hotel that cost—and this nearly made Olivia faint—five hundred dollars a night. In the elevator on the way up, she whispered to him, "Did you know it was going to be that much?" and he burst out laughing.

"Do you know how much we're going to earn this week?" he asked.

She went back in her mind to the session with Mr. Bezin and frowned doubtfully. Mystery Harker's jewelry had earned them about a quarter of a million dollars. She thought she ought to figure out how many robberies they would need to do, a year, to stay in that hotel for 365 days, but her mind gave up. It was simply *tons of money*, more money than her father, for instance, had earned in her lifetime.

"Why the cheap cars, then?" she asked finally, weakly.

He shrugged. "People notice expensive cars, and they look at the people who are driving them. Nobody's curious about the driver of a Ford Focus."

The room they were given on the twenty-eighth floor overlooked all of Manhattan. It had a picture window that went all the way down to the floor, a little dizzying if you stood right

next to it. That night they were making love with the Empire
State Building in the background, its lights so close that Olivia
kept imagining walkways from one building to the other.

In the morning, they went out and bought Olivia a few days'
worth of what Paul called "high maintenance rich girl clothes."
It was a long day of dressing rooms and salespeople, whom Paul
drove away with a fiery impatience that made Olivia smirk. "He's
only doing his job," she said to him after he'd snapped, "Could
you find a new friend, please?" at a particularly clingy salesman.

"I'm only doing *my* job, and he's getting in my way," Paul said
carelessly.

In one store he slipped into the changing room after her and
played the game of undressing and dressing her, fondling her in
passing until she was burning and dizzy with lust. Then, in the
middle of pulling off a dress that he'd judged too baggy, he
pressed her up against the wall. She felt his hard-on then—which
had become the center of her world, the first thing she thought
of when she woke in the morning—and he had to cover her
mouth with his hand as he slid his cock into her, riding her up
against the wall. She watched him fuck her in the mirror, trans-
fixed by the movements of his strong buttocks driving into her
from below, and the glimpses of his wet dick, rosy and thick, as
it slipped into her tight pussy. At last he pressed her flat against
the wall, his cock seeming to lift her up as it went deeper into
her than ever before, opening her wider and wider. She felt it
jerking as he came in a rush, and she came at that instant, her
cunt squeezing every last drop out of him as he held her against
the wall with the pressure of his firm body.

They bought thousand-dollar dresses that contained only

a couple of ounces of fabric, and spindly shoes with six-inch heels that were miraculously as easy to walk in as sneakers. She spent the afternoon in a salon where every hair on her body was either trimmed, shaped, highlighted, or removed altogether. The only thing Paul declined to buy her was new underwear. "No one wears the stuff anymore," he said. And then added, under his breath, "Or you don't."

Back in the hotel room, she dressed up for him, first in a slinky red jersey dress that clung to her breasts; then in a halter and shorts that could have doubled as a bathing suit; then in a lacy white V-neck dress cut so revealingly that she had to stand up perfectly straight to keep from exposing her breasts completely. Paul chose this white dress as the costume for the job, and made her hold still while he dressed her in the sapphire earrings and pendant he had kept back from Mr. Bezin. Then he had her step into a pair of blue high heels, and knelt down to fasten them around her ankles. And then he was leading her over to the bed again, where he promptly bent her over and began to fuck her from behind. And, as it always did, the sex seemed like her real life, from which she had been distracted for much too long by ridiculous trivialities.

Flying on a fake passport terrified her much more than she expected, and the stares she got in her red jersey dress didn't help matters. She realized with chagrin that the skimpy, pricey clothes they'd bought in New York were now the only clothes she had. No T-shirts, no sweatshirts, no baggy jeans. She was now a full-time temptress. Paul's arm around her waist provided a certain buffer against the male attention. And every time she looked at him, she felt elated. His glossy black hair, the masculine beauty of his face, and the power of his body, evident in even the slightest move he made, gave his expensive suit the look of a disguise. When the Canadian immigration official stamped her passport—with far more attention to her cleavage than her documents—and waved her on to join Paul, she noted the look of easy confidence on Paul's face, as if he controlled all the airport officials and policemen and ordinary men in the world. As if he were compelling them to kneel at her feet and do her bidding.

The hotel in Toronto was even grander than the one they had stayed at in New York. The room was so large that the elegant chairs and the massive walnut four-poster bed seemed lost in all the space. There was an orchid on the desk; the bath soap had oatmeal and rose petals mixed into the cake. The little welcome kit waiting on the bed included a sampler set of liqueurs and a box of truffles. Olivia was deeply disappointed to notice that the other guests in the lobby looked absolutely ordinary. She had half expected them to be wearing crowns.

The jewelry store was two blocks down, and was an equally elegant, imposing place. A few exquisite diamond-and-gold confections were on display in the window, with an ostentatious lack of price tags. The interior was Spartan, consisting of long glass cases presided over by two beautifully dressed men with an air of frosty respectability.

The younger of the two men closed the store at night, and

therefore became the target. He was a slim blond man with a serious air, and a definite hint of shyness—so Paul reported with glee. Olivia wasn't allowed on the reconnaissance expeditions, lest she be recognized later.

On the following day she had to go to the store alone for the prep run. Paul prepared her meticulously, inspecting her from all angles in her halter top and shorts, mussing her hair, sending her back to the shower to wash off all her makeup. At the last minute he called down to the concierge to get suntan lotion. When it came, he stripped her again to slather the lotion all over her. "You just walked in from a day in the park—that's the concept."

Olivia began to laugh at his seriousness. "Do I have to find my motivation? Who *is* this jewelry-buying girl? What is at the heart of her need for jewelry?"

He smiled at her sarcastically and made her yelp by suddenly slipping two fingers into her pussy.

"Oh, don't start that . . . unless . . ."

"What is at the heart of her need for jewelry?" he repeated. Then a wicked light appeared in his eyes and he said, "Hold still. I think I have an idea."

He got down on his knees, squirting more lotion on his hands and spreading it over her shins and then up her legs, working it into the soft flesh of her inner thighs in gentle circular motions. As he reached the place where her thighs met, he dipped both thumbs into her cunt, spread it open, and began to lick her with powerful, thrusting motions of his tongue.

She cried out and almost lost her balance. His tongue was plunging into her and then flicking up over her clitoris hard, playing back and forth over it until she could barely stand. She put both hands into his silky hair to steady herself. He began to work his thumbs into her, one after the other in a back-and-forth motion that made her knees buckle. Meanwhile his tongue had softened its attack and focused on the very tip of her clit, where it tickled maddeningly. It was as if he was holding her at a precise distance, or holding her orgasm just out of reach. But finally she felt her pussy let go and the coming hit her hard. It was like falling and falling. The effort of staying on her feet made the intense waves of feeling course down her legs, the tensing of her muscles taking on the dark sweetness of orgasm. When she came back to herself, he was laughing into her, looking up at her with that wicked light even brighter in his eyes.

"Now I think we have your perfume exactly right."

Walking down to the store, she was deliriously aware of the slushy wetness in her crotch, hypersensitive in the tight shorts. It wasn't just that everyone was looking at her; everyone was taken aback by her, it seemed. Women as much as men. She kept telling herself that whatever they might think, this outfit had cost twelve hundred dollars, U.S., and— Well, what did Canadians know about fashion? Still she felt almost as if she were streaking, and she arrived at the jewelry store in a strangely heightened state. All her bare skin was energized by the attention of passersby, and she felt the painful nub of her clit singing out again in her shorts; the two points of her nipples were hard and alive, bobbing in her halter top.

When she went into the store, the bell on the door made her jump, and then she found herself smiling in embarrassment at the young blond man who was the target of her clothes, her suntan lotion, her lushly wet pussy. He looked at her with an absolute lack of expression, which almost made her lose her nerve. But then she saw the other man—a middle-aged bald guy with a supercilious quirk to his lips—bearing down on her. She had to do this. She had to prove herself. She couldn't let herself be sidetracked.

Ignoring the bald man as if he were completely invisible, she swept through the store straight to her mark, toying with Mystery Harker's sapphire pendant in a show of coy anxiety that *almost* concealed her real anxiety.

He said, with a slightly tense formality, "Can I help you?"

She looked at him a little uncertainly and said, "I guess. I'm just looking around . . . you know."

He took a half step back, and she realized that was the wrong move. After a cursory inspection of the display case in front of her, she said, "Wait. . . . Actually, I'd like to see these brooches."

"Which tray?" he said, without a flicker of surprise.

She pointed without paying much attention, choosing on the basis of how big the stones looked at a glance. He pulled a ring of little keys out of his pocket, and her heart immediately fixed on them. In a flash she knew she was going to get those keys. She was going to get the keys, and she was going to get the contents of the display case. She was born to do this; it was going to be child's play.

Five minutes later, she had—per Paul's instructions—taken

half of the brooches out, inspected them from various angles, and left them lying on the counter. The blond man—or Matt, as she had discovered his name was—had passed judgment on various brooches, each of which she held up to her right breast with a dubious air. He dutifully examined her right breast again and again, and made generally admiring noises without ever shedding his air of professional sangfroid. Finally, deciding to try a brooch on for real—a little silver dog that was carrying a sizable diamond in its mouth—she feigned difficulty with the catch.

"Could you help...? I can't get this at all."

At this, she was gratified to see a pall of consternation cross his face. And when he said, "Of course, miss," his voice had dropped an octave and acquired a certain husky misery that Olivia knew of old.

He managed to pin the brooch to her without copping a feel at all—she was almost proud of his forbearance. Then she studied the brooch in the mirror with a slightly hangdog air. Now she was ready to prepare the ground for the evening. She said a little too softly, "You can call me Megan. My name's Megan."

He just smiled politely.

And she added, with a wounded note in her voice, "I'm buying myself consolation prizes today because my boyfriend just broke up with me." She looked suddenly, meltingly, into his eyes. He looked down but then seemed to feel that he was being insensitive. He manfully looked back at her face.

"I'm sorry," he said, again with that husky difficulty.

"Oh, it's not so terrible. I just need to take my mind off it.

So . . ." She looked down at the brooch and sighed. Then she said abruptly, awkwardly, "Maybe a ring . . ."

Ten minutes later she left the shop, having chosen a ring that was—what a shame—one size too small; it would have to be resized. Could she come back at six thirty to pick it up? Oh, they closed at six? But she was leaving town. . . .

Of course an exception could be made. She gave him a down payment and left the shop with a tingling sense of victory, visions of gemstones dancing in her head.

She showed up that evening in her white V-neck dress, without the sapphires, and spent about ten minutes trying on necklaces with Matt's attentive help. Then she paid for the ring in cash— with a (she hoped) charmingly ditzy disclaimer about how she'd ruined her credit— "I'm such a shopping addict." She put the ring on and smiled with pleasure. Then she asked Matt out for a drink.

She added, "I just have to go by my hotel room to pick up something. You can come up with me. There's an amazing view."

His eyes dipped toward her cleavage in a strong indication of the amazing view he hoped to have when they got into the hotel room. He said politely, "That sounds like fun."

She followed behind him with fawnlike innocence in her eyes while he locked up the store, pulled down the security wall, locked that, and put the keys in his pants pocket. And as they walked down the street, she touched Matt's arm confidentially and said, "You know I only came in your store because I thought you were cute."

He smiled at her with a helpless rabbit-in-the-headlights look, and said, "No—really?"

"Really," she said. "I like the ring, but what I really wanted was you."

If there was one thing Olivia had never found difficult, it was separating a man from his pants. With Matt, it would prove as simple as getting down on her knees in front of him in the hotel room and saying, "Take these off." When he let them down, she pulled them off over his shoes and tossed them as casually as she could to one side. Then she was nuzzling his already erect cock through his underpants. If he was tempted to wonder why she had thrown his pants toward the closet door, he was easily helped to forget about it. A command to "Close your eyes" was the next step. Then she got to her feet and kissed him with one hand stroking over his head, his forehead, his shut eyes . . . the other pulling down his underpants and finding his naked cock. A few seconds later Paul had slipped out of the closet, taken the keys, and was out the door.

At the slight noise the door made closing, Matt opened his eyes for a second, saw Olivia's rapt face, and shut them again. She left her hand drift down the shaft of his penis, and her heart was suddenly gripped with an insistent desire. She had had her lips against his glans, she could feel his hard-on against her mouth. . . . She heard in her head a dim replay of the planning session she'd had with Paul.

"Just get his pants off and then you can pull back. Make out with him, keep him at arm's length. I'll only be gone ten minutes, and once I get the pants back to you, you can get cold feet and get rid of him."

"But what if he won't stop?" Olivia had said.

"He won't try to force you in a hotel. Don't worry." Paul smiled with only the slightest edge of anxiety in his face.

It had never occurred to either of them that it might be Olivia who wouldn't stop.

She fell to her knees, and her mouth fastened greedily on the tip of Matt's cock, the delicious taste of his precome making her moan gently with satisfaction. Then she was taking his whole cock into her mouth and throat, the hardness of him, the urgency of his attack, wiping away any thought outside of sex. She took turns sucking hard and then letting her mouth go soft so that he was sliding past her wriggling tongue with only the faintest pressure. He was muttering, "Oh, my God . . . thank you . . . oh, my God."

Then she couldn't stand it anymore. She let his cock slip out of her mouth and was standing up to pull him onto the bed with her. They fell side by side and Olivia pulled her dress up with one hand, showing him that she was wearing no panties. The motion itself skewed her dress enough that one breast came spilling out of the top, and Matt seized it immediately in his hand, murmuring "Megan . . . Megan, you're so beautiful . . . ," And he was reaching between her thighs. She gasped as his fingers found her naked, wet pussy, sliding across her clit and into her with tense hunger. Then he was on top of her, his cock pressing against her clit, then reangling to find the opening of her vagina. The resistance of her tight pussy gave way only gradually—or else he was taking his time, letting his dick sink into her inch by inch, as she gasped and held as still as she could, concentrating on the feeling. And as he finally filled her completely, pressing in to his full extent, she heard from the street the first angry notes of the jewelry store security alarm. She said instantly, instinctively, "Oh, God, Matt. Fuck me."

And he did. He fucked her hard, needy, and rough in a way she wouldn't have expected. Her cunt tightened rapidly into a blinding hot orgasm, increasing both her wetness and her sensitivity threefold. He was squeezing and twisting her tits, and the feeling of his big cock entering her again and again was maddening, driving her past orgasm and into a different, deeper kind of coming that made her heart pound. She found herself writhing under him, her hips reaching up to bring him in deep with every thrust, her cunt clutching his dick in wrenching spasms of pleasure.

Then Matt said, "God...I can't...It's so good." He thrust into her one final time and came himself, his hand convulsing on her exposed breast.

At that moment, Paul slipped back into the room—and froze in the doorway. Olivia couldn't see him clearly from where she lay, but the simple body language of his outline gave her the message nonetheless.

Of course, she and Paul had agreed that when it came to business, jealousy should not get in the way. But Olivia already suspected, as her body tensed again—this time in fright and chagrin—that there were limits to that tolerance. And as Paul slipped into the closet again, a bulging carryall full of gems over one shoulder, she shut her eyes to put off finding out what anger, hurt, or betrayal would show in his beautiful eyes.

Chapter Ten

Lee stretched and let her biology textbook slip off her lap and fall shut beside her on the silk upholstery of Olivia's living room sofa. She checked her watch again: five thirty. Olivia should be arriving any minute, unless her flight from Austria was delayed. Lee tried to cheer herself by imagining Austria, and the ski chalet Olivia had been selling this week, but the image was shrouded in the boredom occasioned by an hour of studying for biology finals. The majestic view of Manhattan's Central Park from Olivia's penthouse apartment, which Lee usually adored, had likewise become tainted. Somehow cell-membrane chemistry had got mixed up with skyscrapers and black diamond pistes in a mishmash through which Lee could only feel resentment that, yet again, she wasn't allowed to come on the trip.

She would have thought Olivia was just cheap, despite the

ungodly sums she obviously earned in her real estate business. But Olivia paid for Lee to have her own apartment downtown, paid Lee's tuition at Columbia, paid Lee's credit card bills every month, and bought her presents on top of that. It certainly wasn't every college junior who got a Cartier diamond necklace for her birthday—not that Lee had anywhere to wear such a thing. But the one thing she would have liked best—to go along with Olivia on her trips, at least during the summer—was not allowed. "I'll be working," Olivia would say. "You know I love hanging out with you, Lee, but I wouldn't have time to hang out with you on these trips. They're not vacations."

"It would be a vacation for me," Lee would say. "I can manage to have fun without you, you know. I won't get kidnapped."

But on this one point Olivia was firm. Lee could be as spoiled as any girl in New York—but she would do it in New York. And so Lee had never even been out of the United States. At least, not until her little escapade this spring—but, God willing, Olivia would never find out about that.

She had first met Jake in the bar across the street from Olivia's place, shortly after being told by her sister that she was not going to go to Mexico for spring break, not as long as Olivia was paying the bills. "I know what happens at those resorts." That prim phrase sounded so weird coming from Olivia that it almost made Lee laugh. But the next moment she realized Olivia was trying to take the place of their father. Though neither sister would bring his name up in these arguments, his spirit was always in the background. Still, it seemed unnatural for a sister to be so humorless about spring break. Olivia knew Lee wasn't a virgin, after all. Did she really think something unspeakable would happen to her if she was let loose among a lot of drunken college students? In fact, what did she think Lee did on Saturday nights if not hang out with a lot of drunken college students?

So Lee had been in a rotten mood when she went into Flanagan's across the street. She'd sat at the bar and ordered a straight whiskey, just to make the point (to the nobody who was watching) that she was a complete grown-up. It did pass through the back of her mind that a *complete* grown-up wouldn't have thought being able to buy drinks was such a big deal (she had just turned twenty-one in February, and the thrill was still fresh).

She was miserably imagining the whole holiday she was missing, her mind perversely lingering on exactly those aspects that would alarm her sister most. She *definitely* would have gone topless on the beach. All year round she suffered for having small— but pretty—breasts that disappeared in clothes; what was the harm if she showed them off just once? There would *definitely* be a drunken hookup with a stranger, who would *definitely* be a football player who was into her for all the wrong reasons. She would *definitely* . . . Here she began to embroider and paint the entire scene. . . . It would be a cheap motel room with a flashing light in the window. With all her usual inhibitions forgotten, she would make him hold still while she straddled him and plunged down on his cock, taking it deep inside her. He would be groaning and reaching up to fondle her breasts—the breasts that would have drawn him to her on the beach. Then he would be plunging up into her from below, his thick cock hammering her as he . . .

"Hey, are you drinking alone?"

Lee jumped. The stranger who had accosted her was startlingly good-looking. His blue eyes seemed almost uncannily brilliant against his deeply tanned skin and black hair; and he had the sculpted features of a Hollywood heartthrob. He was wearing a polo shirt, but there was something about him, a potent physicality, that made the preppy look seem like a disguise. Immediately she found herself staring at his biceps, his strong forearms—he must be an athlete, she thought. Then she saw the look of coolly appraising intelligence in his eyes and changed her mind. He could be something on Wall Street, perhaps, or a doctor.

What she knew for certain was that he was far too sexy to be talking to her, at random, in a bar. Lee was the sort of girl guys fell for *eventually*, after knowing her for months—if they weren't distracted by girls whose charms were more obvious. She had a disarmingly pretty face, but her hair was a nothing shade of brown and her body slender and graceful rather than eye-catchingly curvy. Because her sister bought her clothes, furthermore, she dressed conservatively. Now she was wearing a calf-length tunic dress in a thick lined cotton that left everything to the imagination. A man like this should have walked right past her on his way to—well, Olivia.

"Oh, well . . . I guess I am drinking alone, if you put it that way." She laughed nervously. "I mean, no one's meeting me. That's redundant, right?"

"Be as redundant as you like," he said.

They began to talk then, and he was as charming as he was gorgeous, if that was even possible. Actually, Lee found, it was hard to tell how charming a man was when he looked like this.

It was hard to think about anything but his face, his body, what his arms would feel like if they were around you, pressing you against his chest. He was saying something utterly, maddeningly fascinating about his business interests in Europe and about how pretty her hair was, and all she heard was, *Maybe I'll sleep with you. Maybe you'll get to touch me naked, tonight.* She was laughing at everything he said and trying not to stare too obviously. She was drinking three whiskeys in a row and getting dangerously lightheaded. She was thinking of how to invite him to her apartment without it being possible, even slightly, that he would say no.

And at the end of it he suddenly put his hand on her shoulder—lightly, familiarly, in a seemingly thoughtless gesture—as if he didn't know that touch would send wildfire through her entire body. As if Lee would not melt to the core of her being and freeze again, praying that he would kiss her.

He didn't. He simply looked her confidingly in the eyes and said, "Would you do me a favor?"

"Of course," she said without thinking.

"You don't know what the favor is," he pointed out, and gave her a smile that almost made her reach out and *make* him kiss her.

She said, "I don't need to know what the favor is," and then took a deep breath, shocked by her own daring.

He laughed. "You're so much like . . ." Then he seemed to catch himself. He shook his head and the hand was gone from her shoulder.

"So much like what? Who?" she said with a plaintive note. (He must be made to touch her shoulder again. He must!)

"Listen, the favor. I need someone to come with me to London for a few days. Do you think you could be my date?"

Lee took a minute to make the decision, but it was purely for show. There was never any doubt what she would say, and she was still convinced that any heterosexual girl—or homosexual man, for that matter—would have made the same decision. "No, I really *meant* 'of course,'" she said breathlessly, her eyes laughing into his. "So, of course." Just as any rational girl in New York City would have said, Lee was deeply convinced.

But she wasn't quite ready to argue the point with her sister, or to tell Olivia everything that had happened as a result. Therefore, Olivia still believed Lee hadn't spoken to her over spring break because she was angry about Mexico—not because she was in another country and didn't know how to conceal the fact from Olivia's caller ID.

Now Lee was woken from her reverie by the annoying little two-note tune played by Olivia's intercom. She froze, irrationally feeling that someone had arrived to expose her—as if Olivia had hired a telepathic spy who had been lurking in the lobby downstairs, waiting for Lee to *think* the wrong thing. Then she realized how dumb that was, and went to the intercom with a rueful smile on her lips.

She picked up the receiver and said, "Hello?"

"Hi, Lee?" the doorman said. "Is your sister there? I didn't see her go in."

"Hi, Frank. Olivia's not back yet."

"Gotcha."

She heard Frank repeating to someone that Olivia wasn't back, and then an indistinct deep voice responding. Then Frank came back on the line: "Hi, Lee? Gentleman still wants to come up. Says he had some business with your sister, but he'll talk to you. Should I tell him to wait?"

"Why would he talk to me if he has business with Olivia?" Lee said.

"Yeah, he said he wanted to talk to Olivia. Now he says he wants to talk to you," Frank said in a disapproving tone that was obviously directed against the "gentleman," whoever he was. Lee smiled to herself. Frank had always been overprotective of both girls. He had two teenage daughters and tended to regard Lee and Olivia as older versions of his girls, hazardously unprotected in the big city. In any case, there was no way Lee was going to let this opportunity slip—if only because it was bound to annoy Olivia.

"No, it's okay, Frank. Send him up."

Hanging up the receiver, she went to the full-length mirror next to the front door and frowned slightly at her attire. She was in old cutoff jeans and a T-shirt, clearly not the thing for welcoming business associates. On the other hand, she was just the kid sister. She was distracted for a minute by her own face. The clear, almond-shaped blue eyes, the delicate nose, and the pale pink lips had a precise beauty that always comforted her. Even if she wasn't that striking, she was undeniably pretty. For the thousandth time, she considered bleaching her hair and rejected the idea. It would seem like she was trying to look like Olivia. She knew men preferred her sister—there was nothing she could do about that. But at least she could cling to her pride. Then the doorbell rang and she started guiltily.

The first thing she noticed about the man she let in was that he towered over her. He was perhaps six foot three and, unlike many tall men, was broad-shouldered and brawny enough to make that height seem natural. His face had an angular handsomeness that instantly appealed to her, and he met her eyes in a direct way that made her instinctively smile.

"Hello, I'm Nicholas Taylor. Perhaps your sister spoke to you about me?"

The surprise of his British accent distracted her for a moment. His voice was also unusually deep, and she realized a man's voice alone could make him attractive, or *more* attractive in this case, *devastatingly* attractive in this case. By the time she answered, her face felt hot. "No, she doesn't always tell me things," Lee said. "But come in. Sit down. I'm Lee."

He followed her in, looking around the apartment with a marked interest that made Lee wonder for a second whether Frank had been right and he intended to rob the place. She followed his gaze, envying once again her sister's good taste. The furniture was modern, low to the floor, with clean, rectangular outlines. Both furniture and rugs were in a range of greens, from olive to lime to mint, a subtle variation of tones that played off one another without ever quite clashing. Then there was the gleaming maple flooring and the white walls with a painting here, a photo there. Lee's favorite was an eight-foot-by-eight-foot black-and-white photo of the view from Olivia's window itself, in winter. You could look from the view itself to the photo and somehow it made the glorious view more present, more impressive.

He said, "A beautiful place. Does she own it?"

"Of course. You know she's a Realtor," said Lee. "Well, of course you do. You must be one of her clients?"

Nicholas looked at her with faint surprise in his eyes. It was rapidly replaced by his previous impassive cordiality. "I'm not exactly one of her clients, but we'll get to that."

She noticed a slight distortion in his consonants that suggested English might not be his native tongue, and immediately wondered if he was one of Olivia's European friends. Again she felt the keen unfairness of never getting to have European friends, and she resolved to make this man her friend . . . if friend was really what she had in mind.

They sat down, Lee on the sofa where the biology book still lay, and Nicholas on an armchair opposite. She crossed her legs with a consciousness of his eyes on her, and although his face remained polite and distant, Lee knew somehow that he was admiring her.

Then they both sat in silence for what felt like an eternity. At last Lee said, and was alarmed to find her voice coming out weak and frightened, "What did you want? I mean, if you're not one of Olivia's clients."

He said, "I don't want to alarm you."

"But you *are* alarming me," she said, with her natural candor. "I'm getting alarmed, anyway."

"I'm sorry."

"So *stop* alarming me."

At this, he began to laugh. His laughter had the same bass gravity as his voice, and she again found herself smiling at him without knowing why. Then he seemed to force a look of seriousness back into his face. He said, "I would very much like to stop, Miss Stewart, but I don't think I can."

She bit her lip. She realized she should be worried, but something about the way he said it made her feel deeply gratified, as if he'd been asking her out. "So go on alarming me, then."

"Well, with your permission," he said, smiling again. "I think you may be concerned to hear that I work as an investigator for the insurance company that covers the possessions of Mr. Ralph Axton."

Lee looked at him with a faint chill passing over her. "Well, I know Ralph Axton. I know him a little. But listen..." She looked superstitiously at the door, trying once again to figure out how long Olivia would take getting in from the airport. "It's just that... my sister doesn't know that I know him. She doesn't know I was ever in London, actually. So if Olivia comes in, could you pretend...?" She made a face. "Maybe we could talk somewhere else?"

He shook his head. "She does know, I'm afraid."

Lee swallowed. "She does?"

"I told her."

"Well, why would you do that?" said Lee, distressed. "I mean— how do you know Ralph? You're an insurance person of some kind?"

He regarded her gravely for a minute. She saw a dawning amused realization in his eyes. Then that his eyes were an odd pale green that went all too well with his cool demeanor. "You don't know about the gems, do you?" he said.

"The gems?" Suddenly Lee felt faint. A vague misgiving that had been lurking in the back of her mind now appeared as a definite shadow, and then a huge black blot. "Gems? What gems?"

"That's incredible. You don't know."

At this moment the door flew open and a turquoise leather suitcase was thrown in. Then another. A third was wheeled in behind a mussed and red-faced Olivia, who immediately froze to gape at the two of them.

"Welcome back to New York, Miss Stewart," said Nicholas casually.

Olivia took a deep breath and let it out, possibly counting to ten. Then she said, equally casually, but with an edge of spite, "Mr. Taylor. Is there any reason I can't throw you out of my apartment right now?"

"Because it would be to your benefit to talk to me."

"I meant a legal reason."

"I know." He smiled. "I've been having a very enlightening conversation with your sister."

"Funny. That's what I object to most," Olivia said. "Close the door on your way out, please, Mr. Taylor. I'll come to see you at . . . What was the company again?"

He stood and took a card out of his pocket, laying it on the glass coffee table with a nod to Olivia and a smile to Lee. Then he left briskly, closing the door, as requested, behind him.

The instant the door closed, Olivia grimly said, "We'd better talk."

Lee's first night of acquaintance with Jake had ended disappointingly chastely. Toward the end of the evening, he'd seemed distracted, and she felt a miserable conviction that he'd found her boring after all, and she would never hear from him again. On the sidewalk outside Flanagan's, he had kissed her good night—

on the cheek—and promised to e-mail her with details of the London trip. Three days passed without word, and she had begun to forget the whole thing—or at least to try to forget it. Since he'd said they would leave in four days (which, by then, meant the following day), she finally figured he was just another guy giving her a bullshit line. But why would such a gorgeous man have to give anyone bullshit lines? And why hadn't he tried to take advantage of it, when obviously—wasn't it obvious?—she was ready to do anything for him or with him.

The night of that third day, she was trying to forget it in her bathtub. She was lying up to her ears in lavender bubble bath, listening to a suitably self-pitying emo playlist—when her door buzzer went.

Nobody ever visited Lee unannounced. Lee lived in a third-floor walk-up, and unannounced visitors would have been a hardship. If anyone rang her doorbell at ten p.m., it was probably a drunk looking for someone else. And she would have to run down three flights of stairs, dripping wet in a bathrobe, in order to find that out. So, on any other night, she would have lain in the bathtub cursing the annoyance under her breath and waiting for it to go away. Tonight...

She was in her bathrobe and down the stairs with the buzzer still ringing in her ears. And in the doorway, there was Jake, looking a little flustered and even embarrassed. He said, "Oh, no. I dragged you out of your bath." He was wearing an untucked shirt over a pair of jeans, but he looked just as fresh and perfect as he had the last time—as if he had been especially prepared by a team of experts to be irresistibly attractive to Lee.

"That's okay," she said, a little out of breath from her rush down the stairs. "I mean, that's fine. Do you want to come up?" She heard herself sounding overeager, and hoped it would be likable rather than just pathetic. She never could hide her feelings.

"I can come up, but I can't stay," he said. "I was coming to ask you if you can leave tonight."

"Oh. Oh, that's . . ." She blinked at him. "Of course."

"It's going to be a strange trip." His voice was low and urgent. "I'm going to have to ask you to take certain things on faith. But I promise you won't get hurt." He smiled. "In fact, I promise you'll have a good time."

Her heart pitter-pattered madly as she tried to quell her grin. "So you mean, I shouldn't ask questions?"

"I know it sounds ridiculous."

"Can I get dressed?" she said, glancing back up the stairs.

He laughed. "Not only can you get dressed," he said. "But I've brought the clothes for you to get dressed in."

"Oh . . . that's . . . I mean, it's really not necessary." And for the first time, Lee had serious reservations about the whole adventure. She could all too easily imagine the headlines. MANHATTAN GIRL WENT WITH KILLER WILLINGLY. Or: CANNIBAL VICTIM LURED BY GIFTS.

Still, twenty minutes later she was in a cab with him, headed to the airport, wearing a little slip dress that he'd brought with him in a garment bag. At his behest, she'd brought no clothes of her own. "I'll dress you for this trip," he'd said. "You won't need anything, really, but yourself." Her basic toiletries were in a little Louis Vuitton overnight bag he'd provided. The shoes—little Prada loafers—were perhaps one size too big.

And as a pledge of his earnestness, he'd put a bracelet on her wrist, the contact of his fingers on the sensitive skin of her arm making her flutter inside helplessly. The bracelet was a little cuff encrusted with alternating gray pearls and white diamonds. She asked him, trying for humor, "What do I have to do to earn this?"

"Whatever I say."

Here Olivia broke into Lee's story, with a red-hot intensity of anger. "Did he sleep with you?"

Lee frowned at her and a spirit of rebellion rose up in her. "I don't see how that's any of your business."

"Whose business would it be, then?"

"Mine." Lee put her nose in the air, scowling. "And, um, his. Ours."

"Ha!" Olivia shook her head. "You think you know what you're talking about. You're like a child."

Lee stared at her, with her mind groping again for an impossible answer, straying in a forest of preposterous guesses. "Wait. Do you know this guy, Livy?"

"Let's not even say I know him," Olivia said in a low, hoarse voice. "Let's just say I hate him and I'm going to break his neck if he's touched you."

Lee was exasperated. "I'm twenty-one, for Christ's sake. I *like* men touching me."

"Take it back!" Olivia said with sudden, high-pitched fury.

Then Lee began to giggle irrepressibly. "Take it back?" she said.

Olivia stared at her uncomprehendingly for a second and then her face, too, twisted into a foolish grin. "Oh, well."

"Yes, Olivia, I take it back," Lee said, with her hand up in a Girl Scout–oath gesture. "I *do not* like men touching me. Especially good-looking men who take me on their private planes to Europe. That's my pet hate."

"Private plane?" Olivia said, with a renewed irritability. "Don't *tell me* he has a private plane now."

"So you do know him."

"Oh, God. Just go on with your story."

The private plane had actually been Ralph Axton's. And when they boarded it—Lee feeling as if she were still in her bathtub, improbably deep in an improbable lavender emo daydream—Ralph was there, lying on a leather sofa that was bolted to one wall, fast asleep with a huge marmalade cat fast asleep on his chest. He had red hair—to match the cat, she couldn't help thinking—and a lean, spare body that looked especially endearing the way he lay with one arm hanging off the couch.

"Ralph Axton, the future Lord Axton," Jake had whispered into her ear. "And *you* are my girlfriend, Jenny."

She squinted at him.

He said in a low voice, "This will be a lot more fun if you just play along and see what happens."

So she did. When Ralph Axton woke up and was introduced to her, she let herself be introduced as Jenny without blinking. She let the cat crawl into her lap and smiled at both men impartially. Ralph immediately opened a bottle of wine and poured her a glass just in time to spill some in her lap as the plane took off. Then he dabbed at her thighs with a napkin while Jake growled at him, "Back off, Ralph. I have my eye on you."

Ralph said, "Oh, no harm done. Purely friendly, isn't it, Jenny?" And he tried to catch her eye in a conspiratorial way, while she kept her gaze fixed on Jake.

They got through two bottles of wine while Ralph and Jake chatted and sniped at each other. At first they seemed to know each other well, but she finally worked out that they'd only met a few weeks before, at some horse race. There was a dispute over who had chosen some winning horse and who had merely placed his bet based on the other's superior knowledge. Then disputes about French foreign policy, the relative merits of baseball and cricket, and whether a future Lord could be considered unemployed. With the amount of wine that was being poured, the starry sky outside the plane's window, and the pale clouds below, she couldn't follow it all very well. All she knew was that Jake had slung his arm around her waist familiarly, and that at some point, when they arrived wherever it was—London? Austria? heaven?—she would share a room with him. After all, she was his girlfriend, Jenny.

Ralph was endearingly funny, and almost as good-looking in his fair-skinned, lean way, as Jake was in his dark, more muscular way. He kept flirting with her, suggesting that she give up Jake for him. "Do it sooner rather than later. I say it for your own good. Anyone can see he's going to break your heart."

"I think I'll risk that," Lee said, smiling uncomfortably.

"No, you mustn't take such a terrible risk," Ralph said authoritatively. "It would be wrong of me to allow it. As soon as we arrive in London, you shall marry me and bear my children."

"Yes, bear the children immediately after landing," said Jake. "Get it out of your system."

"He mocks me," Ralph said with dignity, "out of insecurity."

At this moment the cat, purring on Lee's lap, reached up one paw and pressed it passionately into her breast, the claws making her wince.

"There, Louis has marked you," said Ralph. "You now belong to me."

"I'm going to mark *you* in a second," said Jake, and both men laughed companionably while Lee detached the cat's claws from her dress.

The attention and the wine made her almost unpleasantly excited, her mind dimly imagining both men moving toward her, how Jake would hold her still and kiss her while Ralph's lips moved down her throat, and his hands tested the tender peaks of her breasts. He would pull the straps of her slip dress down— perhaps she would struggle and Jake would have to force her arms behind her back. He would murmur, "Don't try to fight it. You're here. You've already made up your mind. . . ." Then her naked breasts would be bare to the hungry eyes of both men. Ralph would begin to suck her nipples, his tongue tickling their tips, his teeth fastening on them gently, until she was squirming with arousal. Jake would be sliding a hand up under her dress, his fingers sliding inside her thighs, finding her pussy, its wetness.

He would pull her legs open as Ralph opened his fly and pulled out his long, hard dick, ready to enter her. . . . She would be held down to accept being used, fucked ... first by one man, then the other. ...

But time passed and Ralph fell asleep again sprawled on his couch, while Lee nodded against Jake's shoulder, dreaming of orgies. At last, Jake led her to a second leather couch at the rear of the plane. He pulled her down beside him and, in the roar of the plane's engine, began to talk to her again confidentially as they lay with their bodies pressed together in the narrow space, their arms around each other. He murmured into her ear, "You're being a good sport about all this."

"I can't complain so far."

Then she was dazzlingly aware of his hand spreading against her slender back, the movement of it down over her waist, stroking and cradling her, pulling her body snug against him. She realized she was holding her breath.

He said into her ear, "You get prettier. The more I look at you, the prettier you get."

"Was I ... I wasn't pretty enough before?"

"No. That's not what I said." Then his lips lightly touched her throat, just beside her ear, and the kiss made her hot all over. He said in a low voice, which mingled with the airplane's rumble, "I want to kiss you. Can I?"

"Please," she said, breathlessly.

His mouth moved onto hers, and they were kissing as his hands began to roam gently down her back, tracing her ass and moving on to lightly grasp her upper thighs and ever so slightly spread them against him. As her crotch made contact with his, she shivered and clung to his shoulders. The mere sensation of his body being so much larger than hers, so much stronger, made her whimper inaudibly, helplessly. She felt the bulge in his jeans pressing into her with that specific seeking gesture and pressed back, her hips arching forward to meet him, her hands now feeling the muscles in his back. For a moment they were grinding together, and then—stunningly, horribly—he had pushed her away.

"Let's . . . We shouldn't do this."

"You mean, because Ralph's there?" she said. He didn't respond, but a few minutes later, he gathered her against him again, this time loosely, tenderly. She let the desire in her body ease, relax into a general sense of expectation, the feeling of lying in his arms while the plane bore them both onward over the sea. And she had fallen into a boozy semisleep in which she lost consciousness of everything but his body against hers, when the plane began to tilt downward, downward, and finally came in to land at London.

If there was one thing Lee would never have expected in an aristocrat's London home, it was that it would be messy. It was a better class of mess, she had to admit. An antique divan had three fur coats left tumbled on it, with a plate on top, which bore the remnants of some sort of strawberry cake. A trail of expensive women's shoes was left at the front door, where the owner had obviously taken them off on arriving home, and never picked them up again, pair after pair. There was at least two weeks' worth of newspapers disassembled on the rug by the fireplace, with an ashtray spilled over the lot. Beside the rug an enormous stuffed cougar lay on its side, frozen in midsnarl, and a second marmalade cat, the twin of the first, was nestled on the cougar's neck happily, as if it recognized the family relationship.

Where Lee would have pretended nothing was wrong, Jake immediately said, laughing, "Can't you get someone to clean this up? It's a disgrace, Ralph."

Ralph yawned. "Oh, I think I gave her the week off. My parents and sister are away, you know. I don't like people lurking when I'm here by myself. They spy and tell stories to the tabloids. And then, of course, if I *don't* do anything depraved, I'm so conscious of disappointing them."

Then Lee couldn't help interjecting, "This is all from a week?"

"Oh . . . I suppose a few days," said Ralph carelessly. "I don't remember when I went to New York at all, now."

The room Lee and Jake were to stay in was almost incongruously spotless. It was an anonymous room with a grand bed, whose headboard was painted with a scene of a Greek goddess hunting deer; it looked suspiciously Renaissance to Lee, and she tried not to think about what damage she might do to it as she let herself fall back onto the bed. Ralph, passing by the doorway, called out pleasantly, "Last chance, Jenny. I know you are *very* self-sacrificing, but I think even Jake will not blame you if you come with me at this point."

"Good night, Ralph!" she called back, and then revised it to: "Good afternoon, I mean," because although she desperately needed to sleep, in London it was one in the afternoon. Then Jake firmly closed the door and began—as if it was nothing, as if her heart was not beating a hole in her chest as she watched—to undress.

First it was the shirt, which he unbuttoned while yawning and saying to her, "I hope Ralph isn't getting on your nerves."

"No," she said without knowing what she was saying. He had thrown the shirt on a chair and he was beautiful. He was perfect. He had those washboard abs, and the hair on his chest was fine and dark, a faint *T* over his cushiony pectoral muscles. But it was more than that; it was the whole shape of his body, the graceful sweep of his broad shoulders, the perfect golden skin. . . .

He was opening his jeans, and for an instant she actually shut her eyes superstitiously. Then she opened them just in time to see him unzip his fly and shift the jeans off with a twist of his hips that made her faint with lust.

"Do you like him? Ralph?"

"Oh. Yes. Yes, he's fine," she said.

His jeans were on the floor. He stepped out of them and she was dying. She couldn't move. He was going to— He had to, didn't he?

Then she found herself saying, with her miserable goddamned straightforwardness, "Hey, Jake? Are we going to have sex?"

He froze. She froze.

He was in his briefs, looking at her with an expression she couldn't read. With no expression. With such a handsome face that all you could think about was what he looked like. Then you had forgotten to look at his expression. All you had remembered was *not,* under any circumstances, to look at his dick.

She looked at his dick. Oh, God, she could *see his dick.* And it was . . . not quite hard, but stiffening . . . halfway there. . . .

He said, "I can't . . ."

"You can't?" she said, with utter disbelief.

"I'm sorry," he said, and he was ducking, grabbing his jeans from the floor. "I can't."

"But that's impossible!"

"I'm sorry. I didn't think you would care...."

She blurted out, "Care? How could I not care? And anyway— you're almost naked!"

Then, to her horror, Lee burst into tears.

Here Olivia interrupted Lee's story again, saying sanctimo- niously, "But of course, he was right. He shouldn't take advan- tage of you." Her face showed a contentment that filled Lee with disgust.

"Oh, to hell with that," she said. "It was leading me on! He was ... I mean, it was cruel."

Olivia shrugged. "You don't know what his reasons might have been," she said primly.

"Well, I hope it wasn't because he had herpes," Lee said, sud- denly losing her temper, "because he *did* fuck me, after all."

Olivia's face went pale and then clouded over with a disgust even greater than Lee's of a minute before. She swallowed. At last, Olivia said, with venom in her hoarse voice, "Did you make him do it?"

Lee stared at her sister in disbelief. "Do you really think I have to make men sleep with me?"

"But he said he wasn't going to!" Olivia said.

"Well, he was comforting me. You know, I was crying and ... it just happened."

"You tricked him," Olivia said. "Crying—it's the oldest trick in the book."

"What are you talking about?" said Lee. "Why does this upset you so much, anyway? Is this your boyfriend?"

"This is my *enemy!*" Olivia said, and then she burst into tears herself.

Lee managed just in time to stop herself from saying that Olivia could cry all she liked, but Lee wasn't going to sleep with her. Oldest trick in the book! She had to actually hold her breath to keep from saying it, but she stopped herself. Then she slowly let out her breath and said the right thing for a change. "Hey, Livy. Are you okay? Do you want to tell me what's going on? I don't mean to upset you. . . ."

"No," Olivia said miserably, wiping tears away with the back of her hand. "Just finish the story. I'm sorry . . . I'm sorry I keep interrupting."

Jake had first embraced her and kissed her on the forehead. He had told her how beautiful she was, and that if she knew why he was doing it, she would understand. Lee had said, unforgivingly, "But there was no call to take your clothes off . . . and you kissed me on the plane. . . ." And no matter what she did, she couldn't stop crying. She had been waiting for him for three days, then for an eternity over the Atlantic Ocean, and then for a longer eternity while he stripped, and then—brick wall.

Finally he managed to get her to lie down. He cuddled her spoon fashion from behind—carefully keeping her clear of his groin—and murmured into her ear, "I'm sorry. I'm so sorry, Lee. I think men forget sometimes that women . . . really want them."

"Of course we do," Lee whispered, half to herself.

"It just seems vain to think so. Do you understand?"

"I guess it was vain when I thought you wanted me," Lee whispered. "That was what was really vain."

"Don't be crazy. Why do you think I kissed you on the plane?"

"You were leading me on," Lee said miserably. She was already half asleep, she was so tired. And she found herself saying, "If you don't make love to me, I'm never getting out of this bed. I'll starve here."

He laughed into her hair. "Lee, that's ridiculous."

"I know," she said sleepily. "Just hold me. No, really hold me. Hold me like you did on the plane."

So he was holding her close, and she was dropping off to sleep, dimly aware of his bare skin against that flimsy slip dress, of his arms around her; dimly aware of the surprising fact that the plane didn't seem to be moving at all. And then she was dimly aware of his hard-on pressing against her thighs from behind.

The next second she was keenly aware of it. And of his hand pulling her dress up, his hand pulling her panties down. His dick pressing between her thighs, finding her slit. Its head slipping over her pussy as he thrust it in between the soft space at the very top of her thighs.

She parted her legs and was gritting her teeth, afraid that if she cried out, he would come to his senses and refuse her again.

There was his cock, slipping past her clitoris until she was half mad with the pleasure of it. She couldn't stop herself from reaching down and letting her hand touch the tip of his cock as it slid forward. Then she was gently grasping it as it came, again and again, spreading the slipperiness of her juices mixed with his over the tip, then spreading it over her own clit. He thrust again and . . . again . . . and then his cock caught in her from behind. He was pressing it inside her.

It went in impossibly deep, making her cry out, forgetting her resolve to stay silent. And he was fucking her; he was actually thrusting his dick into her. She reached back to feel his body, the muscles at his waist moving under the smooth hot skin. His dick sliding in and out of her, going in deep and pulling back, faster and faster until she was clinging to the bed, gasping as he beat into her rapid-fire. His hands were stroking her breasts, his fingertips reaching in under the dress. It went on and on for seemingly forever—an eternity in which he fucked her faster, deeper, than anyone could possibly stand, and the feeling was so overwhelming that she had seemingly forgotten to come, had forgotten that anything in the world could feel better than this, could feel *more* than this.

And then *he* came, with a blinding surge of force as he drove even deeper, more finally, into her. That set her off, and at first she didn't even know what was happening to her as the orgasm wiped her out, seeming to throb out from her cunt and fill her to her fingertips, to the soles of her feet.

And as she lay, drained and lost in pleasure, not knowing how much time had passed, not knowing if she was awake or asleep, she thought she heard him murmuring, "Darling . . .

Olivia." But then she was dreaming, and in her dream she knew that had been a dream. He couldn't have said that. He had no way of knowing Olivia; Lee had never even mentioned having a sister.

She woke just as the sun was beginning to set. The room was dark, with a faint rosy glow against the curtains. Jake was standing over her, wearing a suit and tie with a white shirt so immaculate it seemed to glow in the dark.

She sat up, disoriented, half remembering the sex, half remembering him rejecting her. "Are you leaving?" she said, frightened.

"*Shh,*" he said. "Not yet. Don't worry."

He sat down on the edge of the bed and put one hand on her calf, stroking it as if to quiet her. She continued to stare at him, gradually gathering in her mind everything that had happened: the flight, her crying, the sex, the muttered "Olivia"—though that part, of course, hadn't really happened. At last she said, "This has been so wonderful. Is it over?"

"It's almost over. Now I have to collect my favor."

"It would be too good to be true, I guess, if this was already your favor."

Then they both looked at the bracelet on her wrist. In her sleep, she had been resting her weight on it somehow, so that her wrist was a little sore on one side.

He said softly, "You're so sweet. I'll never forgive myself if this hurts you in any way."

"No biggie," she said even more softly.

Then they were smiling at each other in the dark, as if
they'd known each other forever.

At last she said, "So what's the favor?"

He went to his open suitcase in the corner and pulled out a
white silk robe, shaking it out and inspecting it for creases.
Then he looked at his watch. He took a deep breath, and when
he looked at her again, he was all business. "There isn't much
time. What I need you to do, Lee, is very simple. Change into
this. Go downstairs. You will find Ralph Axton by the fireplace,
smoking, with his cat. Keep him there by the fireplace for an
hour."

Lee swallowed. "What if I can't?"

"You can." He smiled. "Even if you weren't as lovely as you
are, he wants to sleep with you to get back at me. But if something unforeseen happens, and he moves toward the stairs—
scream."

"Scream?"

"Start changing your clothes now. Sorry. I don't mean to rush
you, but I have to rush you."

She stood up and pulled the slip dress off over her head. For
a split second she was bitter; he was seeing her fully naked for
the first time. Did he even care? She kept herself from looking to
see if he was looking, and pulled on the robe as quickly as she
could. "I'm not sure I can scream. I think I'd be embarrassed.
I mean . . ."

"Then you'll have to succeed, won't you?" Jake said.

She looked at him then. He was gazing at her in an achy way
that made her certain he *had* watched her undress. "Is that your
clever way of manipulating me?"

"No, it's my stupid, primitive way of manipulating you." He looked at the bracelet on her wrist, with a slightly apologetic, gentle air. Then he took the watch off his own wrist and handed it to her. "Whatever I say—remember, you promised?"

She took the watch and, after a moment's consideration, put it on her other wrist. Its weight made her notice the weight of the bracelet, and she couldn't help imagining herself in manacles. But she said with as much good grace as she could muster, "Do I get to know why?"

He looked at her with no expression whatsoever.

"Are you after some sort of secret papers? Are you a spy?" she said, and laughed, then felt foolish. Perhaps he was a spy. It was no more unlikely than anything else that had happened.

"I'm doing something you don't need to know about, so you aren't going to know about it. It wouldn't help you at all to know. And we're running out of time." He pointed to the watch. "An hour exactly. When the hour is up, make an excuse and leave. Then don't let him see you leave the house, but leave the house by the front door. Turn right and walk to the corner, where there will be a car waiting to pick you up. A black Mercedes. The driver will be waiting for Jenny."

"In my robe?"

"That's up to you," he said, smiling. "But don't waste any time. The car will take you to Heathrow Airport, where I'll be waiting for you at the Virgin Atlantic check-in with a plane ticket and your passport."

"My passport . . ."

"The same one that got you here. You can keep it as a souvenir. I'll see you in an hour," he said, and then he was out the door, leaving her stroking that pearl-and-diamond bracelet, wondering how she had come so far in so little time. Only ten hours had passed since she had been soaking in her bathtub, trying to forget all about the trip to London that was never going to happen.

When she got downstairs, she found Ralph Axton sitting cross-legged on the floor by the fireplace, smoking, a marmalade cat in his lap, a newspaper open in front of him. He was wearing a bathrobe himself, which might also be silk; in this light Lee couldn't tell. As she walked in, he looked up with no surprise at all.

"Have you finally seen sense and changed sides to me? Clever girl. Come sit with me and have some champagne. I know there's a bottle of champagne under these newspapers somewhere. I lost it there myself. . . ."

She came forward, feeling the swish of the silk against her thighs. "I woke up before Jake. . . . He's still asleep."

"What a shame. I miss him already," said Ralph. "But please sit down. Louis and I will both be insulted if you don't."

She knelt down and managed to sit on the floor without exposing herself, while Ralph and his cat watched her, both with the same sleepy, pleasant gaze. "I don't think I want champagne," she said. "You know, I just woke up."

"Isn't champagne considered a breakfast drink in America?" Ralph said.

Then Lee reconsidered. The hunt for the bottle itself would

buy her precious minutes. "All right," she said, and added hastily, "If it's right here. I don't want to make you get up."

"Enchanting. Finally a woman who understands me." He
began to fling sheets of newspaper around noisily, much to the
cat's annoyance. At the moment the champagne bottle was revealed, unopened on its side, the cat had finally had enough and
bolted up the stairs. Lee watched it vanish into the shadows and
wondered what it would find up there. What in fact was Jake
doing?

Ralph leaned forward and grabbed the bottle. "No glasses,"
he said sadly. "And tepid. I am an execrable host."

"Do we need glasses?" said Lee brightly. "In America, we
seldom drink from glasses."

"You are a liar," said Ralph. "I have just come from America,
and it was rotten with glasses. Just for that, I think you should
give me a kiss."

Lee tried to coldly stare him down, but he ignored this completely. He put the bottle to one side and moved toward her with
a surprising speed and grace, like a cat pouncing. At the last second, she decided not to react in any way, and he kissed her on the
lips with a gentle emphasis. Then he pulled back an inch, looking at her face with an affectionate deviltry in his eyes.

"There, you got your kiss," she said, with what she hoped was
chilling indifference.

He smiled. "And now you get yours."

And he kissed her again, lingeringly, letting his tongue play
over her closed lips. After a minute, Lee's lips parted without her
consciously deciding to open them, and for a moment his tongue

was in her mouth, and she was kissing him back . . . Then he was suddenly sitting back where he had been, picking up the champagne bottle and loosening the cork.

The cork popped, and he immediately put the bottle in his mouth, catching the foam as it came out. Then he handed the bottle to her, and she swigged, still half in that kiss, achingly conscious of the cool silk on her naked body. The bubbles tickling in her mouth made her want to kiss more. She supposed that was what champagne was meant to do. Perhaps she could kiss Ralph for an hour. They would kiss and drink champagne; it would seem like no time.

Ralph took the bottle back from her. "You are a really very lovely girl. It's a pleasure trying to seduce you. I promise not to blame you if you resist, but you must promise me that you won't resist." He took a swig from the bottle, looking at her dreamily all the while.

"I'm not making promises today. I've found that they come back to haunt me."

"Meaning that you've made promises to Jake. But you see, that's making promises to the wrong person, and is bound to end badly." He reached out and caught her ankle lightly in his hand, pulling her foot into his lap.

"What are you doing?" she said, smiling.

Now he was stroking her calf, his long fingers trickling over the skin with wonderful delicacy. "I'm used to stroking Louis. I need to pet someone in order to think clearly."

"Couldn't you just think unclearly?" she said, and moved to pull her foot away.

But he grasped her ankle again with a surprising strength and firmness. "If you resist, I shall tickle your foot. I am a genius at tickling."

"Give me the champagne," she said, laughing at him.

He handed her the bottle and returned to stroking her shin, and up over her knee to her thigh. She drank and, as she did so, surreptitiously looked at the watch. Ten minutes had passed.

"Am I boring you?" Ralph said pointedly.

"What do you mean?" she said when she had swallowed her wine.

"You were looking at what appears to be Jake's watch."

His voice had a hint of steel in it now, and suddenly she wondered if she was safe with him. *Scream,* she thought. *I just might have to.*

He went on. "No, it's very rude of you, and I think I will have to confiscate the watch."

He put out his hand and waited with a confident smile.

"I can't give you Jake's watch," she said in a faltering voice. She was almost certain Jake wouldn't care about the loss of the watch itself. But if Ralph took the watch, she would have no way of knowing when an hour had passed.

"I'll give it to Jake later," Ralph said. "I have no use for Jake's watch."

"Then let me keep it."

He sighed. "I'll have to wrestle you for it, won't I? I'm sorry, but I get very childish about these things."

She said, nervously, "Don't be silly. I can't give you—"

"But I am silly, beautiful girl. I'm silly as all hell."

And then he had pounced on her again, grasping her wrist and unclasping the watch effortlessly. Lee grabbed his fingers and twisted them back frantically. He had begun to laugh, and he pushed forward, tumbling them both over onto their sides. The champagne bottle tipped over, spilling on the newspapers as they wrestled. Lee attempted using her nails, and he caught first one of her hands and then the other. She was still struggling as he forced her onto her back and rolled on top of her. Then he was kissing her again, pinning her arms up over her head. Her robe had been pulled open in the fight, and she felt the fabric of his pressing against her belly, her thighs, her pubic mound. Silk, definitely silk.

Scream, she thought. But she was kissing him back. And then the skill he brought to the kiss was mesmerizing; she hadn't known that kissing could be that good. Meanwhile, with surreal clarity, she felt his hard dick through the cloth of his bathrobe, pressing against her thigh.

She thought, faintly but with absolute certainty, *Fuck screaming.* At least this man had the courtesy to seduce her, instead of needing to be seduced.

When he began to force her thighs apart with his knees, she shut her eyes and let him. He let go of one of her hands to pull his robe open. For a second she felt his bare cock pressing against her pussy lips, the nakedness of it thrilling. Then he was inside her, fucking her.

Later, Lee would try to remember exactly what it was he had done. It was something to do with a perfect physical intuition, a kinetic intelligence like an athlete's, but applied to a very specific goal. His cock went into her with an even, particular stab that never failed to press into and rub against her clit, then, gathering speed, diving so deeply into her that a noise escaped from her every time. Then it had pulled out past her clit again with a subtle zigzagging motion that drove her half insane. And again and again and again, slightly different every time. She felt her orgasm coming almost immediately, but when she was on the brink, the first sweetness of it gathering deep inside her—then he paused, with his cock all the way inside her, teasing her with its bulk and hardness. He pulled her robe farther open and ran his hand down over her breasts, saying, "I haven't seen you properly yet. I have to see you. . . ." And while he looked at her, his hand went down to her pussy and his thumb found her clitoris and began to play with it, teasing out the beginnings of a second and different orgasm. She found herself stroking his chest as if imploring him to let her come this time. She was biting her lip with the intensity of her need, as he kissed his way down her neck and grasped one nipple in his lips, sucking it with a complex and delicious motion that sent an arrow of new pleasure after the ones running through her cunt.

She began to murmur, without knowing what she was saying, "Please . . . fuck me. Please, I let you fuck me. Please just finish it, please. . . ."

He let her nipple free and kissed her on the mouth again. Then he was saying into her ear, "You *are* very beautiful. I don't think I want to let you go. If I fuck you, will you leave Jake?"

"Of course, of course I will," she said, not knowing what she was saying, or if she meant it, or if it mattered.

Then he was thrusting into her again, with his fingers still flashing back and forth over her clit, and she was coming, her whole body arching against him as he came, too, driving into her with a focused savagery that made the whole world flash white and black as Lee almost lost consciousness.

"And then . . . well, the hour was up." Lee shrugged while Olivia stared at her in consternation.

"So you left?" Olivia said. "With . . . what did he call himself?"

"Jake, you mean?"

"Oh, right. Stupid name."

Lee shrugged. "Well, yes. I told Ralph I needed to shower before Jake woke up. And I ran upstairs and changed and then . . . the car was there. It was pretty funny, somehow."

"And 'Jake' was there at the airport?" Olivia said angrily, as if being there at the airport were a heinous crime.

"I *really* wish you would tell me what all this is about," Lee said. "Yes, he was there at the airport. And he gave me the ticket and passport, but he didn't come on the plane with me." At the memory, she couldn't help making a little forlorn grimace. The flight had been very strange and lonely, and she couldn't appreciate the luxury of first class at all, coming right after the private plane. The worst part was that she felt certain she would never see Jake again. She kept remembering how she'd promised Ralph to leave Jake. Well, she had, although it wasn't her decision.

And in the days that followed, something told her not to attempt looking up Ralph Axton on the Internet, not to try to contact him. Something to do with jewels. Some subconscious line her mind had drawn between the insane piece of jewelry

Jake had given her, and whatever he'd been doing while she let Ralph seduce her in front of the fireplace.

Olivia said with bottomless disgust, "I would kill him if I could be sure there was a hell."

"Well, while you're at it," Lee said with another flight of temper, "tell him I'd like to hear from him. Maybe *he'll* tell me what all this is about."

"No, he won't," Olivia said carelessly. "And, basically, you'd better forget all about it, give me that illegal passport, and start studying again. One thing I can promise you is that you'll never see Jake again. Or that creepy insurance cop, or..." Olivia searched in her mind for other people Lee would never see again.

Lee offered, "Ralph?"

"Well, just *hope* you don't see him again. Christ!" Olivia said.

"How do *you* know these people, Olivia? You're being pretty high and mighty, considering."

Olivia stood up and began to pace, fuming. "I know these people because I have to know these people to pay for your education, and your rent, and..." Olivia found about fifty other things she had to pay for, and listed them all in a crescendo of irritation. She was down to the parking ticket Lee had gotten the last time she borrowed Olivia's car, when Lee's eyes strayed to Nicholas Taylor's business card on the table.

Now that she looked at it, it wasn't a card—it was *two* cards, one on top of the other. The top one was slightly shifted to the left, just enough that you could see it if you looked closely. In a moment, Lee had taken it and slipped it into the pocket of her shorts, while Olivia obliviously continued to pace and give non-sensical reasons for doing whatever she liked while Lee was supposed to stay at home like a nun.

"... and the final thing is that I would never forgive myself," Olivia wrapped up, "if I let you get into any trouble. You're my responsibility, Lee, and you are *not*, I repeat *not*, going to waste your abilities."

At this Lee got to her feet and grabbed her biology text-book. "I'm going," she said with a dignified (fake) calm. "And incidentally—I'll waste my abilities however I want."

Chapter Eleven

"Impulse control," Paul told Olivia. "That's the key to survival in this business: impulse control. Without that, you're not a jewel thief at all, Olivia. You're an inmate. A prisoner. A convict—"

"I get it," she said irritably. "Let's move on."

It was a month after the lucrative, but personally disastrous, escapade in Toronto. Olivia had shooed the jewelry store guy out, with a garbled excuse. As soon as the door closed behind him, Paul came out of the closet, and he and Olivia stared at each other, listening, until they heard the elevator in the corridor open and close.

Then Paul said, with poison in his voice, "You actually fucked that guy in front of me."

"It just happened," Olivia said, stunned and humiliated. "I don't know how it happened."

"I can tell you how it happened. I had to watch it."

"Paul . . . don't. It was just on the spur of the moment. I mean, we were stealing those . . . the stones, and I was frightened, I guess. I don't know how it happened."

" 'Spur of the moment,' " he spat out. "Why does that suddenly sound obscene?"

"Paul." She looked at him desperately, feeling the whole world slip through her fingers. She said, "I love you." Then she blushed and felt the weight of the words. She had always believed that the man should say *I love you* first, but this was a special case. And of course they loved each other; it was so obvious it hadn't been necessary to say it out loud. It was in every touch they exchanged, every look, in the easy way rapport turned into sex and . . .

"Well, I don't love *you*," he said coldly. "I don't love you at all."

Her blood turned to ice. Her heart flipped onto its hate side in an eye blink. "You *liar*," she said. "You nasty, cruel, fucking *liar*."

From that moment on, there was hardly a day's peace for Paul and Olivia.

In the month that had passed, they had flown to Bali, where they had spent two weeks in paradise, fighting. They fought on a white sand beach with palms swaying overhead; they fought while they drank cocktails on a terrace overlooking a bright blue sea. They fought in the Jacuzzi at their five-star hotel, and they fought on the way to the airport to fly to Thailand, where they fought in Buddhist temples and seedy bars and on bicycle rickshaws.

Whenever they weren't fighting, it seemed to Olivia, they

were having sex. They made love in an intense silence, as if they were both afraid that a single word would break the spell, and the fight would begin again as if it had never ended. But while they were making love—or lying in each other's arms afterward, spent and entwined, her lips against his strong throat, him breathing softly in her hair—it was bliss. It wasn't just that she had never felt that way before. She had never known feelings like that existed, feelings that made physical pleasure feel mystical, magical, larger than life. And there were also hours when they talked like best friends, and made each other laugh, and kissed again and again. But all it took was for the conversation to take a wrong turn—any mention of infidelity, jewelry stores, or Canada was deadly—and they were snarling at each other again.

Now they were fighting in a suite at the Westin Excelsior in Rome, by a window overlooking the Via Veneto; Olivia was sprawled on a bed of unholy softness, Paul in an armchair of absurd luxuriousness. A three-hundred-dollar bottle of white wine sat in a bucket of melting ice on a trolley between them. On another trolley sat an equally expensive bottle of wine, empty, among the remnants—half-eaten pastries, stale croissants—of their continental breakfast. It was noon, and they'd been arguing since nine in the morning.

"Anyhow," Olivia said wearily, "didn't you tell me when we first met that you were no good at impulse control? Wasn't that why you took me with you?"

"Well . . . ," he began, with a sarcastic twist in his voice. Immediately she was sure he was going to say something nasty about wishing he hadn't taken her. She steeled herself, already feeling the poison dart in her most sensitive spot.

But instead he sighed and gave her a rueful smile. "Well, Livy, you know what? Perhaps impulse control isn't everything."

She laughed with surprise and relief. "I'm glad you took me, too," she said. "I think our fights are ..." She was stopped by a qualm, and shook her head, smiling as lovingly as she could.

"What? What are our fights?"

"Okay. They're dumb. Because you're jealous of me, and that's dumb."

He looked at her with fatigued irony, as if he couldn't be bothered to point out how right he was to be jealous.

She said, "I mean, because all jealousy is dumb. Either I love you or I don't. And I do. I don't want to cheat on you. It was just—"

"Poor impulse control," he said heavily. "I get the point. And, speaking of poor impulse control, with all this pointless argument, we're going to be late for our meeting."

That day they were going to pull their second robbery, stealing a briefcase full of uncut stones from a diamond smuggler who was staying in this same hotel. It was a job that had come through a friend of a friend of a friend of Mr. Bezin. The smuggler, a Belgian called La Chasse, had wronged someone, or said the wrong thing, and therefore had been set up. It was something to do with Bezin's Norwegian nemesis, Tordahl, who was, in Mr. Bezin's words, "Growing rich on my life's blood, Mr. Paul. Though I know Tordahl is very dear to your heart, so I do not want to offend."

"I have nothing to do with Tordahl," Paul said crossly. "Stop kidding me about it."

Bezin said to Olivia, "It only breaks my heart that an honest man like Paul should deal with a person who lives by lies. Yes, Paul, I am afraid your Tordahl is a Creature of the Lie . . . a typical Norwegian."

However murky the backstory, the plan for the theft was simple. Paul was going to pose as a buyer. Once the diamonds were produced, Olivia would pull a gun on the man and keep it trained on him while Paul bound him hand and foot. That would buy them enough time to escape with the gems. The refreshing part of this job was that once they were clear of the smuggler, the risk was over; no one would be notifying any authorities. Their bags were in their rental car, ready to be driven to the airport where they would fly to Buenos Aires—for no better reason than that Paul had never been there before.

Olivia couldn't quite get used to the fact of the gun, though. It was too apallingly real—a heavy, cold object that *felt* like it could kill someone. It had taken her half an hour to be trained to hold the thing credibly, even unloaded. In her handbag, it felt like a chunk of cold bad luck. Paul had agreed to leave it unloaded for the job; it was extremely unlikely the smuggler would have a gun, given the fact that jewel smugglers spent half their lives in airports, trying to avoid calling attention to themselves or to the contents of their luggage. If La Chasse did pull a gun, Paul said, Olivia should throw hers on the floor and beg for mercy. Then (this was at nine that morning) Paul suggested that in a worst-case scenario, she offer her favors in exchange for their freedom. That was when the fight had begun. Three hours later, it was time to leave, and in fact, they were going to be a few minutes late for the meeting Bezin's friend's friend's friend had arranged in the hotel.

Paul grabbed the briefcase they were bringing—supposedly a briefcase full of cash with which Paul was going to pay for the diamonds. In fact it contained nothing but newspaper. The trick was going to be to get the smuggler to show his goods before they were forced to count out any cash. They went out and down the hall to the elevator, Olivia mincing along in the high, high heels and miniskirt she was wearing to play the part of Paul's bimbo girlfriend.

It turned out the room they were meeting La Chasse in was the twin of theirs, one floor above. When the door to the room opened, Olivia was fleetingly distracted by the surprise of seeing their exact same room, with the same curtains and wallpaper, the same upholstery on the same chairs.

That was rapidly replaced by her surprise that the person who opened the door was a woman—an Asian girl in a miniskirt just as tiny as Olivia's own, with lush black hair that swept over her shoulders to waist length. The girl put out her hand to Paul, saying in labored English, which was barely intelligible through her French accent, "Allo, I em La Chasse Nguyen. Is it Mr. Paul—" And here followed such an extreme mangling of Paul's most recent phony surname that Olivia couldn't remember offhand what the name was supposed to be.

Paul then responded in a flood of French, while ushering Olivia ahead of him into the room. Olivia moved forward numbly, the familiar surroundings comforting her, but in an uncomfortable way. She wasn't sure she wanted to be comforted when in a few minutes she would have to point a gun at someone and appear menacing while wearing stiletto-heeled sandals. Point it at a girl, furthermore, which seemed like disloyalty. It was betraying her own kind. It was nearly cannibalism. Also, the French might as well have been nonsense syllables for all she understood, leaving her with the uneasy sense that she had no idea *when* the gun should be produced. It was surprisingly demoralizing.

To add to her distress, Olivia couldn't help noticing, as they all sat down——Paul on the bed this time, and she and La Chasse in matching armchairs——that this girl and Paul were getting along a little too well. Paul was gazing into La Chasse's clear brown eyes raptly, and the two of them were bantering back and forth like old friends. Left out so decisively, Olivia had time to inspect La Chasse, and had to admit that the girl was unpleasantly pretty. And in a way that was the opposite of Olivia—a slinky, kittenish way that made Olivia feel bovine and ridiculous. She remembered for the first time in weeks that her eyes were too close together, that she had a potbelly, that she was ugly and stupid and . . .

"What is she saying?" she suddenly blurted out.

Paul and La Chasse both turned to stare at her. Paul said, with an alarming kindness in his voice, "She's onto us, I'm afraid. The game's up."

Immediately Olivia was furious; clearly Paul just didn't want to steal from this girl because she was hot. "That's not possible," she said.

"Listen," said Paul. "You should appreciate this. La Chasse was *dating* that friend of Bezin's——"

"He wasn't Bezin's friend. He was the friend of the—"

"Whatever. The point is that this is a case of jealousy." Paul smiled at her soothingly. "Like you, La Chasse likes men to an unusual degree. And as she's been telling me, she never *promised* fidelity to anyone. She had an open relationship—like ours."

"Who said we had an open relationship?"

Paul ignored her and went on. "So we've come to an agreement."

He smiled at Olivia with that frustrating, unnerving kindness, and then turned to La Chasse and said something in French.

La Chasse replied in a low, caressing voice and began to unbutton her blouse.

"No . . . ," Olivia said. "You *can't* be serious."

"There's nothing serious about this," Paul said. "It's fun. It's inherently not serious." And he got up from the bed and bent over to kiss La Chasse on the mouth while she shrugged her blouse off onto the armchair behind her, revealing high, round breasts with deep russet nipples. Paul immediately began to fondle them, his hands forming over them and squeezing gently, then moving to allow his fingertips to squeeze and tickle her nipples. La Chasse arched her back, and Olivia saw the flash of her tongue between their joined lips.

Her mind was racing, trying to come up with a way of explaining why this was unfair, totally unfair, and he ought to stop it *right now.* But her mind just went in circles of distress, while Paul began to unbutton his own shirt, revealing that sleek golden physique she knew so well, and wanted painfully every time she saw it. Even now. She longed to go forward and pull him away from the other girl, press him against her . . .

La Chasse stood up and pressed Paul against herself. Their bare torsos slid together, and Paul made a deep, soft growl of desire. His hands pulled up La Chasse's skirt and then molded to her tight, round butt, pulling the cheeks gently apart as he pressed her against him, his hips arching into her. He was actually lifting her slightly off the floor, grinding into her.

Olivia shut her eyes, trying again, vainly, to think. She should leave. She shouldn't leave under any circumstances; if she did she might never see Paul again. She should . . .

Her eyes snapped open, and she tried to ignore the developing scene of Paul and La Chasse (damn, La Chasse was completely nude now, and so beautiful, her body a deeper gold than Paul's, and so slender and pretty. . . .) as she turned around and scanned the room until she saw a briefcase, the same size as the one Paul had brought, but with a shinier finish to the black leather. It was sitting on the floor beneath the window with the view of the Via Veneto. It leaned against the wall with what seemed to her a cheeky air. It seemed to be winking at her and saying, *Cheer up! You and I can still cause some trouble!*

She got up with a hangdog slump to her shoulders, hugging her handbag as if she was too depressed to care about how she looked, and stumbled toward the window, looking out a little bleakly as she fumbled her handbag open. When she turned around, she froze for an instant, halted by the picture of Paul perched on the edge of the bed with his pants around his ankles, while the naked and clearly gymnastically talented La Chasse was poised above his naked erect cock.

The cock was that deep mauve, that ideal thickness, that— La Chasse sank down and took it all inside her, her back arching again as she cried out. Then Paul was fucking her from beneath, and Olivia could see his shaft moving in and out, the balls pressed up against La Chasse's pink slit. . . .

"Excuse me," Olivia said as loudly as she could. Her voice was weak and hoarse with what she suddenly realized was lust. She swallowed and made herself say more coldly, "Stop it right now."

La Chasse, still rising and sinking on Paul's dick, looked over her shoulder with an expression of contained ecstasy. Her face stilled and became nonplussed as she saw the gun Olivia was aiming directly at her head. Paul was looking at Olivia in combined amusement and horror. He said something in French and La Chasse froze, scowling at Olivia. Paul chose that moment to shove up into her again, and La Chasse's features blurred with pleasure, then cleared once again and she said in her mushed-up English, "What you do-eeng? You want what?"

Olivia picked up the briefcase and said, "Are these the jewels? I came for jewels, not a sex show."

Paul said—still fucking up into La Chasse with even strokes that made Olivia inadvertently breathe in time with the movements of his cock—"Why don't you open it and see?"

"Stop that," Olivia said with a mounting desperation. "Stop it."

La Chasse turned away from her again, leaning down to Paul with the air of someone abandoning a pretense of polite attention. Olivia crouched down and opened the briefcase. At first all she saw were frilly underpants and bras. Digging among them, though, she exposed a further layer of plastic bags in which rough stones glittered. She slapped the briefcase shut and got up, walking with it toward the door, past the bed where Paul was reaching up to pluck at La Chasse's nipples. La Chasse had put one hand down to her cunt and was feeling the motion of Paul's dick in and out of her with her fingers while using a thumb to play with her own clit. . . .

Olivia lost it. Dropping the briefcase next to the bed, she aimed the gun at Paul this time and screamed, "Goddamn it, listen to me! This is so mean! How can you do this?"

Again the couple stilled and looked at her. Paul said evenly, "You forget, Livy, I know the gun's not loaded. And I've already told La Chasse, so *you're* the one who should stop."

Olivia stood staring at him, pale. At that moment, La Chasse cried out and began to move more frantically on top of him, obviously coming. Her face was intent and flushed, and she tensed from head to toe, straining to drive Paul's dick deeper into her, deeper, moving her hips around to get at every inch of her orgasm. Then she had collapsed onto his chest, licking her lips, her eyes dull and happy. She said something to Paul and reached one hand out toward Olivia.

Paul laughed and said, "Livy . . . do you want to join us instead of standing there looking shocked?"

Olivia stared for another long minute, biting her lip and trying to ignore the surging desire in between her legs. Then she gave up—very consciously gave up, thinking clearly, *This is what I'm going to be like, from now on.* She reached back and unzipped her dress. She unhooked her bra and pulled her panties down. Then, feeling comfortably naked, as if nudity were a warm bath she had slipped into, she crawled onto the bed.

La Chasse raised herself off Paul and fell to one side, leaving her hand still circling the base of his cock lovingly. And Olivia found herself mounting her lover in front of the other woman. She took his dick in her hand, and pressed the tip of it against her clit for a second, whimpering faintly at the incredible relief she felt. Then he had grabbed her hips and driven his cock up into her. La Chasse's hand was raised up against Olivia's pussy, and a second later, her fingers were playing over Olivia's clitoris while Paul fucked Olivia with delicious force from below. Olivia was conscious of La Chasse watching her breasts tremble, her dark eyes filled with a drowsy appreciation. Olivia's cunt was already tense. It was like a pang of bliss into which Paul was thrusting, and she kept picturing La Chasse's orgasm, the tension through her body, the collapse.

Then suddenly Paul reached up and grabbed her by the waist. He moved her onto her back, turning with her to rest on top, and positioning her with her ass on the edge of the bed. La Chasse's hand fell away, and Olivia was staring up into Paul's eyes, the intensity of them reminding her of all the angry words that had passed between them. In a low, grudge-filled undertone, he spoke. "I do love you, Olivia. I love you so much I can't forgive you."

Then he had slipped his dick out of her again. She let out an involuntary sigh of disappointment. But before she could say anything, he was pressing the tip of his dick into her anus. She gasped—it was something she'd never done before, and he knew that. They'd talked about it; it was something they were going to prepare for, because . . . Now his dick was spreading her excruciatingly. He was forcing it in as she breathed, "Wait. . . . Wait. . . ."

Then he was sliding inside. There was an incredible feeling

of violation and of sexual fulfillment mingled. He was *fucking her in the ass.* His dick opened her again and again, and she found herself staring at his face, clinging to its familiar beauty as her body seized into orgasm after orgasm, coming in a diffuse and profound way that was new to her, that made her afraid and grateful at the same time.

He had said he loved her. He had said he loved her. And she clung to that as well, in the instant of dizzying lost control when she realized Paul had one hand inside La Chasse, and that La Chasse was lying right beside her with her legs splayed, her hips arched toward another orgasm. Then Olivia realized that she loved that fact. It made her come again, and again, and she cried out Paul's name without knowing she was doing it.

The three of them showered together afterward, and for that enchanted span of time—the two hands, male and female, soaping her breasts; Olivia spreading lather over La Chasse's slender waist and over her smooth, round ass; then pressing for a lightning moment of love against Paul's muscular chest, feeling his cock half hard again in the cleft of her thighs—for those minutes, Olivia was entirely happy. Everything was going to be all right. Jealousy was dumb. It was as dumb as her basically comic waving of the gun in the faces of La Chasse and Paul; it was as dumb as—she couldn't think—as all the other wonderfully dumb things that were sex and love and Paul.

But then, as they all dressed, just at the last minute before she and Paul left, Paul said something to La Chasse in French. La Chasse laughed and glanced at Olivia with an expression that could have meant anything. That could have meant, among other things, that La Chasse and Paul were laughing at her.

Olivia felt a knife in her heart. And when she and Paul left, she smiled at La Chasse blindingly, and picked up the wrong briefcase. She walked out of the hotel room carrying all of La Chasse's jewels, leaving their own newspaper-stuffed case behind.

In the elevator, Paul put his arms around her and held her without speaking. They walked through the lobby with their arms around each other. With every step, the briefcase knocked against Olivia's shin like a reminder that everything *wasn't* all right. And, in confirmation of this, as Paul handed their parking ticket to the doorman and they waited on the sidewalk for their car, she found herself saying, "I suppose that thing with La Chasse could be a regular thing. Something we do, you know, regularly?"

Paul tensed a little but then pressed her against him. "If you like. I don't know . . ."

"But do you like? That's all I wanted to know."

"Well, of course."

"Fine. So you don't *actually* need me, do you? You could just go back upstairs to her."

"Oh, Livy." He laughed. "Now you're as crazy as me."

Then their car—a nondescript, economy-sized Fiat—was driven up. As they got into the car, Paul turned to her with tender disquiet in his eyes. "I know that was over the top, what I did back there . . . but you did seem to like it, afterward. And of course, it wasn't planned." And he smiled nervously. "Poor impulse control?"

"It's okay. I had a bit of poor impulse control back there, too."

"I guess," he said, pulling into the frenzied traffic on the Via Veneto. "I guess you maybe went farther than . . . let me go farther than you really wanted . . . ?"

"No, I'm okay with that," she said. "But I seem to have stolen La Chasse's stones."

He sighed, and a smile played around his eyes, although he continued to focus on the traffic. "I know, Olivia."

"You . . . know?"

They both began to laugh, and he was saying, "It wasn't planned. It was just—"

"Poor impulse control!"

"Exactly!"

The next month was the honeymoon period of their relationship. They found an apartment of insane luxury in Buenos Aires, with a rooftop swimming pool surrounded by a garden of palms and tropical flowers. They didn't do any work at all then. On an ambitious day, they drove out to the beach. On a lazy day, they stayed in bed until sunset, making love and making love and making love again. They swam nude by starlight, chasing each other underwater and then coming up to find their tumblers of champagne on the edge of the pool.

Then the night before they left Argentina, they went out to a nightclub, where Olivia found herself, at the end of a few hours of sweaty dancing and unrestrained drinking, somehow kissing someone who, when she pulled back to tell Paul that she loved him—wasn't Paul. Paul had left the nightclub, and she had to find a cab and go home alone. In the plane the following morning, her miserable hangover was made intolerable by Paul's angry, brooding silence.

Although they stayed together for another year, the honeymoon never really returned.

On the plus side, in that time, he taught her every aspect of the business, as well as how to order wine and to play golf, tennis, and various casino games. He even tutored her in the rudiments of French. On the minus side, they were in a state of constant, exhausting war. There was an episode in which Olivia got too chummy with a target, and Paul burst into the room and punched the poor man in the jaw, effectively scuttling the job. There was an episode in which she threw a pearl necklace out of a tenth-story window to protest his flirty conversation with a maid. There were screaming matches and long, delirious days of making up. There were Dear John/Jane letters written and then torn up. There were promises and threats and tears.

Olivia gave him good cause for his jealousy time and time again, suffering from poor impulse control with the scion of a jewelry empire, a busboy, and a plainclothes policeman. After the busboy incident, she woke up in the hotel room alone, with no jewels, no money, no passport, and no clothes. Paul left her there for the worst six hours of her life, before returning shamefaced, miserably apologetic, pleading insanity. After that, she opened her own numbered bank account, and began to make a backup plan for the day when Paul actually left her. Even at that point, it never occurred to Olivia that she might be the first one to leave.

Chapter Twelve

It took Lee ten whole minutes to make up her mind to go visit Nicholas. During minute nine she was still walking toward the subway station to catch her usual train home. As minute ten ticked to its close, she was waving for a cab and giving the cabdriver the address from Nicholas' card.

The office was in an elegant five-story art deco building, in the midst of a forest of skyscrapers. The lobby was vast and grandly empty, with a few black leather armchairs on an expanse of black marble floor. Lee went up to the security guard with a quailing feeling, unhappily conscious of her cutoff shorts. What if Nicholas hadn't meant to leave two cards? It seemed a little far-fetched to think he had, now that she was actually here. She didn't have anything to tell Nicholas, either. It was she who wanted

information from him; and she wasn't even sure the information
was what she most wanted.

Still, she made herself go up to the guard and ask for Nicholas Taylor, giving her name with a confidence she was very far
from feeling. She gave her name and the guard had picked up the
phone when Nicholas appeared beside her, looking down at her
with that cool and serious calm.

"It's very good of you, Miss Stewart," he said. "Why don't
you come up to my office?"

And then she meant to say something sensible; even "Sure"
would have done it. But instead she looked at him with her body
responding as if he'd kissed her for the first time. She said,
"I just came to see you. I don't care about the gems."

He looked at her with a pointed patience and repeated, "Come
up to my office."

Then she was following him across a further expanse of
black marble, which seemed to stretch forever like a black sand
desert while her legs became weaker and weaker. Why had she
come at all? Why did she have to say that stupid thing? He led
her into an elevator paneled in reddish wood. The elevator doors
closed. He was about to press the button for the fourth floor,
but he turned toward her. Then their eyes locked.

Lee knew her eyes were wide with misery and longing. His
eyes seemed to drink some of the longing from hers. A minute
passed and they were still just looking at each other. Then the
doors began to open. Nicholas pressed the CLOSE DOORS button
with one hand; with the other hand he pulled Lee against him
and kissed her. Her head dropped back and she was standing on
tiptoe, her body molded against him, and that specific weakness

she'd been feeling had turned into blazing energy. She had never been so conscious of her body. At the same time, she was agonizingly conscious of his body, trying to feel its contours through his suit, and her hand moved shyly up to his shoulders. He was kissing her—and then he wasn't.

He stood back and pressed the button for the fourth floor. Then he was looking down. His demeanor was entirely changed; he looked dazed and somehow his hair was slightly mussed, though she didn't remember touching his hair.

He said softly, "I'm sorry about that."

"About what?" she said, in a dream.

Then the doors opened and she followed him down a hallway, through a reception area where a middle-aged woman in office garb greeted him, only to be completely ignored. He ushered her through a door like all the other doors in the hallway. Inside was an office paneled in the same reddish wood as the elevator; the office was large enough to fit a long conference table as well as a desk and chair. He came in behind her and shut the door.

Their eyes met, she took a step toward him, and they were kissing again. He pressed her against the door and his hands were exploring her body, running up her hips and then lifting her T-shirt to touch her breasts. The suddenness of it was almost paralyzing, and she found herself passively resting against the door, letting him do what he wanted, her hands weak against his chest. Then he had opened the top button of her jean shorts and stopped, murmuring into her ear, "May I?"

"Yes, yes . . ."

A moment later she was naked, and he had walked her, kissing her all the while, back to the conference table, where he lifted her and laid her back, kissing down her throat to her breasts. Lee was lying on the cool wood with her eyes shut, hardly believing it was happening. He was kissing her belly now, the near-tickling sensation awakening echoes deep inside her. Then she felt his lips hot against the lips of her pussy, the sudden insinuation of his tongue into her making her tense and inhale sharply. Then he was licking her, his tongue slipping inside her and then flipping incredibly rapidly over her clitoris, making her squirm involuntarily with pleasure. She felt the heat of her orgasm gathering and intensifying. She was going to come, now, with this near stranger, in an office building in the middle of—

Then he stood back and he was opening his fly. She looked up at him with a fearful hunger, and then he was bending over her again, kissing her so that she tasted her own juices on his lips. He rested his cock's length on top of her slick, wet pussy, while her tongue found his and she moaned into his mouth. Then his cock had found her opening, and pressed there, teasing her with just its very tip. He whispered into her ear, "May I?"

She said, "Yes . . . please."

Then he thrust into her slowly, letting her feel every inch. She found herself spreading her legs to give him easier access, the size of his cock now making her whimper with a kind of desperate satisfaction. And he had gone all the way in, his cock filling her to the depths. He pulled out just an inch and went back in again, savoring the feeling of being all the way inside her, letting his cock move from side to side so deep that she couldn't help being slightly afraid through the pulses of sheer pleasure. When he began to fuck her for real, in hard sure thrusts, she gasped and her hands reached up to find his jacket, pulling him toward her without knowing what she was doing. At the same time, she began to come, and his thrusts rang into her orgasm, bringing tears to her eyes as her cunt spasmed over his cock.

It seemed to go on forever, and he seemed to be sinking deeper into her, and deeper, finding every impulse of pleasure she possessed and calling it into resonant life. She was murmuring his name, lost, and needing him to stop, and frightened by the knowledge that he eventually would. And at last, he thrust so deep inside her that her body protested; her cunt was like a scream even as the bliss peaked and tingled down her legs and up to the tips of her breasts. Then he was coming, and pressing her to his chest, holding her to him and moaning in a husky, low voice, "God . . . Oh, God, Lee . . ."

Gradually the world came back into focus. Lee opened her eyes. Nicholas was looking down at her with tousled serenity. He said, "This might sound funny. But I think I have a crush on you, Lee."

"Oh. That's good," she said. "That's a good word for it. I have one, too." Then she said, "Oh . . . wait. I should say that's ridiculous because we just met."

They smiled at each other a little foolishly. Then he kissed her again, a lazy, thorough kiss that made her relax completely, feeling his weight on her as a wonderful drug. Then he moved up off of her and he was pulling up his pants, rearranging his clothes with an expression of bemusement. She hopped off the table and stood, looking around, half expecting the room to be transformed by what had just happened.

It was the same very formal office, with no clutter and nothing out of place. There were a desk lamp with a green shade; walnut venetian blinds; a silk rug on the floor woven with a design of russet quail and mauve grapes. It was almost insultingly circumspect and clean.

"So would you like to take a seat and tell me what brings you here?"

"Do you want me to get dressed?"

"No," he said simply.

They smiled at each other again, and he added, "But of course you can. It just wouldn't be my first choice."

She hesitated for a moment, and then went to sit naked in the armchair in front of his desk, crossing her legs primly. He sat behind his desk and regarded her with a resumption of his professional face, in which only the faintest glimmer of sexual reminiscence remained.

"What brought me here," she said. "I have to think."

"Take all the time you need."

"Oh . . . oh, God. Of course." A horrible chagrin ran through her, and she glanced at her shorts and T-shirt on the floor with regret. Perhaps she would have found this easier with clothes on, after all. She steeled herself and said, "Listen, Nicholas. Is my sister some kind of criminal?"

"Yes," he said easily, without any change of expression.

"And . . . Ralph Axton?"

"Had half a million dollars' worth of jewels stolen from his home the night you stayed there." Nicholas smiled as if this was likely to be pleasant news. He clarified, "Of course that's not the resale value to the thief. As stolen goods, they might go for two hundred thousand or even less."

Lee took a deep breath. "Well," she said with light sarcasm, "that's not surprising at all. That's the sort of thing that always happens to me."

"I know very well that this never happens to you." His face looked tender again. "It's my job, after all, to know that kind of thing."

"But I'm guessing it happens to Olivia." A note of envy crept into her voice. It was absolutely typical of Olivia, somehow, to turn out to be a jet-setting jewel thief instead of a mundane Realtor.

He looked at her with almost hapless sympathy. "She's become of some interest to me for that reason, yes."

Lee said, "Oh, hell. And you know I have to help Olivia, no matter what. I don't *want* to . . . ," she said with more bitterness than she expected.

He laughed, but then looked away, his eyes veiled with remorse and worry. He said, in a lower tone, "I shouldn't have done what I just did."

"You mean, we shouldn't have had sex?" she said. "But at least we got to do it once. That might be the last chance. . . ."

"I know."

"Yes. I can't go out with you if you put my sister in prison," Lee said flatly. Only after she said the words did their full import sink in. Then she was looking at him with helpless misery, her arms crossed tightly under her breasts. "Oh, hell. I do have a crush on you."

"Lee——"

"No, wait. Let's just get this over with. When I went to London, I was with a man called Jake Wythe."

"No, you weren't. You were with a man called Paul Breakness. Jacob Wythe is one of his aliases."

"Well, whoever he is, Olivia said he was her enemy. What does that mean?"

For the first time, Nicholas seemed taken aback. "I don't know. As far as I know, she was still working with him two days ago."

"Working with him?"

He gave her a whimsical look, and she blushed deeply, remembering what she had done in the Axton house. "Oh, you can . . . I don't need to know the details."

"I suspect you already know them."

"Stop it. Yuck." Lee shook her head. "So I guess they're lovers and so on." She shook her head in amazement. If a gorgeous man took Lee off on a private plane to London, seduced her, involved her in a plot to purloin a nobleman's rubies—*of course* it had to be because he was secretly after her sister! "I know it's probably tactless to be upset. But if you only knew. I've spent my whole life as a cheap Olivia substitute. I get her leavings."

Nicholas met her gaze evenly, calm again. At last he said, with restrained and somber passion. "I can't see how that could be true. You're much more beautiful than your sister. I'd like to take you home and make love to you every night."

She inhaled sharply and put her hand to her mouth, trying to stop the smile that immediately appeared on her lips. "But we've just met," she said. "That's what I'm supposed to say. So I'm saying it."

"But if you didn't want to hear extravagant things from me, you should have put your clothes back on."

"That shouldn't make a difference," she said, but her voice was wispy and hoarse. She cleared her throat and said, "Okay. I accept your extravagant things. I guess I feel some extravagant things. Don't ask me what."

"Lee, I have an idea." He sat forward, looking at her with a resumption of his previous cool intelligence. "I'm not a policeman. I'm not actually responsible for law enforcement, per se. My only responsibility is to safeguard my company's interest in certain jewels, not the safety of all jewels. So—if we can recover the property of the Axtons and the Fremberg-Asps, there's no reason that any of this should go any further."

Lee sighed, trying to imagine persuading her sister to give up hundreds of thousands of dollars' worth of jewelry. Olivia wouldn't even tell Lee what was going on; clearly she didn't value Lee's opinion. Lee would have to try, nonetheless, she supposed. Still, it was a lot to worry about, right now, coming on the heels of all the discoveries about her sister, about the trip to London, and incidentally, about the uncertain future of Lee's college fund.

"I have an idea, too," she said finally. "My idea is that we pretend you never told me this, and we have sex again now. Can we try my idea first, and *then* your idea?"

He stood up, and without saying anything further, crossed the space between them and lifted her from her chair. In another minute, they were on the rug, all thoughts of jewels, crimes, and consequences far, far away.

Chapter Thirteen

Olivia phoned the number Paul had left in the Fremberg-Asps' safe as soon as Lee left the apartment. She was prepared to shout at him, to threaten him, to throw it in his face that he'd slept with her sister. . . . What she wasn't prepared for was to have the phone go straight to voice mail, and for the voice mail to say "Hello, Olivia. Meet me at 144 East Ninety-first Street, tomorrow, at four in the afternoon." Then it bleeped. All her planned speeches flew out of her head, and she hung up in a flurry of anger and longing.

Now, as Olivia approached the address Paul had given her, she balked in uncertainty. It was a pretty little four-story building in the heart of the Upper East Side, with plaster moldings of seahorses and dolphins on the facade; perhaps it had once been some kind of maritime institute. Now it bore a tasteful plaque proclaiming it to be the KARTEN INSTITUTE FOR PHIL-ANTHROPIC HEDONISM.

After some deliberation, she realized that although she would never have foreseen this, it was exactly the *kind* of thing she would expect from Paul. She went up to the door and, seeing no doorbell, lifted the heavy brass knocker and pounded on the door three times. It was only after she'd finished that she realized she'd been grasping a knocker in the shape of a penis, and pounding it against two brass balls.

She heard frantic footsteps, running one way, then the other. There was a girl's voice shouting, and then laughter from what sounded like four or five people. The girl scolded them, and then finally the door was opened by a tiny blonde wearing a bikini top and holding a throw rug around her hips. "Hello!" she said, "I'm Bella. I'm so sorry. I'm supposed to be answering, but everything just got out of control up there." She waved vaguely in the direction from which Olivia had heard the laughter. "And— Oh, do you mind nudity?"

"Well, no," Olivia said.

"Thanks!" the girl said and dropped the throw rug. She was naked on the bottom, but what was more startling was her pubic hair, which had been dyed bright red and shaved into a neat valentine. A black line had been tattooed around it to emphasize the shape.

Olivia made a conscious decision not to stare; she wasn't ready to make polite chitchat on this particular topic. She said, "I'm here for Paul. . . ." Then she balked. There was no knowing what last name he was using, or whether he was in fact called Paul.

The girl frowned and turned to call back toward the "out-of-control" room, "Hey, do you guys know Paul?"

A woman's voice called back, "In the Yellow Room."

"Oh . . ." The girl cocked her head at Olivia and said, "Two flights up, and it's the first room on the left. It's not actually yellow anymore," she said confidentially, "so don't be misled."

"I won't be," said Olivia. "Thanks."

She set off up the stairs, and the blond girl disappeared again, untying her bikini top as she went.

On the first landing, Olivia paused to stare at a huge stained-glass window, which replaced an entire wall. It represented figures she guessed were Adam and Eve, to judge by their fig leaves. But they were kissing each other in a very unrepentant way, and Adam had his hand on Eve's bare breast. A single clear pane in the center, which was almost exactly Olivia's size, showed a courtyard behind the house, filled with flowering trees and polished white stone paths around a huge fountain. But what really stopped Olivia and held her attention were several tiny white horses grazing under the trees. At first she was baffled, trying to figure out if the horses were too small, or the chairs by the fountain wildly oversized. . . . Then a man appeared from a doorway below and strolled out, completely naked. A horse trotted up to him and raised its head to be petted on the nose. It only came up to his hip. It took Olivia a minute to remember that there were such things, miniature horses, in the world. Then she wondered what sort of institute would create a courtyard to accommodate them. "Philanthropic Hedonism" didn't suggest miniature horses to her, but then she supposed hedonism was in the eye of the beholder.

She went on up the stairs, with a certain weariness now. It

was bad enough to be forced to confront Paul. She'd even briefly considered forgetting about the Fremberg-Asp loot and getting on with her life. But with Nicholas What's-it pursuing her around the globe, she thought it would be best to lie low for a while—if not to look for another job altogether. But first of all, she needed to ensure that she had the money for her mortgage, for Lee's tuition, for their health insurance and the payments on the BMW—it was maddeningly, heartbreakingly expensive to be Olivia. In fact, she often reflected that no one could really blame her for stealing. She was only struggling to pay her bills like any other middle-class American.

Anyway, it was bad enough to be forced to confront Paul, without his deliberately rubbing it in her face that he was having more fun than she was. He didn't have any family to take care of; he had no responsibilities at all. And as she turned down the hallway and approached a blue door, which had the words YEL-LOW ROOM stenciled on it in red, she felt a sudden violent nostalgia for her first year with him, before her father had died, before she had been the one who bought the plane tickets and planned the robberies—when *she* had been *Paul's* responsibility. She shook her head to clear the annoying daydreams, and knocked on the door.

"Olivia?"

His voice paralyzed her for a moment, and she realized she wasn't ready to see him at all. Her legs felt weak, and she had to count to ten to quell the urge to rush in and throw herself into his arms. And surely his voice had sounded anxious—lovelorn—too? Finally she mastered herself and said with a forced chilliness, "Can I come in?"

Then he opened the door. He was more beautiful than she'd remembered; taller than she'd remembered; sexier than she'd remembered. An athletic man of six feet with black hair—now cut short—and piercing blue eyes. His face was covered in stubble, which made him look annoyingly even prettier, ravishingly sloppy, as if he'd been in bed with someone for two days and hadn't had the chance to shave. His tan was the same; so was his muscular body—on display in a white wife-beater and shorts, which she was sure he'd chosen to flaunt himself in front of her.

Olivia was dressed in the least sexy clothes she owned—baggy jeans and a man's light blue Brooks Brothers shirt that had originally belonged to a lover of hers who always held a special place in her heart because she hadn't stolen anything from him. They'd only dated for a couple of weeks, but the fact that it was actual dating, and not preparation for a job, still made her sentimental. He was named Jason, or Aaron, she thought. It was probably one of those two names.

"Well, you look terrible," she said. "Have you been wearing yourself out in the cause of Philanthropic Hedonism?"

He ignored the waspishness in her tone. "Did you see the horses and bunnies?"

Despite herself, she was intrigued. "I saw the horses. There are bunnies?"

"White bunnies. And cockatoos, actually. Though the cockatoos keep escaping, so perhaps there aren't any cockatoos at the moment. It's a real shame; I spent two days teaching one of them to say, 'Olivia Stewart stole your jewelry,' and then it flew off and got eaten by someone's Doberman."

"That is a shame," she said. "Because that evidence would really have held up in a court of law. You would have been off the hook."

"Oh, it's not that. I do it all from cheated love," he said, and bowed to her slightly, the gesture seeming all the more mocking combined with his sloppy clothes. There was something about it that made her painfully notice his body again. She found that she couldn't quite remember what his chest felt like under her hands, the shape of his belly and the sweep down to the triangle between his thighs . . . and she wanted to remember it. She wanted to just check and see. . . .

"Can I sit down?" she said stiffly.

"Sit anywhere," he said, and waved at the bed, which was the only seating in the room.

Walking over, she noticed a little alcove in the wall with a thick metal pole in it; there was a hole in the floor below it, and in the ceiling above as well, and she realized that it must be a fireman's pole. Paul saw her looking and commented, "Yes, the place is full of things like that. That one goes up to the room of the proprietress—Blue Karten."

"Oh, Blue Karten, of course," Olivia said. "The oil guy's daughter."

"The late oil guy's daughter. Now the fourth richest woman in the world. And the most depraved, I think."

"Second-most depraved, after me," Olivia said stiffly, sitting on the corner of the bed. It was covered with a grand bedspread embroidered with some bacchanalian scene—genitalia and limbs entangled in a knot she couldn't immediately make out.

"No," he said, and a shadow crossed his face. "I have all the respect in the world for your depravity, but Blue is in a class by herself."

"She's not sleeping with the miniature horses, is she?"

"No," he said, and sat beside her on the bed. "You would?"

Olivia laughed, and was touched to see a spark of fondness in his eyes. She looked down at the floor. "Well, let her be the most depraved, then."

"Blue's pretty impressive," he said, with a languid reminiscence in his voice. "Anyway, the fireman's pole is there so that Blue's lovers can escape speedily from her room. It leads down directly to the garage, so you can slide down, get into your car, and race off into the night."

"Like the Bat Cave."

He smiled at her for a moment, and Olivia felt that old electricity between them.

Looking away awkwardly, she said, "You wouldn't think she'd need all that. I mean, who is she hiding all these lovers from? If she's—"

"Oh, her mother, partly. The mother doesn't know, and wouldn't approve."

"But the plaque on the door?"

Paul smiled. "Blue told her it was left over from the previous owner."

His eyes showed a frank admiration of Blue's audacity, and Olivia was struck by a familiar pang of jealousy. But she didn't even want him! It was so unfair! She forced her face to remain impassive. "Partly her mother? What's the other part?"

"Oh, she's sometimes got a boyfriend who thinks she's faithful to him."

"Well, it's a good thing you're not like that, anyway. *You* won't be taken in." She made herself smile casually, but every nerve in her body was straining to hear him say that he *wasn't* Blue's boyfriend.

"Yes," he said. "It is."

Then he was going on about what an amazing establishment the house was: "Like a medieval court." Blue Karten had a populous entourage assembled in the various rooms and apartments of the building. Her hairdresser and dermatologist lived there, as did three ex-boyfriends and an ex-girlfriend. How "ex" they were depended on Blue's mood, how jealous her current boyfriend was, and the medication she was on (prescribed by the doctor who lived in the basement apartment). Various other lovers either lived on the premises, or appeared and rang a special concealed doorbell, which paged Blue on her cell phone. "There are some fairly extreme scenes here. Blue likes to have sex in public, for one thing. Her favorite thing is to have two men fucking her—she's a double-penetration girl—while a party goes on around her. Though her parties are more like orgies. At one of her parties, she had a cloakroom where everyone had to leave all their clothes before coming in."

As he spoke, Olivia was burning inside at the idea that Paul had invited her to *his new girlfriend's* house. And he hadn't said anything about a job yet. This Blue Karten might be his version of Jason, or Aaron, someone he actually *liked* as a *person*, an idea that Olivia suddenly found ridiculously unprofessional, even faintly immoral. It was one thing for her to feel that way. She was younger than he was, and a girl. He should know better, and she was rehearsing ways of expressing her disdain when he suddenly said, "But you must be wondering about your jewels."

"They're not my jewels," she said scornfully, hypocritically— she'd been furious all week about his having stolen *her jewels.*

"André von Fremberg-Asp thinks they are. He's told me many times how you did him a favor by stealing the jewels, because they got the insurance money. He likes to think of you wearing them, apparently." His face had set in a grim disgust she knew of old. "He hinted that you had some carnal knowledge of one of the strings of pearls, but I didn't like to press for details."

"And you told him," she said irritably, "that I couldn't have stolen his jewels, and that's ridiculous, because I've never stolen anything that you know of, and . . ." Here she found herself unaccountably short of breath.

He said, "I am really eating my heart out about that cockatoo."

"How do you even know André?"

"The pearls still have your smell."

She stared at him, at a loss for words. He sat there being beautiful as if he were doing it on purpose, smothering her with his perfect lips, with his strong body. He was only a few feet away, and he was looking down at her shirt. Suddenly she wished violently that she'd worn one of her halter tops; you couldn't see anything in this stupid shirt of Jason's, or Tarquin's, or whoever it was.

She imagined Paul pressing her back onto the bed with one

hand, spreading her legs. He had the pearls in his other hand, and he was rolling them down her body, the round cool stones tripping over her nipples while he kissed her and his cock....

He said softly, "If you want the jewels back, Olivia..."

"If I want them back?" she said, far away.

"I want *you*," he said. "I want you again. I want you now... for starters."

She could hardly breathe. "You want me to prostitute myself for them?" she said angrily. She couldn't help it; she couldn't give in to him, even though she could feel that her face was vulnerable now, full of the old habit of relying on his protection.

His smile was almost bitter. "But what else have we ever done? What did we think we were doing?"

"I could steal them from you."

"Let's not play that little scene again," he said. They both looked away, distracted by memories. Her mind was still playing the scene with Paul and the pearls. He was putting them over her neck, as he always did after a heist, dressing her in their loot. She was lying back on the bed as his cock found her, pressing into her and making her tell him that she loved him... although she didn't anymore. She didn't—she was over that now.

Then he said, suddenly, "I shouldn't have let you go. I've regretted it ever since."

She laughed sourly. "Obviously. All four years, you... Oh, Paul, let's just leave it."

"I can't leave it. You were so young, Livy. I was wrong to blame you. You hardly knew what you were doing. You were a *virgin*." He tried to catch her eye. When she wouldn't look at him, he sighed. "I can't let this drag on anymore, Livy."

"You have your heiress and I have ..." Here her face filled with righteous anger. "I have my sister you dragged to London and fucked and got mixed up in a crime!"

"God, Olivia. None of that was planned. I just saw her outside your house and followed her. One thing led to another.... I'm sorry."

"Impulse control," she said bitterly.

"You shouldn't have left me, anyway." He tried to hold her gaze, but she looked away. "You shouldn't have stolen from me, and you shouldn't have left me."

"I had no choice," she said, in a voice that was lost and forlorn.

Paul and Olivia had last been in a bedroom together four years ago. It was a fifty-dollar room in a Lucky Inn just outside of Penntucket. They were there so that Olivia could see her sister and her father for the first time in a year. Her father was still six months away from his fatal heart attack, and already more or less reconciled to the idea that Olivia was going to be a Realtor and would never finish high school. To make him feel better, she had put on a massive engagement ring, and Paul had agreed to play her fiancé, although he could only appear in her family home, and never anywhere in town. There was too much risk that he would be recognized.

It was already a stroke of luck that none of the people who had seen Paul walk out behind Olivia had realized that she had run away with him. Of course Olivia's father had never publicized her departure. The people who later found out that Olivia had left town would have no inkling that it was the same night that Mystery Harker's jewels had left town. If Mitch Stewart, for his part, ever learned about the jewel heist, it would never occur to him that it could have anything to do with his daughter. He lived in a world of electricity bills that couldn't be paid, hardware shipments that didn't come on time, worries about his kids' report cards. He had never known any of the private beach Penntucketers, or been sorry that he didn't know them. If there was one good thing about Olivia's suddenly leaving, in his opinion, it was that it had taken her away from those people, who were liable to give her wrong ideas, and make her unhappy with the modest life in front of her.

Lee was sleeping over at a friend's the night Paul came to dinner. Olivia couldn't help suspecting that her father had wanted to keep Lee away from them, in case Paul turned out to be some kind of sex fiend. He would probably never get over the fact that Olivia had run away with Paul—there had been no slow progress of Paul coming to the house to take her out on dates, then coming to dinner, then asking for her hand. And although he seemed to genuinely like Paul, Olivia wondered if her father would ever trust either of them again. And he knew such a tiny fraction of their real depravity.

On the positive side, put in this situation, Paul turned out to have wonderful manners. Olivia kept thinking of his deeply respectable parents, and imagining him being taught how to say "please" and "thank you," and to defer to his elders. He evinced an inexhaustible interest in her father's hardware store, and insisted on washing the dishes after dinner. Mitch told her in confidence that Paul seemed like a "fine young man."

Olivia, watching Paul make polite conversation with her father, realized once again how much she loved him. And that he really loved her. Paul had nothing to gain from making her father like him. It was something he could only be doing to make her happy. And, sitting there in the good-girl dress she'd bought especially for the occasion, with that chunky engagement ring gleaming on her finger, she couldn't help feeling sad that it was all a charade. She and Paul couldn't even go to a restaurant in town without risking his freedom. They would always be on the move, or even on the run. They would never have a home; they would never have children together. Their only friend was Mr. Bezin, if he could even be counted as a friend.

When they left her father's house, Paul drove them down to the public beach where they'd first met. The parking lot was closed for the night and they had to park the car at a strip mall and walk. It was a chilly October night, and they were the only people out. They walked with their arms around each other, the wind to their backs. Olivia tried to remember seeing Paul for the first time there, but the windswept, lonely scene was so different that she couldn't call the image to mind properly.

They were standing together looking out over the ocean. There was a full moon that night, and it made a sparkling path across the waves and a pearly one up the wet beach. Paul had one arm around Olivia. They stood silently for some time, in a sentimental accord. In their year together, they had learned each other's moods, and often they communicated best when they were silent.

It was Olivia who spoke first. "Thank you. That was hard, I know."

As if he hadn't heard her, he said, "Marry me."

Then she was looking up at him while he stared off over the water.

"Are you kidding? Paul?"

"No." He swallowed. "I'm not kidding at all. There's no reason we can't."

"Under whose name? I mean, is there anywhere you can get married without getting arrested?" she said, laughing nervously.

"Anywhere you like," he said. "I haven't done anything wrong under my real name in years. It's all those other Pauls who are the bad boys." He smiled at her and said, "I never wanted anyone to appear at my parents' house asking questions."

"But what's the point of getting married, for us?"

"What do you mean?" His face clouded over. "The same point as there is for anyone else."

With him scowling at her, she found it hard to remember everything she'd been thinking at her father's house. She knew it had made her feel romantically doomed, and exceptional in some tragic way . . . but in the face of his incomprehension, that had gone all murky, and she was left stammering, "But if we got a house . . . I mean, we can't stop moving around. So we can't be, you know, like most married people."

"I didn't know you wanted to get a house. But we can, if that's what you really want. We have more than enough money." He kissed her on the forehead and said, "You know, we don't have to keep doing robberies."

At this, a shiver went through her, and she saw the whole thing clearly. It wasn't that *they* couldn't settle down. It was Olivia who couldn't settle down. She couldn't give up the thrill of the robberies, that moment when the gems were first in her hands, and the world seemed charged with adrenaline and sex. Mornings in hotel suites, plotting the next heist over a breakfast of strawberries and champagne; flirtations with men when you were secretly figuring out a way to steal their keys, to break into their house, to trick them; the next exotic R and R stop—Fiji, Tahiti, Hong Kong; every whispered endearment and every red-hot fight and every time his hand had snuck up her dress and found the crotch of her panties and lightning had gone through her. . . . She was in love with that whole life, not just with Paul.

She turned to him and kissed him. He hesitated at first, but then her lips found that current of mutual need that united them, and his mouth fastened on hers intently again, he pulled her against him. She unzipped his coat and pulled it round her; she slipped her hands under his shirt and over his silky skin. As always, the firmness of his body, its latent strength, made her feel a little drunk. She was instantly desperate to have him inside her. They knelt down on the cool sand together. He was pulling at the dress she'd put on to see her father, which covered her to the neck. Finally, he just tore it open and pulled her bra down, bending to kiss her breasts, to hold them again. His hands felt freezing cold, and she almost pushed him away. But then she shut her eyes and made herself hold still, the cold coursing into her breasts, and awakening an answering heat inside. They fell into the sand together, the wind stroking them with its cool, soft fingers, and the crashing of the ocean sounding like the sound track of their desire. She shifted herself down to kiss his chest, her tongue teasing over his nipples and then down his hard belly.

As always, his muscles flexed in response, and he had pulled open his belt, freed his cock, before she could do it. Her lips found the hot broad tip of it and her tongue instantly played over it, tasting the sweet drop of precome there, revisiting the exact shape of it. Her pussy twinged as if he had thrust into her. Then she was slipping her mouth down along the hard length of it, savoring the fineness of the skin, the tensile firmness of it, the slight upward curve of it from the base. He groaned and his hips arched, sliding his dick deeper into her mouth. Again her pussy spasmed as if he was fucking her already, and she pulled up her skirt and yanked her panties down, finding her cunt with her own fingers. With her other hand, she cradled his balls, squeezing them and using them to gently pull his cock deeper into her throat. His cock pressed into her throat and then retreated, pressed in and retreated, and with each thrust she let her tongue play along the sensitive underside. Meanwhile, she had slipped a finger into herself and found her own wetness, using it to moisten her clit and stimulate it with first one finger, then two sliding rapidly past each other. At last, he pulled his cock out of her mouth and reached to pull her up beside him. He moved on top of her and a second later he was inside her. She let herself scream once, sharply. As he fucked her, the wind intensified, adding a note of chill and wildness to the feeling of him pounding into her, underlining his desperation. When she came, the biting wind seemed to raise the feeling up; it had a keen knife-edge that made her cry out again. And he instinctively pressed his hand over her mouth, holding her down as he came, too, his dick slicing deep as the spasms of his orgasm made it jump inside her, hitting the keenly tender point of her own orgasm and opening it into hotter flame. And in her mind, she was shrieking that she would marry him, she would do whatever he wanted, she was his and no one else's. Nothing else mattered.

But when it was over, when they were lying silently together on the beach, his coat pulled around them against the wind—she said nothing. His hand still lay loosely over her mouth, as if it were a symbol of the thing that stopped her from saying she wanted to marry him, too.

At last he said, "I guess it was a stupid idea."

And although she knew exactly what he was talking about, she said "What? What was a stupid idea?"

He began to pull his clothes back into place, to detach from her. And he said, "Nothing. I was talking to myself."

"So you see, you were already *planning* to leave me," Paul said, lying back on the royal blue bedspread on the waterbed in the Yellow Room. "It was only a matter of time."

"That's not true," she said, distant and sad. "Not true."

"Listen." He sat up, and the closeness of him made her sick with longing. "I want you to do a job with me, for old times' sake."

She swallowed. "You need help with something?"

"I need you to do a job with me," he said almost petulantly. "In exchange for the Fremberg-Asp jewels."

"So you don't want me to sleep with you? It was about a job?" She smiled at him weakly.

He touched her cheek with the tips of his fingers, and even

that contact made her shiver. He said, "I want to sleep with you *now*. In fact...I won't even tell you what the job is until you promise to sleep with me."

They sat there, his fingers to her cheek, his beautiful eyes fixed on her face. Then he let his fingers glide down to her mouth and trace her bottom lip. She pulled back suddenly and said, "I promise."

He swallowed and said, suddenly gruff, "Can I kiss you?"

She leaned forward as he leaned forward and their lips met naturally, with that old consensus of flame. The heat flowed through her body and she felt like herself for the first time in four years. Then she was pushing him away, tears in her eyes. "Just tell me what the job is," she said, her voice strained. "I don't know if I can really do this."

"You can," he said. Then he spoke rapidly and evenly. "Blue Karten is getting married in a week's time. On the occasion of her wedding, Blue's mother is giving her all the family jewels. Handing them down from one generation to the next. Most of them are nothing special, but there is a particular princess-cut pink diamond that one of Mr. Bezin's friends has her heart set on. We'll be getting three-quarters of a million for that piece alone.

"The night before the wedding, the jewels will be there." He pointed to the ceiling. "In a locked chest in Blue's bedroom. The lock is a joke, and Blue is basically counting on no one knowing that the jewels are going to be in her bedroom while she has her bachelorette party downstairs."

"She's not marrying *you*, is she?" Olivia said.

"No, dummy." He gave her an exasperated smile. "Why would I marry Blue?"

"But you slept with her?"

"Did you sleep with Fremberg-Asp?"

"Is that a rhetorical question?"

He started to laugh. "I wish it wasn't a rhetorical question, but now that you mention it, is the Pope Catholic? Did you sleep with Fremberg-Asp? Does a bear shit in the woods?"

"So you slept with her, anyway," Olivia said, trying not to laugh.

"And you're jealous."

"And *you're* jealous," she said.

"It's been four years, I don't have any time left to be jealous. I have to fuck you again."

She felt a dawning fear of him, of the power he had over her. "No, wait. I'll get the Fremberg-Asp jewels back?"

"Yes, whatever you want, Olivia," he said impatiently.

"Wait—"

"No, angel. I'm sorry. I'm not going to wait."

A moment later he was entangled with her, his big arms wrapped around her; his chest flattened her large breasts as their bodies met and fit together. She felt again the precise joy of slotting into him, like a key into a keyhole, or like the moment when a safe's combination lock snicked into place, and the door fell open. He was kissing her and his hands were opening her shirt, her jeans, pulling her clothes away as easily as if they were made of tissue paper. For a moment she had stiffened, the fleeting idea of resistance had crossed her mind, but then she was helping him peel her clothes away, kicking her jeans on the floor and pulling up his shirt to feel the delicious hard curves of his body again. She followed the soft line of hair that ran down his belly to his jeans, and then he was pulling his jeans down, kicking them off, and she had his sweet dick in her hand. As she touched it, the memory of a thousand fucks came flooding back, and her body was overwhelmed with a heat that came to a point in her pussy and sent it into a mini-orgasm, a little tweak of lost control. Then she felt the shock of his fingers at the opening of her pussy, finding that tweak and spreading it deeper. He thrust three fingers into her and let his thumb slide up over her clit. As the fingers penetrated, the thumb ran up until he was wiggling the base of his thumb against her, pressing in hard. She answered him with her hips curling into the force, riding his hand while she pulled his other hand to her naked breasts. Somehow when he touched her, it was as if she could feel the appreciation he had for her tits, the firm overripeness of them, the rounded shape.

Then he moved on top of her, as he had a thousand times before, back when the world was young, before anything had ever gone wrong. He paused with his cock against her clit, his fingers still inside her, moving gently, making her pussy clench and long for him for real. "Olivia, do you still want me?" he murmured.

"Paul, just fuck me. Don't ask stupid questions, for God's sake. . . ."

And he was inside her, fucking her with such perfection that immediately she felt raised above every stupid trivial thing that had happened in the last four years, up into a sky in which every event was a blissful sensation that blinded her and changed her. Olivia felt as if her body was being transformed from flesh into pure pleasure that was all a form of love, and it made the room spin; it made her call his name without knowing where the pleading, husky voice came from. And through it all beat the firm relentless driving of his cock, its familiar straightness and hardness finding a mysterious need deep inside her and hitting that point again and again until everything she had ever wanted came true in an overwhelming orgasm. She clung to him as he came in her and clung to her.

Then he was kissing her face, her neck, the top of her head. She said softly, half sobbing, "You shouldn't have made me do that...."

"Yes, I should have," he said with absolute confidence. "You're mine, as far as I'm concerned. You can't change that."

"You can't make me...." Then the worst part of it came back into painful focus for her, and she pulled away from him sharply, sitting up on the bed. Looking around the room, she now noticed the drawing on the walls: erotic sketches from various countries and periods, all of which seemed to mock her and degrade her now. "You slept with my *sister*," she said.

He took a deep breath and shut his eyes for an instant. When he opened them again, they were helpless and tired. "There's nothing I can do to change that now."

"No," she said coldly. "There isn't."

"Livy, I never even intended to *talk* to your sister. I was trying to work up the nerve to talk to you. But then I saw her going into the bar opposite your house...."

"And the rest just happened," she said.

"You know what it's like when you get caught up in a job."

And she did. For a moment, she was with him, in the flow of a job that was part con artistry, part plain theft. You took opportunities as they came, and while the fever was on you, nothing else mattered. But she shook it off, insisting, "This is different. If it was only once, fine. But you have a habit of attacking me through the people I love."

"Olivia. That's not true."

"You can't tell me it's not true. That's *how we broke up.*"

It had taken her almost a year to piece together what exactly had happened the day after Paul had proposed marriage to her. All that year, she'd gone back and forth in her mind, trying to figure out if she'd been right to leave him. And at the end of it, she was left knowing that, right or wrong, she couldn't forgive him.

The afternoon of that day, Olivia had gone for lunch with her father and sister. Paul was going to be left alone in the Lucky Motel for four hours. He was planning to watch a movie on cable, make some phone calls, and "plan our next vacation in a place you won't like, to get back at you for deserting me."

Except that he never went back to the Lucky Motel.

Some madness took hold of him. Perhaps it was misguided nostalgia, a longing to see the place where they'd first met. Perhaps it was one of those cravings to tempt fate by going to the one place where there was the most danger. Perhaps it was just a stupid whim, born of having too much time on his hands.

Whatever the reason, immediately after dropping Olivia off, he drove to the Harkers' house. He didn't get out of the car. He just pulled over to the side of the road and stared. He lit a cigarette and rolled down the window. He was staring at the house as if it were haunted by the ghost of his true love. It didn't matter to him—as he told Olivia later—that Mystery Harker might look out her window and see him. He didn't think she would be able to recognize his face from that distance and angle, but even if she did, the whole point of acting on impulse was that one took insane risks. In putting himself into danger, he was making some kind of sacrifice to fate.

So he didn't move when he saw Athena Markleby walking toward the car. She came forward very evenly, unhurried, picking her way across the lawn between the Harkers' house and the Marklebys' in high-heeled shoes. She locked eyes with Paul and the two of them stared at each other while she walked up to the open car window.

Her first words were, "So, where is she?"

"Who?" he said.

Athena smiled. "Why don't you come up to the house? Nobody's home until eight."

There was a long pause. Paul stared at her, trying to understand why she had approached him, why she hadn't simply called the police.

At last, Athena said, "I'm sorry. Do you know who I am? I know who you are, of course."

"Who am I?" he replied.

"From my point of view, you're the other man," she said. "However perverse that sounds."

"I accept your invitation," he said. The madness had completely taken hold of him by then.

"Thank you very much. Why don't I get in and you can

drive me back to the house? These shoes are really no good to walk in."

Athena Markleby spent the next hour confiding in him about her love for Olivia. Her tone was always dignified and calm, even when she was telling him about the nervous breakdown she'd had when Olivia disappeared. She described making love with Olivia at Mystery Harker's party, not realizing that he had witnessed it. He got the feeling that she was confiding in him because she recognized that he loved Olivia, too; she was treating him as a kindred spirit, out of an intense loneliness. They were sitting together on a sofa in her bedroom, and she was behaving as if all this were completely natural, as if this were how one dealt with thieves in the best families.

Paul tried to match her candor; there was a nobility in her behavior that made him respond, above and beyond the need to convince her not to call the police. But all the while, two things were distracting him, preventing him from fully responding to her distress.

The first was his continuing obsession and growing bitterness with Olivia's response to his proposal of marriage. He kept thinking of ways to take it back, to tell her he'd been joking, he'd been testing her. *I would never marry you. I'm not even in love with you anymore,* he wanted to lie. But even in the fantasy, something inside him wept, and he wanted to get on his knees and beg her to stay with him, not to cheat on him anymore.

The second thing that kept distracting him was a familiar

glitter from the dresser to his left. At a certain point, his curiosity unbearably aroused, he stood up to stretch and saw that, yes, there were four or five pieces of jewelry there, necklaces and bracelets strewn over the dresser's surface among discarded panties and stockings. And at a glance, they appeared to be of extraordinary quality.

"So I've been thinking about you a great deal, Mr. Breakness," Athena was saying.

Paul sat down, looking back at Athena's face and forcing an empathetic expression onto his features. He said, hoping that she hadn't already told him this, "You recognized me from the party?"

"Among other things. Everyone knows your face, in this part of town. The police came door to door, leaving pictures of you. But most people don't know Olivia left with you." She ran one hand through her thick auburn hair and sighed, giving him a desolate smile. She added, "They don't know because I never told anyone."

"You were so sure she'd left with me?"

"Olivia had been pining for you; she told me about it. When she hadn't come back by the following night . . ."

"You must hate me, then," he said.

"Don't worry. I can't turn you in, because Olivia is your accomplice. She would go to prison, too—am I right?"

He smiled bleakly at her.

She said, "We were planning to live together, you know. I should be in New York at this moment, sharing an apartment with my lover. Tough luck, isn't it?"

"There are many kinds of tough luck," he said.

She appraised him again, her eyes full of warmth and the honesty of her own pain. At last she said, "I won't pretend, Mr. Breakness. I'm glad if you've suffered." Then for a long, fraught minute, she studied his face with intense and critical intelligence. At last, she said, "Olivia is still with you, isn't she?"

"Not for much longer," he said, without knowing why. And then, out of nowhere, he was hopelessly aroused, drunk on the situation, on the slender and beautiful girl in front of him in her summer dress, on the exposed gems that he already knew he was going to take. "Can I hold your hand?" he asked.

She gazed at him impassively. Then she put her hand to her lips and kissed the palm before stretching it out for him to hold. "For Olivia," she said.

He held her hand loosely, weaving his fingers into hers and then withdrawing them, drawing his fingertips against her palm lightly. Her dress was strapless bottle green cotton with a full skirt. She had pulled her feet up onto the sofa to sit cross-legged, without taking off her green high heels. He was leaning slightly forward, and their joined hands were resting on her knee. Through the fabric he felt that knee more and more keenly. He began to imagine himself stroking her leg, up past the tender inside of her knee, up the underside of her thigh and . . .

"Give me something else for Olivia."

He moved one finger and began to caress her leg with it, ever so gently. She held his gaze but said nothing.

Impelled by some instinct he could never have explained, he moved forward and snagged a finger into the elasticized top of her strapless dress. He felt her breathing quicken as he slowly, slowly, tugged the dress down. The swelling tops of her breasts were exposed, and at last the tender, pointed nipples came free, already beginning to harden at the tips. Here he stopped and took one breast in his hand, squeezing it gently. He tenderly pinched the nipple between his thumb and index finger, and she breathed in sharply, looking at him with a deliberate passivity. By now his dick was fully hard. He had to shift a little to relieve the pressure in his jeans, and then she saw him doing it, and saw the bulge in his crotch.

Athena put out her hand and covered the bulge, letting her hand rest there loosely at first. To Paul, the faint pressure was almost unbearably tantalizing. He found himself fighting the urge to cover her hand with his hand and press it down harder, fucking up into it from below.

Athena met his eye and paused for a moment, as if seriously considering what she was doing for the first time. Then she seemed to come to a conclusion that satisfied her, and she found his zipper and pulled it down. She found his dick and maneuvered it out of his open fly. Then her hand was stroking it lightly, the fingers barely resting on the hot skin. At the same time, she pulled her dress all the way down and he was squeezing both of her breasts. It was perversely exciting that all this time her serious green eyes never left his; she seemed to be daring him, or else unflinchingly completing her forfeit in a wager. He wanted to ask her if she was sure, if she was all right. But something told him that she might be insulted. So he moved forward, kissing her, guiding her onto her back on the broad sofa. And she was pulling her skirt up, spreading her legs. When his cock found her wetness, he was too far gone; she would have had to scream at him to get him to stop. He continued to look into her eyes as he sank his dick into her, slowly, feeling her tightness as his dick invaded it. She swallowed and then said, "Thank you," with her same cool politeness. Her voice was only faintly hoarse.

"You're beautiful," he said. "And you feel incredibly good."

He let his dick slip deeper into her by stages, monitoring the expressions on her face, which were blurring into a kind of helpless passion, finding their way from sadness into the sexual. She was watching him likewise, her eyes seeming to fight the trance of sex to remember who he was, where she was.

And she said, in a whisper, "Fuck me like you fuck her."

He almost balked then, but at that moment, he felt her coming. And he lost control again, fucking her with long, sure strokes that made his dick more and more sensitive as he went. He could feel the intricate reactions of her cunt, the spasms that racked it as she arched back and clung to the sofa behind her instead of to him. Watching her face, he caught the intensity of her surrender—it was sex as pure escape, as rebellion against the way life cheated you. It was a glass of ecstasy drunk in defiance of all the tragedy in the world.

He came with a fainting intensity. Then he clasped Athena to him, letting his cock lie gradually slackening inside her as he stroked her head and kissed her on the lips for the first time. Gradually she relaxed and embraced him back, her slender arms feeling tentative, careful, as they encircled his waist. And she said again, with gratified courtesy, "Thank you."

In a minute, she was fast asleep. He lay for a long time watching her, the pixieish face pouting slightly in sleep, the freckled shoulders hunched up protectively into her waves of red hair. At last he realized if he didn't leave, he would be late meeting Olivia.

He disentangled himself from her carefully, gradually, taking care not to wake her. But it wasn't until he turned away and his eyes fastened yet again on the jewelry she'd left on her dresser that he remembered what he was planning.

Paul glanced back at her sleeping form. Already, he realized, he was being careful not to breathe too loudly; his body had shifted into a wary posture.

And he thought, *As long as I don't tell Olivia, no harm done.*

He lifted each piece slowly, soundlessly, from the dresser, and slipped them into the pockets of his jacket. Athena slept through-out, her slim arms curled around the space where he had been a minute before. When all the jewelry was in his pockets, Paul leaned down and kissed her hair, holding his breath.

Then he went downstairs, got into his car, and drove back to the Lucky Motel, just in time to be there when Olivia arrived.

Two days later, Olivia was looking in his suitcase for a T-shirt she had lost, and saw an odd sparkle inside one of his tennis shoes. She reached in and pulled out a bracelet. She recognized it immediately. It was the first piece of "real" jewelry Olivia had ever tried on herself, a simple thing made of one strand of dia-monds and one of rubies. In between the stones were delicate silver A's.

She and Paul were in a hotel suite in Boston, spending the night before they caught a flight out to Monte Carlo for another job. It was a job Olivia had especially looked forward to, involving a whole brat pack of rich kids who liked to gamble and get too drunk to know where their belongings were. Olivia had discovered that she had a penchant for gambling, and a positive knack at card playing; her carry-on case was stuffed with primers on blackjack and baccarat, which she had planned to read on the plane on her way to a delicious and daring fortnight in the Grand Casino. . . .

Olivia sat on the floor with that bracelet in her hand and ran through possibilities. Of course Athena could have sold the bracelet. He could have stolen it from someone else. . . . It could have happened before. . . . No, no matter how she figured it, Paul had gone to see Athena. And he had slept with her. And robbed her. And he hadn't told Olivia.

He was in the other room, watching a movie on TV, and by the time he missed Olivia, and came to look for her, she was gone. She had taken two of her suitcases, Athena's jewels, the jewelry from the last heist, his wallet with all of his ID, and both of their plane tickets. As he ran outside, he saw the rental car, with her tearful face in the window, wheel and pull out onto the main road.

Chapter Fourteen

When Olivia got home from Blue Karten's, comprehensively mussed and not sure if she was ecstatic or despairing, Lee was lying in wait on her sofa. She had her biology textbook with her again, although a keen eye would have noticed that she was still on the same page. As Olivia came in, Lee sat up and said, "Livy, I have to talk to you."

Olivia looked at her and found, to her chagrin, that her first reaction to her own sister was jealousy. The idea that Lee had slept with Paul eclipsed everything else, and she was irrationally annoyed by the fact that her sister was *younger* than she was. She said, trying to sound parental and not envious, "I think I told you not to come here without telling me."

"Yes, you did," Lee said pleasantly. "You're right about that."

Olivia came over to the sofa and sat down heavily. "Okay," she said. "So what is it?"

"Listen," Lee said. "I talked to that detective. The insurance guy?"

At first Olivia didn't react. She just stared off out the window, feeling too beleaguered to even think about yet another problem. Then she said, "Oh, well. I guess when you think things can't get worse . . . So you know everything."

"I know enough. Do you want to tell me your side?"

Olivia made a face. "My side of the story is that I'm a Realtor."

"Oh, come on! You know what? Things could be much worse. That's why I went to see him, to stop things from getting any worse."

"And?" Olivia met her eye now, with a light sarcasm sharpening her features.

"Well." Lee blushed but forged ahead. "Um, the basic thing is, he's an insurance guy, not a cop. And he hasn't talked to the cops yet. So if you give back the stuff that his company covers, you know . . . it doesn't have to be everything."

"Give back . . . ?" Olivia's face lit up with incredulous amusement. "Give back jewels?"

"Oh, be like that," said Lee. "I knew you wouldn't take me seriously."

"No, it's just counterintuitive. It's like putting oil back in the ground or . . . I don't know. It's not that easy getting them."

"Like I said, it's not all the jewels. It's just the Fremberg-Asp jewels and the Axton ones."

"Well, there's a slight problem. I don't have those jewels."

Lee and Olivia glared at each other. Gradually Olivia's features softened. She said, "I've seen Paul."

"Oh." Lee looked stunned. "You mean . . . that's Jake?"

"Yes."

"Right. So you saw him? But then you could get the stuff . . . or are you still enemies?" Lee shook her head. "I don't understand any of this."

Olivia sighed. "Listen. How much does Mr. Taylor know?"

"Oh . . . well, he seemed to think you'd been working with Jake—Paul—for a long time."

Olivia leaned back in her chair, debating with herself. She could barely think; her mind kept returning to Paul, and coming up with reasons she ought to go back to the Karten place tonight. At last she decided to let the whole charade go; clearly she wasn't going to be a jewel thief much longer, and she would be lucky if she didn't go to prison. It was time for Lee to know everything. Maybe she really could help. "Well, I've been working on my own for four years. Before that, I was with Paul."

"Whoa. *Before* four years? You mean, like when you first left home?" Lee's eyes were alight with wonderful speculations, and a broad smile spread across her face. "Ha! He was the one you ran away with!"

"He stole Mystery Harker's emeralds that night. Do you remember?"

"Oh, wow. I haven't thought about that in so many years.

That's so funny. I remember I kidded you about it, but I never really guessed you'd run away with him. God, Livy." Lee sighed. "You have *so much* more fun than I do, it's sick."

"Oh, well," Olivia said drily. "You seem to do all right."

"But are you saying you guys aren't friends anymore?" Lee said. "He seemed very nice when I met him. Oh, sorry. . . . Don't mean to bring that up again."

"We're . . . friends again. But it's complicated. It's not necessarily just a matter of giving the jewels back. For one thing, the Fremberg-Asps needed those jewels to be stolen, for the insurance. If we return them . . ."

Lee scowled at her skeptically. "What about the Axton jewels?"

Olivia bristled. "Well, I had nothing to do with *them*. I mean, maybe *you* should be trying to get those."

"Maybe I should!" Lee snapped.

The two sisters glared at each other with the flash-point enmity peculiar to family members who deeply love each other. Then Lee's face cleared into seriousness. "Don't fight with me. Nicholas is going to get the police involved soon, and then both you and Paul will be arrested."

Olivia shrugged, trying to look unconcerned. She felt sure she could escape from the police one more time. She could even pull off the Karten heist and *then* escape from the police. But this time she wouldn't be able to come back to New York. What she would lose would be her sister. "You know, talking to the cops is frowned on in my line of work," she said softly, trying not to show the sadness that had overcome her.

"Not a cop," Lee muttered. She got to her feet. "Listen, you can do whatever you want. But, as you say, it's Paul who has the gems, and so he's obviously the one I should be speaking to."

"You mean you're in contact with him?"

"No. But I can find him. I'll just go and talk to Nicholas." And then Lee was leaving, her biology book cradled to her chest as if it were a teddy bear she was clinging to for comfort.

Chapter Fifteen

Olivia arrived at Blue Karten's bachelorette party in a bad mood. She'd received an e-mail from Paul in the morning with directions on when to arrive, where she would find him, and her part of the plan. Immediately she'd written back in what she hoped was a casual tone, asking him if he'd seen Lee. She got no response, so she wrote again, explaining that it wasn't that she was jealous; it was really about the insurance detective. No response. She'd written back saying that she wasn't going to write again, she would just see him at the party, but she was really surprised not to hear from him. When he hadn't written back an hour later, she turned off the computer and forced herself to concentrate on showering and getting dressed.

She was wearing a little purple dress that was mostly lace, with strips of satin here and there for decency's sake. With it she wore a pear-cut diamond pendant and matching earrings, which had originally been the property of the First Lady of a certain South American nation. Her rule was: always wear jewels to get jewels. She thought if you were wearing diamonds, people subconsciously assumed you had no need to steal them. Of course this could all be a complex rationalization for keeping expensive trinkets when she could have converted them into money.

It was ten o'clock when she arrived, and stepping out of the cab, she could already hear the party, a complex hubbub composed of two parts hip-hop and one part laughter. In the windows, there was nothing to be seen; all the shades were drawn. There was also a pair of bouncers at the door, who checked her name against a list before waving her to the door.

She went in and followed the noise to the central hall. Here the first impression she had was that she had entered some kind of changing room. While few of the people were exactly naked, no one was exactly dressed, either. Immediately she felt prudish because the business parts of her anatomy were concealed by her skimpy attire. Some people were dancing, but far more had moved beyond that point to making out, heavy petting, and even fucking in the middle of the dance floor. Bella, the girl with the valentine muff, wandered past wearing only a gauzy apron. She was pursued by a tall black man who occasionally, vehemently, spanked her—which she appeared to scarcely notice at all. After each spank, the man smiled blissfully and put his hand to his crotch for an instant. Then he was preparing the following blow. When Bella noticed Olivia, her face lit up and she cried out,

"Darling! How *are* you! Love the coat! This is Jean-Luc." Then she lowered her voice and said, as if it were an embarrassing fact, "He doesn't speak much English."

"Enchanté," Olivia said to the beaming Jean-Luc, who shook her hand with his spanking hand, which felt extraordinarily hot from its activity.

Moving on into the room, she noticed a preponderance of fancy masks, often worn with jewelry and nothing else. One girl was wearing a gorgeous blue feathered mask and a matching little pubic mask, attached to a bright blue G-string. The face mask had been pushed onto the back of her head, however, to allow her to go down on a man wearing a football helmet and the top part of a football uniform, but nude from the waist down. As Olivia watched, one of the few fully dressed people, a nondescript man in a cheap suit, came up on the masked girl from behind, unceremoniously unzipped his pants and kneeled, plucking her G-string aside with one finger to enter her from behind. She jumped in surprise, turned her head around sharply to see who it was and then cried out in ringing British tones, "Why, Jerry! I had no idea you were coming, love!" Then she reapplied herself to the football player's dick and contentedly allowed herself to be railed neatly from the rear.

There were iron rings set here and there in the walls, to which a few hapless people had been manacled. The majority of them was wearing street clothes—or had been before their capture. These clothes had been mostly stripped off them by stray passersby, some of whom paused only to fondle and for a friendly word, others of whom took full advantage. Olivia had just noticed one manacled man who was wearing only a leather hood—the shape of an executioner's hood, but with no openings at all for mouth or eyes—when Paul arrived at her side.

He put his arm around her immediately, almost protectively, and she melted against him, feeling his body's warmth as the only real, effective warmth. All other warmth in the world was like the saccharine of warm, while this was real sugar. She immediately wanted to be naked with him, just as she had at first sight. "You're overdressed," she said.

"You know I always wear a suit to work," he said. He looked at her and smiled. "And you wear stolen diamonds."

Then her heart felt flushed. She laughed for no reason and said, "Here we are, working together."

"And now we can't mention it again. Because the first thing we must do is bring you to Blue Karten so she has a chance to want you."

"I'm ready." They began to make their way through the crowd, curious and lecherous eyes scanning them as they went. Olivia paused as they passed the man in the leather hood. She said, "Why is everyone leaving him alone?"

"Oh," he said. "Well, the other manacled people are staff. That's Sadie, for instance—the veterinarian," he said, and waved at a girl wearing only a shirt, which had been ripped to shreds. Sadie was having her pussy licked while she stood with her face to the wall, her hands bound firmly to rungs far above her head. She returned Paul's wave with a little curl of her fingers, all the while crooning to the man licking her below, "Please don't stop. Please . . ."

"So who's in the executioner mask, then?"

"Oh, that's the bridegroom. A bit of a joke. It is a bachelor-ette party, after all. The idea is that he can't have sex until Blue reclaims him. People have been messing with him from time to time, teasing him, *starting* to suck him off, and then . . . But he's not supposed to come, so they have to be careful. No one wants to be banned forever from Blue's parties."

"So she reclaims him . . . but she's had five men by then? Or what?"

"No, she's being a good girl, just like he's being . . . well, to about the same degree. She's not *fucking* anyone, per se. Then she reclaims him, but with a couple of friends to help. That's us."

"A foursome," Olivia said. "We might not be chosen, though. There are plenty of sexy people here."

"Blue likes me very much. I mean, we're friends, and as well . . ."

"You're a handsome devil, yes, we know."

"I'm a handsome devil she hasn't fucked yet."

Relief coursed through Olivia before she could notice how irrational it was. "You haven't?" she said, trying to be cool. "How did you manage that?"

"Oh, I said I had a groin injury. From skiing. It's tacky but it worked. Blue's crowd is very much the skiing-injury set. But my pretend groin injury was pronounced cured this morning at nine by my imaginary groin doctor. So Blue may have that little debt on her mind.

"Also," he added in a significant tone, "the bridegroom likes you. He does get a vote."

She frowned at him. "Does he know me?"

"Once you've met Blue," he said, "I suggest that you go and see."

Paul led her out to the courtyard, with his arm held firmly around her waist as if to stake a claim. There was reason for this, as she discovered—even with that clear signal, occasionally men plucked at her dress, trying to entice her away from Paul. Their invitations ranged from the frankly icky ("Hey, beautiful, want to try this on for size?" while waving a not-particularly-giant erection) to the uncomfortably appealing (a startlingly hand-some blond man who kissed her on the shoulder blade in passing and said, "Hey . . . catch up with me later . . . please."). As they stepped out into the courtyard, Olivia first noticed the scent of jasmine; the stone walls surrounding the garden seemed to be completely overgrown with jasmine, the white star-shaped flow-ers sprinkled everywhere. Almost immediately she spotted one of the white rabbits, being cradled in the lap of a bikini-clad girl who stroked the animal's back while her head was turned grace-fully to one side to allow her to suck the cock of a tall Asian man. He, for his part, had one hand rather forgetfully resting on the mane of a snow-white miniature horse. It was a scene from some depraved acid-trip fairyland, and Olivia realized that she was faintly shocked—not by the sex, but by the fact that they were doing it in front of the animals. Of course the animals were completely unconcerned, and when she looked at the tangle of flowers in the garden proper, she saw with a faint amusement at her own prudery that a pair of bunny rabbits was also fucking in there—like bunny rabbits. She just hoped she wasn't going to have to play her part in the night's foursome with a tiny equine snorting by the bed.

Everywhere people were having sex—on patches of lawn, on porch swings, leaning up against walls. Olivia had never been at an orgy before, and her first reaction was a fear that she would find herself staring. She assumed everyone would be offended, and think she was really uncool, if she gaped at—for instance— that chubby girl who was sitting on a porch swing and being swung on and off that young man's dick. (Here she found herself staring, nonetheless. The way his long thin cock popped completely free of the girl's shaved pussy and then hit the bull's-eye again unerringly on the next swing— Well, it was virtually a feat of engineering.) But she gradually realized that everyone who wasn't fucking was unself-consciously watching the people who were. She even heard a man commenting to his friend, "She's not deep-throating correctly, that girl. She's going to hurt herself."

Then Paul cleared his throat and nodded toward what Olivia could only think of as a throne—a giant heavily upholstered chair, big enough to seat three people, which sat underneath a trellis thickly overgrown with ivy to form a neat canopy. The girl who sat in the throne, naked but for a tracery of pink pearls around her neck, upper arms, and belly, had dyed her long, thick hair an intense blue that matched her big kittenish eyes. Her skin seemed luminously pale, and her body was flawless—heavy pear-shaped breasts sitting high on her chest, a tiny nipped-in waist, and long, long legs that were no less beautiful for being apparently innocent of the effects of sunlight. She had her legs spread, with one foot up on the cushion beside her, to show a pink slit that was shaved completely, and whose rosy shade chimed with the pearls in a way that emphasized her cunt as an object of beauty. Olivia sighed with mingled admiration and hopelessness. There were some girls you couldn't compete with, not physically. She found herself wondering if that perfect body was what had turned Blue into such a legendary libertine. Blue would never have to worry about what she looked like; she would never have to worry about a man not wanting her, unless he was so devoutly gay as to find all girls repellent. Being naked in front of people would always be a flattering experience for this girl; she was unforgettably lovely.

Olivia said, "Hold on just a second. I think I need to . . ."

Paul stopped beside her, and when he turned to look at her, his face lit up in a tender, secretive smile. "Are you intimidated? I know she's strange."

"If anything's intimidating me right now, it's how beautiful she is."

"Yes. But so are you. You just don't know. What she looks like to you . . . you look like that to other people."

"Oh, that's . . . silly. But sweet." She was tugging one strap of her dress down, letting it fall so that her right breast was exposed. The hanging cloth looked sloppy until she pulled her arm completely free and tucked the strap inside the bodice. Then the dress could have been designed to be worn that way: the one breast fully exposed, the other apparent in hints through the violet lace.

He said, in a light conversational tone, "But you know you have the most beautiful breasts in the world?"

She grinned at him then, looking up from her fiddling. "So this looks all right?"

Fleetingly, he reached out and shaped his hand to her exposed breast, his hand closing over it with a needy appreciation that made her catch her breath. A heartbeat later he had his arm circumspectly around her waist again, saying, "Back to work, sugar. We don't have much time left."

With a delighted smile Blue Karten watched them coming, her elegant posture and outlandish hair making her seem like the queen of an underwater kingdom holding court. As they came up, she stretched her hand out to Paul and he put it to his lips. He kissed first the fingers themselves, and then an enormous pink pearl ring she was wearing. She said, "You're buried in clothes! You are really incorrigible."

"I just came in what I had on," he said. "This is my date, Olivia."

"You see, Olivia understands etiquette," Blue said, her eyes going immediately to Olivia's exposed breast.

Paul said, "I would love to talk more about my faults, but I really have to go and ask a favor of Bella. So I'll leave you two to get acquainted. . . ." And without so much as a glance to Olivia, he was moving back through the crowd.

"Oh, God!" Blue said. "He's deadly! Does he in fact have sex? we ask ourselves."

"Do you want an answer to that?" Olivia said.

"Oh, no. Not a *verbal* answer from *you*." Blue sighed with a friendly look at Olivia's exposed breast. "But if you could get him to tell me himself, nonverbally."

In her imagination, Olivia was suddenly stroking Blue's body, and Blue was licking Olivia's nipple, her heavily fringed blue eyes half shut, while Paul . . . She felt a sensual smile touching her lips. When she came back to reality, Blue was smiling at her with a smokiness that made a prickle run over Olivia's skin. In an hour, that fantasy would come true. Olivia said, "Do you want him so badly?"

"Now I've forgotten who we were talking about. It's you I want, beautiful girl. Wasn't it always? Come sit with me." Blue smiled beatifically and cocked her head. Then she shook her hair back over her shoulders, detaching an aquamarine tress from where it had caught over her breast. Again, Olivia was startled by the woman's beauty. "Would you consider that, or are you as impossible as your friend?"

"Well, I *am* impossible . . . ," Olivia said, frowning as if pondering the question.

"Unfuckable impossible, or impossible in some harmless way?"

Olivia smiled then, and was actually considering hopping up onto the throne when someone grasped her arm firmly from behind. She turned, a little shocked, and was more shocked to find it was Athena, wearing a chic black dress that swept the floor but was absolutely see-through.

"Livy," she said breathlessly, "I didn't know you were going to be here." And she said to Blue, "I'm sorry, but can I steal her? We haven't seen each other in years."

Blue smiled with a shrug of friendly condescension and said, "Just send her back to me. I'm absolutely infatuated."

Athena put her hand in Olivia's and towed her off behind the fountain. They sat on the rose marble wall at the fountain's edge and Athena said confidentially, "You looked like you needed to be rescued. Blue swoops on people." Along the inner edge of the fountain were wineglasses, and Athena now took one and dipped it into the fountain. "Pinot grigio," she explained. "Californian and not bad at all, though the stone adds an aftertaste."

"I didn't need rescuing, exactly," said Olivia. "But it is incredibly good to see you." She took a glass for herself and dipped it. The wine did have an earthy tone in it that wasn't exactly wine-like, but pleasant nonetheless. And Olivia found herself drinking off the whole glass with a sudden impetuous thirst. Once it was gone, her head cleared, and she smiled at her old friend with newfound calm. "So what are you doing here? The last I heard from you . . ."

"I know, I'm supposed to be in Paris. But I met Blue there, and you know . . . She hired me. I'm doing her PR."

Olivia burst out into irrepressible laughter. "Oh, no! Athena! But I'm . . . working."

"Oh, hell." Athena's mouth twisted for a moment as she absorbed this information. Then she blinked at Olivia with a resumption of her typical feline coolness. "Well, I don't know that, do I? And I have no intention of finding out."

They smiled at each other with that renewal of their old intimacy that always occurred when the two met. Although they seldom saw each other, the things they'd been through together had left them with a rapport as strong as that between people who share a bed and have breakfast together every morning.

Athena had known about Olivia's unconventional profession ever since the night Olivia left Paul. Olivia had driven directly from the Lucky Motel in Boston to Athena's house, showing up on her doorstep at three in the morning, holding the purloined jewels in both hands. Athena was sitting on the front steps, smoking a cigarette, wearing green silk pajamas.

Olivia came out of the rental car and walked across the lawn barefoot. "Here's your jewelry. I'm so, so sorry," Olivia said softly, looking up at the darkened windows of the house. "Did he call you? How did you know to wait?"

"No. I've been waiting for you for three days," Athena said, with a soft, sad smile. "I had to see you again."

"I brought your . . . stuff."

"Did he tell you about our conversation?"

"What conversation?"

Athena stood up and put one hand to Olivia's cheek. Olivia turned her head to kiss the other girl's wrist, feeling a vertiginous, sweet nostalgia. It was the scent of dew on the grass, of the ocean behind the house, of Athena's familiar musky perfume. "What conversation?" she said into the tender skin of Athena's inner arm.

Athena leaned forward and kissed her on the cheek. "How much time do you have?" she said into Olivia's ear, her breath hot and secretive in the chill, candid stillness of three a.m.

"I have a plane to catch at nine in the morning."

"Well, then," Athena said. "We have at least four hours, unless I get on the plane with you."

On the drive to Logan Airport, Athena told Olivia all the same details of her heartbreak that she'd told Paul—and how sleeping with Paul had seemed to clear away the necessity for grieving. "It made it possible for me to love someone else, even though it wasn't Paul. I don't know if that makes any sense."

"Not to me," said Olivia. She couldn't imagine sleeping with Paul and not falling in love with him. She sighed. "But I'm glad you're not upset anymore. I did hate myself for just leaving like that. But then I was stealing and running from everyone. . . . It never seemed like the right time."

Athena laughed. "Well, I'm glad I left the jewelry out for him," she said. "I did still want to see you. I don't know if I'll ever stop wanting to see you."

"You mean, that was planned?"

"Of course." Athena laughed. "I knew he would take it, and then you would come and see me. You don't think I'd leave all those diamonds out with a jewel thief in the room out of carelessness? I'm crazy about you, doll, not *stupid* about you."

When they got to the airport, there was a hitch: Paul had phoned to cancel the plane tickets. Athena and Olivia, both punch-drunk with tiredness, became hysterical with laughter at the ticket counter, and it was only through a last-minute attack of conscience on Olivia's part that they didn't buy two first-class tickets to Monte Carlo, but only one. Athena was quietly ready to give everything up for a life of crime, but Olivia wasn't confident enough about her criminal abilities to stake anyone else's freedom on them.

The new flight wasn't leaving until ten that night. So they got a room in the airport hotel and made love all morning, in an open-ended, all-absorbing way that temporarily blotted out Olivia's fears and sorrows. They were drinking sticky liqueurs, prescribed by Athena as medicine for all unnecessary fears. They were kissing and caressing each other and letting comfort turn into arousal and into orgasm and back into comfort again. For a long time Olivia rested her head on the soft inside of Athena's thigh with her hand in Athena's pussy, sometimes simply letting the fingers lie there while she talked, sometimes gently finger-fucking her, and moving her head forward slightly to lick Athena's clitoris in an exploratory mood, feeling a surge of affection and gratification when the other girl whimpered with pleasure.

They slept in each other's arms that afternoon, and in the evening Olivia woke up with the Monte Carlo heist fully formed in her mind. If only she had slowed down Paul enough, if only he didn't corner her at the airport and make some impossible scene, she could get to Monte Carlo and leave again with the jewels before he could get on a plane. It would take him a few days just to obtain a new passport. It should work.

She slipped out of bed and left Athena sleeping. She got up and crossed the room, trying to ignore the hollow terror that went through her at the idea of being alone. To board a plane with a phony passport, to travel across the world with a suitcase full of stolen goods alone, nineteen years old . . . For a moment of sheer terror, she paused, looking at Athena. She could wake Athena and just stay with her. They would get that apartment in New York that they'd always planned to get. She would forget about getting revenge on Paul, forget about gems and heists and all the glamorous gullible people in the world. A normal life: it was there for the taking.

Then she took her cell phone into the bathroom to place her first ever call to Mr. Bezin. From that moment on, she was not just an accomplice: she was a professional thief.

"So," said Athena now, letting one hand dip into the fountain, then raising her hand to rake her long pink fingernails through her fiery hair, "I talked to him."

Olivia swallowed. "Him?"

A little dappled horse came walking up and poked his pink nose into Athena's elbow. Athena stroked his neck. "You know very well who. Are you mixed up with him again?"

Olivia blushed. "Why does everyone assume I'm still interested in Paul?"

"I wonder. Why would anyone assume that?" Athena poked her face forward and rubbed noses with the little horse, who picked up his front hoof and pawed the grass once, in some horsy demonstration of devotion. Then Athena shooed him gently, and he wandered off toward the flower beds, where he began to graze happily. "These horses were my idea, you know," she said.

Olivia laughed. "You're crazy. What are you PR-ing here, anyway?"

"Oh, it's a lost cause, I think. Some minuscule fraction of Miss Karten's blood is Native American. She's Tuskegee tribe, or perhaps it's the Carnegie tribe. Anyhow, she's planning to open a casino here. A combination sex club and casino, if you can imagine."

"Here? This being a reservation?"

"Blue believes she can make it one. She apparently has friends in the government. And Hollywood, and the military, and the Kremlin and the Olympics Committee and Opus Dei— Need I go on? Anyhow, since I've been living here, I've learned not to underestimate her. But I don't think she's a Manhattan Indian, so this one may be beyond her reach."

Olivia caught her breath. "You've been living here?"

"All of Blue Karten's employees live here. We're like a cult," said Athena wryly. "A sex cult, in case you hadn't guessed. And we are a rather handsome bunch, I have to say. It really makes normal life, monogamy, all of that, seem pretty drab."

"Oh, well, I've never tried all of that anyway," Olivia said without thinking. She was looking around for Paul, worried suddenly that her time was running out. Out of the corner of her eye, she noticed that exquisite azure-headed Blue Karten was sitting in between two men whose black hair and brown skin made Olivia fleetingly, painfully imagine that Paul had somehow been duplicated and was kissing Blue's neck twofold, like a bizarre jealousy dream.

"Oh," Athena said, following Olivia's eye. "Those are the twins, Javier and Jorge. She found them in some sort of traveling sex show for the moneyed, 'my-husband-doesn't-understand-my-needs' set. She isn't even paying them. She just gave a lump sum to buy them out of their contract. They've stayed ever since because . . . everyone likes to fuck Blue."

"Do you?" Olivia said in a voice that wasn't hers—was more desperate and childish than hers. She was watching the twins bend to kiss Blue Karten's breasts, moving the pearls aside with hands that looked strong and beautiful . . . and then the hands were up in Blue's hair while the two men sucked at her breasts, and Blue shut her eyes and let her head fall back, two identical golden hands moving in her pearl-pink cunt. . . .

"Olivia," Athena said dreamily. "Of course I like fucking Blue. Perhaps you would even like fucking her, too, before you go off to be married?"

Olivia forced herself to look at Athena. "What do you mean? You mean . . . it's Blue who's getting married. Not me."

"Really? Only Blue?"

"What are you talking about?"

"I told you. I talked to Paul," said Athena. "I had breakfast with him this morning."

"So?"

"I don't think he's going to let you off so easily this time, that's all," Athena said.

Olivia shut her eyes and put her hands up into her thick, soft hair—something she did to reassure herself when she was at her most despairing. *I'm blond and I have big breasts,* she told herself. *Paul must want me. He must still want me. I don't have to be so afraid.* But she said, before she could stop herself, "You're making me want things I can't have."

"Good news," Athena said lightly. "I would never do that."

At this, Olivia stood up suddenly and said, "I'm sorry. I have to go see the bridegroom. Like I said, I'm working." She was

breathless and almost unpleasantly happy—happy in a way that
felt precarious, like balancing on the tiny point of everything
she'd ever wanted.

"Well," Athena said with a patient smile, *"bonne chance."*

When Olivia arrived in the parlor, she was at first distracted by
the presence of a seething mass of naked flesh in the middle of
the floor. It was a tangle of limbs with rhythmic movements here
and there—a proper orgy. Olivia had never seen one before, and
she halted in the doorway for a moment, her breath taken away.
The incredible multiplication of couplings made the activity
into something beyond sexual. These people were involved in a
group effort like a barn raising; there was something selfless, in-
toxicatingly communitarian, about it. It would be so easy to let
herself go and just crawl in ... start with that baby-faced man
there, who was currently screwing an exhausted-looking black
girl, but who would certainly be just as happy to fuck Olivia.
You would start kissing him, she thought, and maybe kiss the
girl as well. Fondling him and her. Perhaps some third person
would find you, enter you, plug you into the mass fuck. You
would work your way toward the middle of the pile, one cock
after another. . . .

Work. She turned with determination toward the place where
she remembered the hooded man as being. He was standing
there still, facing the wall, leaning against it with one elbow.
Another man was standing next to him, and the two were apparently having a casual conversation. The other man—blond, thin,
wearing only boxer shorts and socks—seemed to be telling a

story, gesturing with no apparent regard for the fact that the hood completely covered the other man's eyes and the gestures could not be seen. Olivia, thinking herself into work mode, walked toward the two with a certain drowsy slinkiness, much practiced in the full-length mirrors of the world's finest hotels. She could picture exactly the way her exposed breast would appear, bouncing and trembling; as the blond man looked up, she met his eyes with a particular coquettish sadness that made him trail off midsentence.

She came up to him and placed one hand on his chest immediately. "Listen, I need a private word with the bridegroom. Do you mind terribly?"

"That's awful," said the blond man. "Just when I was thinking I wanted a private word with you."

But he moved away with good enough grace, leaving Olivia alone with the hooded man, whose powerful nudity suddenly embarrassed her, just as meeting a naked stranger would have in her private life. Behind him, she could see that carpet of fucking, and she reminded herself that she had to make him want her.

She put one hand on his arm, and the warmth of it surprised her—as if she'd been expecting him to be a statue. Then she realized that she could touch him however she liked, and he couldn't stop her. He was bound in such a position that he couldn't even have kicked her away very effectively. Something about that intrigued her, and on the spur of the moment, she slipped in between him and the wall, letting her bare nipple trail across his chest.

He said, "Hello?" and she could hear the smile in his voice. "Is that you, Blue?" He had a faint accent, which she couldn't immediately place.

"No," she said, "not Blue." She put her hands on his shoulders and guided him against her gently. He let himself fit into her, and she felt the delicious shock of his naked cock touching her belly, its particular silkiness. She brought her hand around between their bodies and cupped his dick, feeling it already begin to thicken and straighten in her fingers. Then she said, remembering, "Someone told me we know each other."

"You don't know whether you know me?"

Perhaps it was just her imagination, but his voice really sounded familiar, and she even felt a fondness for him—if she did know him, she was certain he was someone she liked. She said, "You don't mind going through this? The being tied up naked . . . it's not embarrassing?"

"It's only fair, you see." His laugh was muffled inside the hood. "Blue did it at the last party, and she told me it was dull, but I wouldn't believe her. Now I believe her."

She tightened her grip on his dick, and found herself tense with desire. She remembered what Paul had said—anything was fair as long as he didn't come. "Is it so dull?" she said.

"You'll get bored with me, too, you'll see," he said. "The best I can hope for is that you suck me for a little while, and then leave me in miserable frustration. Which, since you ask, is the one thing I am finding rather embarrassing."

Then she realized. She sighed and said, "No, I'm not going to get bored with you, André. I promise."

"Who is it?" he said. "I'm sorry. I can only just hear your voice over the music, so . . . if I could touch you with my hands, I think I would know you."

"How do you know you've touched me before?"

"Aren't you one of Blue's friends?"

Olivia stifled a laugh. She remembered Athena saying, *We're like a cult. A sex cult . . .*

She said, "If I tell you I'm not one of Blue's friends, but you have touched me naked just two weeks ago, would you guess? Or have you seduced and deceived many girls in the past fortnight?"

At this he laughed again. "Olivia! Damn you, you have a nerve! You fucked my mother's boyfriend, and you robbed our safe! I was only concealing a certain part of my life from you."

"That you were engaged to be married?"

"First, we only decided to do it for certain this week. And second, it's not even a proper marriage. Not that I don't love Blue . . . and I can hardly begrudge her an innocent desire to be a countess. She'll be a better countess than any *I've* ever met. But she's mainly doing it to help me out. You know the money situation I'm in. . . . Well, this marriage will give me enough credit to start over." He shook his head and laughed again, and she could almost forget that what she was looking at was a featureless piece of black leather. André had obviously adjusted to his situation, and he leaned comfortably into his manacles as he said, "Olivia, I've missed you, you know."

"I thought the jewels . . . I thought the insurance for the jewels . . ."

"The insurance people are making difficulties now. I can't imagine why, but they think I might have been involved in the theft. As if I might have deliberately invited a jewel thief to stay with us. Now that is too ridiculous, isn't it?"

She laughed. "Oh, no—you knew?"

"I would have wanted to sleep with you, anyway. In case there's any doubt."

His cock was now completely stiff in her hand, and she automatically began to stroke it, its heat and hardness making her pussy tingle in jealous anticipation. She flashed on the orgy again, and actually felt the ghost of a cock plunging into her. She found a dewy drop of precome on the tip of his dick and drew it down the underside of his erection with the tip of her index finger. That made his hips strain forward. He made a faint sound deep in his throat and said, "Livy . . . I know I complained about people sucking me and leaving before . . . but would you?"

"Of course." She pressed her lips to his throat first, an affectionate greeting to his familiar beautiful body. Her hand below continued to play with his hard cock, drawing on it more strongly now, in a rhythm of accelerating desire. With her other hand, she couldn't help testing the lush wetness of her own pussy. As always when she worked, she was wearing no underpants, and that feeling of exposure, of easy availability, sharpened her arousal to a point where it was all she could do not to try to tear him free from his bonds and make him penetrate her right here. She looked wistfully at his athletic body—could she mount him? But there was no way. He was six inches taller than she was, and his arms were trapped above his head. There was no way he could lift her.

She satisfied herself with raising her fingers, saturated in her own pussy juices, and thrusting them inside his mouth. He sucked her fingers hungrily, moaning again as he thrust his cock forward, pressing his balls into the heel of her hand.

Then she knelt down and took the head of his cock into her lips. As she tasted the sweet precome—a magical taste to her with all the ineffable charm of fairy dust and love—her pussy spasmed and she reached up to his buttocks to pull his cock deep into her mouth, into her throat. It slid in easily, and again her pussy spasmed as if it was her cunt being entered. And he was fucking her mouth now, his hips pistoning forward while she sucked him hard, her tongue flickering all over the underside of his dick so that he was moaning helplessly, pulling at his manacles without seeming to realize that he was doing so, trying to get his hands free so that he could touch her. So that he could hold her head and fuck her mouth even harder. His cock felt deliciously fat in her mouth, and she could feel every vein of it, the seam between the glans and the shaft stimulating her mouth—and her pussy—in tandem. Putting one hand over his balls and compressing them slightly, tenderly, because by now she was afraid of making him come, she moved the other hand back down to her pussy and dipped two fingers over her clit, once, twice—then found a rhythm that got her a swift, keen orgasm, her mouth convulsing in sympathy, tight over his dick. At the last second, she panicked and pulled her head away, banging her head against the wall in passing as she sat on her heels, holding her spasming pussy protectively with one hand.

He said, "Damn it!" Then he was laughing, but with a definite note of frustration in his voice.

She was still catching the last spasms of her own coming, her hand teasing and holding them as she gasped, "Sorry...the rules."

"Olivia..." He strained against his bonds in exasperation, and even briefly pressed the tip of his hard-on against the wall before giving up. "God. But you don't even know Blue."

"But I want to sleep with you later, André," she said. "You know, when Blue comes to get you. If that's not too uncool to say." She was returning to normal now; she was even able to pull her hand away from her cunt, leaving the last hot impulses to spill into the air. To her faint embarrassment, a few of the members of the orgy were plainly watching her, using her as their pornographic encouragement to coming. She pulled her skirt down with a ridiculous prim gesture and got back to her feet.

André gave as good an impression of looking at her severely as a man could when he was wearing a leather mask with no eyes or mouth cut into it. "Olivia, you're not here to steal the Karten gems, are you? Because this time I can't let you, you know."

"Can't let me?" Olivia pondered and then said, "Well, André, the only way to be certain I don't steal them is to stick close by me, then, isn't it?"

"Ha, ha," he said. "As soon as I get out of these cuffs, I promise . . . Until then, please don't rob my fiancée."

"Until then, I promise." Olivia got on tiptoe and planted a kiss on the leather where his mouth would be. "And no hard feelings if I steal them afterward?"

"Police, yes. Hard feelings, no."

"Deal," she said affectionately.

And she set off past the growing orgy and back to the courtyard, where she was immediately stopped in her tracks by the vision of Blue lying on top of Paul across the seat of the huge throne, her ghostly hair spread over his beautiful bare chest.

Chapter Sixteen

Lee came into the courtyard almost on tiptoe, and froze. It was partly the miniature horses; it was partly the bizarre vision of a cockatoo flapping its wings at a white rabbit that stood its ground, thumping one hind leg belligerently. But it was mainly the fact that at her very feet a young girl with close-cropped orange hair was being screwed fore and after by what appeared to be Latino identical twins. For the first time she wondered if she was really cut out for the life of an adventuress. Perhaps there was a reason Olivia had always wanted her to stay in school.

But then she pulled herself together, tugging a little anxiously at the halter dress she was wearing, whose hemline tended to creep up to reveal a pink half inch of pussy, freshly waxed and absolutely bare. As long as she could hold out until Nicholas got here, she would be all right. As long as . . .

Then she saw Paul.

He was disentangling himself from a woman who Lee guessed must be the hostess—Nicholas had told her about the long blue hair. The blue-haired woman—a woman of such exotic and extraordinary beauty that Lee was caught staring at her, trying to believe her features were really as lovely as they appeared—ran one hand down Paul's chest to his groin, cupped him fleetingly, then turned away and headed indoors. Paul seemed to relax as she left him. He rubbed his eyes, looking around, and froze when he spotted Lee.

She found herself giving him a friendly wave, as if they'd run into each other at the mall. He came toward her with an air of nonchalance, which she was sure was entirely faked; his face anyhow was tense and profoundly unhappy. Reaching her, he immediately took her hand and pulled her into a shadowy corner, saying, "Lee, what the *hell*? What are you doing here?"

"Oh . . . I came to speak to you . . . kind of?"

"Well, don't let Olivia see you. I mean, please don't." Then his face softened. After one last glance over his shoulder to check for an angry Olivia bearing down on them, he said, "And—I'm sorry about London. I should have told you everything, really. But . . ."

"But Olivia would have killed you. Never mind, I had fun." She was having trouble concentrating; she wasn't even sure she had understood what he was apologizing for. Now, before he could escape back into the crowd, she said, "Listen, Paul, I have to give you a warning. And, maybe, an offer?"

She breathlessly outlined everything Nicholas had told her about the Axton and Fremberg-Asp jewels, the offer he had made, the fact that Olivia had refused to help her. "I'm meeting Nicholas here tonight. He's giving me until midnight to get the gems back, and then . . . Do you still have them?" She looked at him imploringly.

"Wait. You want me to give them back to this Nicholas? Or to the owners?"

"Well, it would have to be . . . I guess, the insurance company?"

"Or Nicholas Taylor, whom you believe to be employed by an insurance company—on what basis?"

"He . . . ," Lee stammered and her face grew hot. "No, I've been to his office."

"What sort of an office?"

Lee tried to think. She could clearly picture the office—the perfectly clean, perfectly anonymous office where she'd made love to Nicholas so ecstatically. At last she managed, "Well, it had . . . it was in an office building."

"Yes. Nicholas is a tall man?"

"Um . . . what would you call tall?"

"Lee."

"Oh, okay. Yes." Lee frowned at him. "You think I've been tricked by some con artist—is that it? Because Olivia met him, too—"

"Oh, Olivia!" He laughed with an infectious delight, his white teeth flashing in the dark.

"What?" Lee couldn't help smiling at him. "You're trying to say Olivia wouldn't know?"

"Olivia is a terrific thief," said Paul. "But a good-looking man could tell her that the sun revolves around the Earth, or that children are brought by the stork, and she would believe it absolutely."

"Oh, that's probably true," said Lee. She sighed. "Family trait?"

"A very, very endearing family trait." Paul grinned at her. "So, a tall man . . . anything else?"

"Oh, tall . . . light brown hair."

"Kind of horsy-looking, with weird pale eyes?"

"Not at all," said Lee crossly. "Very good-looking."

"Horsy-looking in a good way, with attractively pale eyes?"

"Oh, okay. That's probably him. So who is he, *Jake*?" she said with snotty ill grace.

"An old friend," Paul said. "That's all. From my life before I made the acquaintance of the Stewart girls. A dealer in stolen goods, for the most part. But occasionally a stealer of the goods, especially when he can rob the robber. Keeps a very nice office on the East Side . . ."

"Oh, to hell with all of you. Anyway, I like him," Lee said irritably. "I just want to know his name."

"I knew him as Nick. But his last name's Tordahl." Paul shook his head at her. "Listen, Lee, I have to go. But bring your Nicholas to the garage at the side of the house at eleven thirty, and we'll sort all this out, okay?"

"Okay," Lee sighed. "Eleven thirty, garage. Go do your grown-up, I-know-everything stuff. And I'll see you then."

He kissed her on the cheek, and then he was gone, navigating through several panicking bunny rabbits and a nude man playing a violin.

Lee stood for a moment, not sure whether to feel comforted or terminally distressed. So Nicholas was just another felon lying to her in order to get some jewelry? She shook her head in the calming darkness. One thing was for certain: she was never going to be prepared for that damn biology test. For a moment, she simply bit her lip in a keen chagrin at the thought that generally she passed for a pretty smart person. And yet everyone had run rings around her, making her sit and fetch and jump through hoops . . . She hoped Paul was right and it really was a congenital weakness for handsome men. Otherwise it looked very much like congenital idiocy.

And then, standing ever so slightly taller than everyone else, Nicholas Taylor/Tordahl/Bullshitter came walking out into the courtyard, spotted her, and smiled coolly. She smiled back with a foolish feeling of lovesickness. She couldn't help it; she actually liked him better now that she knew he was a thief, a dealer in stolen goods, a criminal of long standing. It was much sexier, after all, than working for an insurance company.

As he walked up, she blurted, "I've just talked to Paul."

Nicholas balked. "And from the look on your face, he told you something surprising?"

"Just who you really were. Anyhow, he said to meet him downstairs, at the garage, at eleven thirty. I'm guessing this means you can't have your diamonds, though. So you can go now. I won't keep you." Lee made a face at herself. Of course, she hadn't intended to say any of this. She had intended to play it cool, and trick him into being at the garage at the right moment.

He flinched but held her gaze with only the faintest pall of reproach in his face. Then he said, with a change in his voice that she couldn't interpret, "So, we have an hour?"

"You don't have to be polite," she said. "Besides, I'd rather you just left now than that you sneak out when my back's turned. I'm not going to make a scene. I mean, in case you were concerned." She shrugged and couldn't meet his eye.

She felt his hand on her cheek, and then his breath. He kissed her on the corner of her lips and said quietly, "Lee, do you think I was using you?"

"That's all right," she said. "I mean, I liked . . . the sex."

"Look at me."

With an effort she managed to look at him, but she was aware of slightly squinting, as if what he said next might be so harsh it would hurt her eyes. He was grave as usual, a self-conscious tenderness clouding his eyes. "Everyone has some things they lie about," he said. "Love is not one of my things." He put his arms around her tentatively.

At first she stood stiff in his embrace, but after a minute the temptation of his body was too great. She put her arms around him and let her body sink into his, her head against his shoulder. "What's going on, Nicholas?" she said hopelessly.

"A number of things are going on, but none of them are going to hurt you," he said.

"Are you taking me home after this? To make love to me every night? 'Cause if you're not, I don't want to know." She gave in further and kissed him on the neck. His body against her brought with it a potent memory of fucking in his office. He seemed to be feeling the same thing, because he pressed against her and she could hear his breathing change.

He said, "I can't take you home, exactly. Let's just say I'll be taking you."

She smiled into his neck. "That sounds corny."

"It's not corny. It's evasive. I can't tell you yet and I don't want to lie to you again."

Then he was kissing her, and desire washed away all her curiosity. She was unbuttoning his shirt and his hands were on her breasts, her ass. He was lifting her against him. For a split second she thought, *No, I'm supposed to be dealing with things.* And she thought, *We're in public. I'm going to be like that girl with the orange hair.*

Then she felt his hard-on pressing into her belly, its base pushing against her pussy and grinding deliciously over her clit. And she forgot everything else. She was pulling him against her, willing him to fuck her now. Her back came to rest against the stone wall of the courtyard, and he was pressing into her, dry-fucking her, his dick's length finding her again and again. He pulled loose the bow at the back of her neck that held her dress up, and Lee's only thought was to be grateful that it was that kind of party as he stepped back slightly to let the dress fall to the ground. And he looked at her for a spellbound moment, one hand making its way down her body, over her tingling breasts, to her pubic mound, and then slipping in, finding her clit and sliding one finger into her pussy. She gasped and opened her legs, setting her feet wide apart to give him access. For a tormenting minute he slid one, then two fingers into her, not fucking her with his hand but just feeling her inside, his eyes going distant and drowsy.

By now she was aware of the people milling around just a few yards behind him, of the casual laughter and conversation. There were a few couples in the shadows similarly occupied, but Lee noticed eyes turning toward them, men raking her nude body with their eyes, possibly wondering if they could have a turn. And the thought of it made her whole body hot with awareness, the agonizing sensations in her clit becoming a fire that spread everywhere that the strangers' eyes were fastening on her, wanting her.

Nicholas said into her ear, "I need to fuck you now, Lee."

She just wrapped her arms around his neck and said, inarticulate, lost, "Can you ... like this? Can you just ... ?"

He reached down and lifted her up, first by her ass, spreading her with a delectable sensation of excess, and then, shifting her up the stone wall, he got a purchase on her thighs. She wrapped her legs around him and held on for a breathless second of not being able to wait, of thinking, *Now, now, now.* Then he had opened his pants and his dick was there. There was the flash in which he was actually penetrating her, the shaft sinking in and making her pang all over. Then it was deep inside her, pinning her to the wall, piercing her with intimate thoroughness.

"Oh, God ...," she said, tears coming to her eyes. "Fuck me. For God's sake, Nicholas."

"You know that I want you. You know ...," he said into her ear.

"Please ...," she said, not knowing what he was talking about. "Please."

And he gave in with a deep groan and, holding her against

the cold stone, began to fuck her with minute attentiveness, his dick swiping past her clitoris with every thrust, then thrusting into her from every angle, opening her in every direction and making her squirm as if she were trying to escape. The sensation of being pinned to the wall and helplessly fucked overwhelmed her, and she stared past her shoulder at the groups of people watching her . . . men with intent expressions in their eyes, a generalized public desire for her that was crystallized in Nicholas' big dick slicing into her again and again with sure power.

Chapter Seventeen

E scaping the vision of Paul entwined with her gorgeous rival, Olivia had blundered back through the parlor again, this time feeling unnerved by the ongoing orgy to such a degree that she pulled her dress back into place, covering her breast. Then she went out front and chatted to one of the bouncers, trying to calm herself down, trying to wipe out the image of Paul and Blue intertwined. The bouncer was from Haiti; they spoke in French for a couple of minutes, and it comforted her to remember that she could speak French, even if her accent was pure Massachusetts; she had begun to feel like the awkward townie teenager at the rich people's party again. *I'm a jewel thief,* she told herself. *A hot blond jewel thief who travels the world, stealing . . . jewels.* But at last he told her she was too beautiful to come to a party alone, and where was her boyfriend tonight? She went back inside, feeling utterly despondent.

Now she was sitting on the main staircase, out of sight from both the courtyard and the parlor. The steps were moon-colored limestone with pale blue carpet running up the center, and it was comforting to sit there, with one hand on the cool stone, feeling sorry for herself, ashamed of herself, thinking only of herself. Of course it was wrong of her to be upset. If Paul had walked into the parlor a minute before, he would have seen her sucking André's cock without any self-consciousness whatsoever. But she didn't want to worry about fairness, or other people's feelings, right this moment. As far as she was concerned, for this moment, the world was horribly unfair to Olivia personally. No one understood what she went through.

She had been sitting there for some minutes when Blue herself appeared, as if summoned by Olivia's despair. She walked up to Olivia with a fluid grace that seemed to underscore her nudity, one hand stroking her own breast, and a smile of sleepy delight on her angelic features. Even close up, she was superhuman in her prettiness; the blue hair, the luminous ivory skin, and the strings of roseate pearls made her look like a goddess come down to entice mortals. Olivia instinctively sat up straighter. Again she suffered from that inner fainting feeling: this was The Most Beautiful Girl in the World. The ideal mate for The Most Handsome Man.

"Are you coming upstairs?" Blue said. In the quiet space, Olivia could now hear that Blue's voice was as lovely as her appearance; it had a husky sweet timbre like a low note played on the flute.

"I don't know," Olivia said honestly.

"Well, I can't leave you here, you know," Blue said. "André said you aren't to be trusted. You steal, or lie, or pass bad checks ... something reprehensible." She smiled, looking down at her own breast, the long blue fingernails of one hand tripping over her nipple idly.

"Oh, he told you about all that," said Olivia, with genuine lack of interest. She could have been knee-deep in diamonds at that moment without caring.

"You should come upstairs with me," Blue said, with a sudden intensity, looking at Olivia from under her long navy blue eyelashes. "You'll never be sorry you did."

"I can't."

"Paul won't sleep with me unless you do," Blue said simply, "so you'll have to give in. You would be spoiling the party."

"And here I thought you loved me for myself," Olivia said, smiling.

"I do," Blue said, with that intensity burning out of her eyes.

Olivia caught her breath. The beauty of the girl was mesmerizing. It was difficult to refuse her. For the first time, Olivia had some inkling of the power she herself had over men. It felt different from the power Paul had over her. She could have said no to Paul about almost anything—unless he wanted to fuck her. With Blue, it seemed almost impossible to say no. Her looks were something elemental; it was hard to believe she could talk, walk, eat, do the things ordinary people did. It felt as if the sky had suddenly turned to you and spoken. How could you say no to the sky?

"Paul told me," Blue said slowly, "that you might need to see him alone first. He's up there now."

Olivia felt a spark of agony in her chest. There it was: Paul was already up there. Whether or not she went, he was going to have sex with Blue—of course he was. And once he'd had sex with Blue, Olivia would begin to look chubby, ordinary, clumsy. That was how it began. Within a few weeks, he would be back in the sex cult, living in the Yellow Room, sliding down the fireman's pole in emergencies. . . . Pushing away her paranoid fears, she said, "I can see him alone?"

Blue smiled. "I didn't mean that so seriously about the bad checks." And she added smoothly, "In any case, pretty Olivia, the gems aren't there. They're in a new safe downstairs. So if you'd wanted to be reprehensible, you couldn't do it in my bedroom, which is three flights up. You can't miss it."

Olivia got to her feet, stunned. "Well, that will save me some trouble, won't it?" And she turned and mounted the stairs with a grim awareness of her awkward gait, her chunky hips, of everything about her that made her just another hot blonde with nothing special about her. Another busty girl on the beach, in the crowd at the club, in the hero's past.

By the time she got to Blue's bedroom, Olivia had decided what she had to do. She would tell Paul to forget about her. She would make the point that they'd been apart for four years, and as far as she was concerned, those were good years. Then, before he could make her change her mind (here she had to swallow a fear that he wouldn't try to change her mind), she would step to the fireman's pole and slip down into the garage. Then she could walk away, get a cab, go home. Drink. Tomorrow she could go out shopping.

She had expected to spend some time finding the right room, but when she got to the third floor, the entire floor was a single room with windows running along all four walls. The fireman's pole stood in the center of it. Beside the fireman's pole was an enormous bed, and on the bed was Paul. He was sitting on the edge of the bed casually, naked in a careless way that reminded her painfully of Blue.

"Hi," she said. "The jewels aren't here, you know."

"I know."

She shrugged. "So we've fucked up."

"Not really."

She came toward him, and as always, he looked exactly right to her. There was a nearly empty bottle of champagne at his feet, and he had one leg pulled up on the bed, as if to showcase his strong tanned thigh, with the fine dark hairs along it that she had stroked so many times. She admired—for the last time, she told herself—the lithe grace of his body, his handsome face. She came toward him and leaned over to kiss him on the lips lightly. She was about to begin her speech, preparing a line about how she would always care about him, but . . .

Then she realized what he'd said. "What do you mean, not really?" she said.

"The plan changed." He smiled at her. "But we can't really discuss it right now. We still have to go through with the really painful task of having sex."

"Four-way sex," she said with what she realized was an uptight expression of disapproval on her face.

He laughed. "It won't take long. I promise."

"But, Paul—"

He stood up and took her in his arms, stifling what she was about to say with a kiss. *One last time,* she was thinking as her eyes drifted shut, as her body relaxed against his. And when she opened her eyes, André and Blue were standing at the top of the stairs. They were naked, and André had his arm around Blue's slim, long waist. He had taken his hood off, and she felt the surprise of seeing him, all over again, as if seeing him without seeing his face hadn't counted.

Olivia thought, *The plan changed.* She was suddenly intrigued. What was the new plan? And, before she could stop herself, she had remembered the Kartens' pink, princess-cut diamond that had sold for two million dollars at auction. What would it look like? What was the setting? She realized that she didn't even know if it was set. And without knowing that, she couldn't imagine what it would be like to wear that stone while Paul fucked her later on that night. If she didn't go through with the foursome, she would never find out . . . and for some reason that seemed terribly, terribly, sad. Still, she told herself, the right thing to do was to leave. She should protect herself. The jewels were in the safe downstairs, anyhow; she would never see that diamond.

On one of the matching mahogany nightstands, there were four champagne glasses, one already full and the others empty. Paul lifted the glass that had already been poured and raised it in a toast. "To the bride and groom," he said. He drank it off and then began to pour wine for the others as Blue and André came forward into the room. He handed them glasses, and they both sat on the edge of the bed, sipping champagne while looking quietly at Paul and Olivia. Olivia was conscious of being the only person clothed, the only person standing up.

"Not enough for you," Paul said to Olivia, holding the empty bottle inverted over the final glass. "Do you want me to get you—"

"Yes," said Olivia immediately.

Paul laughed and she looked down in confusion.

"Well, I mean," she said, "I can wait."

"Wait, then," said Blue, reaching up to take Olivia's hand. Olivia came forward, once again feeling hypnotized by the other girl's strange loveliness, her regal poise. Sitting down on the bed between André and Blue, she let André pull down the zipper of her dress, all the while thinking of ways to tell them she was going to leave. She kept her eye on the fireman's pole, imagining the gesture of walking toward it and sliding down, even as Blue pulled her dress down off her shoulders and André bent down to seize one of her nipples between his lips, tugging it gently as he moved his tongue in tiny circles over the very tip. Olivia moaned, and felt Paul's eyes on her, their intent appreciation of her exposed body, which also contained a deeper intimacy, a reminder of their alliance and their long-standing competition. His eyes said that he wanted her more than any other woman because she was his natural mate. His partner in crime. And in that instant she realized that being jealous of Blue—of anyone else—was nonsense. Athena was right. This was the man she would marry. She didn't have to be afraid.

Then André's hand covered her other breast, and she was shutting her eyes; the fireman's pole disappeared, and she forgot that she had ever intended to leave. She kicked her dress to the floor.

Someone's mouth found hers, and she was kissing—who? When she opened her eyes, it was Blue, her thickly fringed eyes half lidded and full of friendly lust. The kiss was startling in its artistry, Blue's tongue playing over Olivia's in such a way that the tiniest caress counted, setting off vibrations through Olivia's body. Meanwhile André continued to play with Olivia's breasts, and his mouth was traveling downward, licking her belly as if he were chasing the pangs of lust that were shooting down from her mouth and nipples to her pussy. Blue pulled Olivia down onto her side on the bed, and Olivia now noticed Paul on the other side of Blue, pressing into her spoon-fashion. His hand was slipping over Blue's thigh as Olivia watched, and then his fingers were turning in, sliding into Blue's pussy. Olivia felt Blue's reaction in her kiss, which intensified as if mirroring what Paul was doing with his fingers down below.

Meanwhile André's mouth had found Olivia's cunt. At first he landed a series of butterfly kisses on her labia, teasing her into spreading her legs to his seeking tongue. Then he was spreading the cunt lips with his fingers, breathing on her exposed wet clit and her spread pussy so that chills went up her spine. And she found she too was kissing Blue with extra intensity, and dimly she felt as if she *were* Blue—perfectly beautiful and in control and fearless, a woman who had never needed anyone but only desired them from above, from a throne. She was transported into a world in which fucking was a delightful fond game, something you did as a matter of course with everyone you liked. And when she shut her eyes, somehow all these things were summed up by the twinkling image of a flawless pink princess-cut diamond.

André's tongue snaked over her pussy then, a rapid intense

tickling that made her clitoris sweetly burn, the sensations washing over it like flames. She squirmed and spread her legs farther,
arching her cunt up to his hungry mouth, begging him for more.
His fingers spreading her made the feeling almost intolerably
keen, and she was instantly longing to come, to let the excess of
her arousal free. And now the hands on her breasts were Blue's;
they were Blue's slim, deft fingers catching at her nipples and
testing the tender firmness of her breasts. The extravagantly
dirty feeling of being made love to by two people—one of them
a woman and a stranger—made Olivia shut her eyes, diving into
a darkness where shame was delight. For a long perfect minute
everything was sensation and sweetness, the waves of bliss from
her pussy and breasts and lips all joining to make her feel as if
she were floating in the depths of an ocean of sex, lost to the real
world.

But then she felt Blue's mouth still, Blue's hands fade away
from her breasts. Opening her eyes, she realized that Paul was
fucking Blue from behind, and the other girl had shut her eyes to
concentrate on the feeling. Blue had raised her slim hands to her
mouth; her teeth were fastened on one finger dreamily. Now
Paul reached over Blue's body to touch Olivia, his hand stroking her throat and over her breast and down. André moved his
mouth away to let Paul's fingers invade Olivia's pussy. She gasped
as she felt André's cock at her slit while Paul's fingers moved over
her, finding the pleasure André had awakened in her clit and
teasing it into full, exquisite flame. Then André's thick cock
thrust into her and the penetration itself made her begin to
come, a flood of aching pleasure that made everything black for

a razor-sharp moment of exploding desire. Her cunt was plummeting through one layer after another of orgasm while André's cock opened her more and more, fucking into her hard. She was gazing at Blue's perfect face, the pink lips parted and the fingers in her mouth loose, quiescent. Blue had shut her eyes and Olivia felt a final, obliterating wave of pleasure before André collapsed on top of her, coming and murmuring her name, and Blue's name, and then just something she couldn't understand. . . .

When her vision cleared, Paul's hand was loosely grasping her thigh, and he was smiling at her; she could see one half of his face over Blue's face. André's weight on her was becoming uncomfortable; he seemed to have relaxed absolutely in coming. Blue was likewise lying with her arms slack and sleepy, her eyes shut, with a look of blissful peace on her sculpted face.

"Is he asleep?"

At first Olivia didn't realize that Paul was talking to her. But he was looking directly into her eyes. "What? What do you . . . Oh."

André's face was smooshed against her shoulder, and she put one hand to it gently. Then she shoved him slightly. "Yes, he's asleep, I think." Then she said, more loudly, "André? Are you asleep?"

"He's asleep," said Paul. "And so is Blue. So . . ."

And suddenly he was rising from the bed, with a look of suppressed laughter in his face. He said, "Do you need help? Do you need me to pull him off?"

"What?"

"You have to get out from under him," he explained. He had

grabbed his jeans from the floor and was pulling them up hurriedly, smiling at her with the pleasure of a little boy who has a secret.

She had barely woken from the trance of her orgasm, and she began to shift André off of her without trying to understand what was going on. He slipped off fairly easily, continuing to sleep with a look of bliss that was uncannily like Blue's. With him gone, she suddenly felt cold and exposed. The delayed shock of what she'd just done hit her, making her feel a little hysterical. She would have liked to make jokes about it, giggle, decompress with a bottle of wine. Sitting up on the edge of the bed, she spotted André's half-finished glass of champagne and bent down to retrieve it, drinking it down in the hope that this would finally calm her down. As she lowered the glass, she caught Paul staring at her in horror.

"What?" she said. "What are you—" Her eyes alighted on the slumbering André, then moved to the unconscious Blue. And—although she still resolutely didn't *want* to understand what was going on—she grasped it all and said, in a weak voice, "The champagne?"

"Get dressed. Get dressed fast," he said.

She found her dress and was tugging it on with a confused flurry in her mind. "But wait—you drugged them? Us, you drugged us. I'm such an idiot." Now she could laugh, as she'd wanted to, but it had lost its pleasantly hysterical edge.

"Yes. Just hurry. You should have five minutes."

"Oh, God. Shoes . . . shoes . . ."

"Forget the shoes! Just go!" he said, gesturing at the fireman's pole.

For the first time she actually realized that the pole went down three stories and ended—in a garage. Concrete or at best tarmac. She gulped. "Can't we use the stairs? They're really asleep." She cringed at the idea of the landing in her bare feet.

"Look, it's perfectly easy," he said, exasperated.

"I don't even know if I want to go with you!" she said. "I mean, I'm not part of this at all. I just had sex! It's nothing to do with me, and if . . . I'll always care about you, but we were apart for four years. They were good years, weren't they? They were okay years!"

"You're babbling," he said, his blue eyes torn between amusement and irritation. "Just go down the pole and we can break up downstairs."

"Oh!" She swallowed again and frowned at the pole in despair. "Oh, the hell with it!" She stepped over to the opening in the floor, trying to quell the pounding of her heart. The pole was shiny, utterly slick metal, and when she looked down, she couldn't tell anything about the bottom. It was . . .

Then she gave up and jumped, banging her hip slightly but catching on and sliding down. At first, panicking, she gripped too hard and progressed with painful slowness through the Yellow Room, where a trio of revelers was enjoying one another in ways that seemed to imply that they were contortionists in everyday life, or at least yoga instructors. Then she relaxed a bit, and picked up speed down through another floor and into the suddenly damp darkness of the garage, where she landed with only the slightest scuffing of the balls of her feet. Then she stepped away from the pole, and bumped into someone who laughed and steadied her by the shoulders.

She turned around and there were Nicholas Taylor and her sister, hand in hand, standing in front of a Mercedes with all four doors open. They were smiling with the beatific ghostliness of figures in a dream. The Mercedes couldn't be real, either... It should be the cheapest rental car possible. And Nicholas shouldn't be here. Lee shouldn't.

"Hello, Miss Stewart," Nicholas said in his cool bass voice. "Welcome to your getaway car."

Then the world began to swoon and waver before her eyes. The last thing she saw was Paul standing over her and asking "Did she hit her head?" Only then did she know she had fallen to the ground, and then she didn't know anything else at all.

Chapter Eighteen

Olivia woke in a deliriously soft bed, with a cool white sheet tucked in over her with a perfect smoothness that suggested that she had been sleeping motionlessly, dreamlessly, like the proverbial baby. A mental image of Blue's blissfully serene face faded as she stretched and felt a wonderfully familiar instability, a drifting feeling that told her that she was on water. *Paul's sailboat,* she thought—but her first glance around disabused her of that idea.

It was a tidy little cabin with a little porthole window showing an expanse of greenish ocean on which bright sunlight glinted. The room was painted maroon, with walnut crown moldings to set it off, and a walnut floor. A table was set with two gleaming white plates and a bouquet of white roses. She was lying in the upper bunk of two bunk beds, and Paul was standing below, smiling up at her.

"I don't want to alarm you," he said. "But we are now married."

For a moment she believed him, and a confused series of emotions flowed through her, which finally resolved into a deep gratitude that they had gotten married without her knowing—she would definitely have fucked it up. Then she rubbed her eyes and said, "Oh, cut it out. That's not funny."

"When we *are* married, will you still tell me my jokes aren't funny?"

"I don't tell you your . . . Oh. Probably." Then she felt the cool slide of a gem into her cleavage and started. "Paul. Is it . . . ?"

She grasped the stone, a pendant hanging on a heavy silver chain. It was a stone so large it really felt like a rock, heavy and cool. If you threw it at someone, you could do real damage. It must have been nearly two hundred carats. She held it up to the light, and its clarity and color—a deep rose that seemed to contain pure white light in its shimmering depths—took her breath away. She smiled up at Paul and said, "Engagement ring?"

"Now your jokes aren't funny."

"It's just high spirits. And incidentally . . ." She caught her breath and looked at him gravely, the happiness inside her feeling more serious than any misfortune ever had. "Incidentally, I will marry you. Whenever you say."

"Ah, but maybe I don't say."

"You have five minutes to say." Olivia knit her brow. "And then I become angry and inaccessible."

"*Shh.* Another bad joke." He came to the bunk and put his

hand up to grasp hers. "I'll marry you anytime you say. We can get the ship's captain to do it. If he speaks enough English, that is."

"Oh, right. Where are we?" she said. "And how did we get here, and how did we get this beautiful diamond? Excuse me—*my* beautiful diamond?"

"First come down and let me pour you some coffee. You can hear about it over breakfast."

So, over eggs and toast, Olivia learned that they had driven away from the Karten house without incident and made their way to the pier, where a certain Norwegian cargo ship was about to set sail for Japan. Nicholas Tordahl happened to be an old friend of the captain, who had spirited him away from the attentions of law enforcement on many previous occasions. Nicholas offered no explanation for this extraordinary helpfulness beyond the information that "Norwegians are good sports." Paul, however, tended to the theory that Nicholas was gradually filling the captain's retirement fund, which was only right, after all.

"But . . . Nicholas? I thought he was some sort of cop. Not even a real cop, but a corporate . . . something," Olivia protested.

"Oh, no. Doesn't the word 'Norwegian' ring a bell?"

"Frankly, no . . . Oh, wait. Wait." Olivia took a bite of toast to fuel her thinking. By the time she had chewed it and swallowed, she had the answer. "Mr. Bezin. His bête noire, what was the person's name?"

"Nicholas Tordahl."

"Ah. So he was right. You *were* dealing with Tordahl!"

"Who is a double-crossing, unprincipled wretch, just as Bezin has always said. And one of my favorite people."

Olivia sighed. Suddenly she wasn't hungry anymore. "Well, that's okay. But there's one thing I *really* don't understand. Just before I passed out . . . I got to the bottom of the fireman's pole, and maybe I dreamed this, but I saw *two* people there. Nicholas and my sister, Lee."

Paul nodded, unperturbed. "Yes, they're in the cabin next door, probably still sleeping. They stayed up late with the captain, toasting old times."

Olivia groaned. "That's exactly what . . . I mean, Lee has a biology test tomorrow."

Paul laughed merrily. "Don't worry so much, Livy. I'm sure the biology test will wait."

"Of course it won't wait! Tests don't wait! Oh, no . . . I can't tell you how hard it was to pay for that school, and to get Lee to study all those years, and . . ." She looked disconsolately out the little round window, through which the sea looked heartlessly pretty and impossibly big. No way to spirit someone across it in time to sit her final.

"Hmm," Paul said, making a bewildered face. "And here it turns out she's perfectly happy without all that. Funny."

"You're just being a bad influence. I know you can't help it, but this is my sister we're talking about. My little sister. It's not me."

"Maybe your little sister knows what she wants."

"That's ridiculous!"

"Olivia." Paul caught her eye. "Are you sorry you ran away with me?"

She stared at him and at first didn't understand the question. Then she took a deep breath and considered it. Although she never would have gotten into a school as good as Columbia, of course Olivia could have gone to college. She could have had a career in what she always thought of as "the real world." She could have earned an honest living and had office friends and gone out on Friday nights. . . .

"I can't say I'm sorry," she said finally. "Because I'm in love with you. And *don't* tell me my sister's in love with Nicholas Turd-whatever, because I'm not ready to imagine that. As far as I'm concerned, she's twelve."

There was a pause, in which they began to smile foolishly at each other. Paul pushed his plate away and stood up. "Listen. Do you want to have some premarital sex?"

"Oh . . . so you *are* going to marry me," Olivia said, with a sentimental lilt in her voice. "But do you promise that we won't buy a house?"

"Promise." He took her hands and raised her to her feet, kissing her forehead.

"And we won't ever have to get up in the morning, or go to an office, or . . . wear sensible shoes?" She molded herself against him, letting her hands find their old sweet routes over his back, up to his shoulders.

"Promise."

"And we can keep stealing jewels?"

"Well," he said, "um."

She pulled away from him and scowled. "We can't. . . . Did something go wrong?"

"Well, Livy, that gem you're wearing is one of the most

famous diamonds in the world. And it belongs to Blue Karten, who's insanely well connected—in Congress, in the White House, in business—"

"Yes, I know, and the Olympic Committee. But why do I have to care?"

"Because I don't mind not having a house. But I don't want it to be because we're both in prison."

"So what do we do? Retire?" she said, as if this were the most preposterous thing she'd ever heard. "Live in some *beach town* for the rest of our lives, trying to impress drunk expats with . . . our glory days?"

"Calm down. You know I would never do that to you. Nicholas and I have been talking about going into a new field."

"Conning honest jewel thieves," Olivia grumbled.

"No. Gambling."

At this, she couldn't help feeling a spark of longing. And a sneaky little voice in her head announced that if it was gambling, she was going to be the best of the lot. She had always had a head for cards. And she could bluff like no one else, if it came to poker. It was . . .

Paul was smiling at her. "I can see my proposal doesn't fill you with *too* much horror."

"Well. I'm willing to discuss it."

"So, premarital sex?"

She put her hand into her cotton bathrobe and cradled the ponderous weight of the diamond again. She would miss the gems, of course. Of course it would be possible to buy them, but that would seem so wrong. They would be like domesticated jewels then, a neutered, boring version of these wild ones. Still, perhaps she could steal one or two. Just as a sideline. She would be *terribly* careful.

"Well," she said, "it is our duty to make love, to inaugurate the diamond. . . ."

"Don't think I didn't see that look in your eyes. And if you think—"

"*Shh.*" She wrapped her arms around him again. "It doesn't matter. Let's just get to know each other again. . . ."

Then she was tumbling into the bottom bunk in Paul's arms.